Wishing on My Father's Star

Holly Hight

Strange Wolf Press

Portland, Oregon USA

Strange Wolf Press
Publishers of quality eclectic fiction since 2012
Portland, Oregon

ISBN number 9 781540 443335
Cover art: Holly Hight
Author photo: Blaine Hight
Cover design: Richard A. Lovett
Interior design: Richard A. Lovett
Editing: Richard A. Lovett
Proofreading: Kristen Dedeaux

For Rune
May you always believe

Myles Lake
1991

My father wakes me just before daybreak, gently shaking me the way he used to when we'd go to the track on Saturday mornings.

"We're leaving, Gina. Up and at 'em." The cold air sneaking in beneath the tarp is razor sharp. I catch a whiff of wood smoke, sagebrush. "It's dawn. Time to get on the road."

I sit up, the words sinking in.

"We're leaving Archer for good."

I don't ask what the rush is, though I suspect it's that restless thing that's always been in my father's heart. I put my coat on over my pajamas and slip out from beneath the tarp, walking stocking-footed to the car, the cold dousing the heat from sleep. I gaze out at Myles Lake, an alkali lake about thirty minutes north of the town of Archer, which I'd once called home. It's beautiful in an otherworldly way. In the blaze of the sun, the water is powder blue, but lifeless, set in the faultless golden hue of desert. There are no trees, not even scrubby stunted ones, so that the impression is one of broad strokes in a simple painting. Above me in the early dawn, white clouds drift by, carried by a cold wind strong enough to rock the car.

We've lived here ever since we lost the house in Archer, changing campsites occasionally, but always somewhere along the lake. I look out at the vista, a palette of mute colors, salt water and stars. *Mine,* I think. One of the last remaining things that's truly been mine.

Dad, in his Stetson, hurriedly folds the tarp and rolls the bags. We're ready to go. The Caddie's gassed up. Our bags are packed. I have so many memories of growing up in this part of Nevada—strife, joy, fear, and sorrow wrapped soundly in my association with the desert's dry tributaries and in the way the hills seem at once both vibrant and barren.

*

As we drive north, away from both the lake and Archer, a sliver of purple burgeons in the east, a hairline of color, barely visible until you look away and then, there it is, obvious. I want to ask what we're doing, but I'm afraid to know. There are too many questions: What about Mom? How will we find her? Tell her we're leaving? Will I ever see her again? Will we ever come back?

I feel his hand on my shoulder, his voice hoarse. "We're gonna make it; you know that, right?"

I think a moment, hope so. Depending on how I look at it, we always have or never have. Until Archer, where we finally managed to settle for more than a few months, we'd lived in a string of places, my life like pearls on a necklace, shining with thin thread between, hoping for that elusive fortune Dad keeps talking about. In the dark, I nod. "What about Mom?" I finally ask.

He hesitates. "We'll see what happens."

"She won't know where we are."

"We'll find her." Dad, the optimist. "Why don't you write her a letter?"

"Where will I send it?"

"Just hang onto it. Keep it in your pocket."

The words float away from me. *Dear Mom—where are you? We're leaving without you and you won't know where we are. How will I ever see you again?* I'm staring out the window, my forehead pressed against the glass. I realize I'm crying.

"Gina?"

I can't face him.

"Gin?" Again, the hand. "We'll be ok." He takes a breath. "And we'll find her."

I imagine her in that vague anywhere. I turn, catch his gaze. "How?"

"I don't know, but we'll do it." He looks at me. "I promise." He turns away and switches on the radio. There's the crackle and hiss of faraway. The trace of a song. Country twang. Loneliness. Archer embodied.

*

That night, we follow an old gravel road and park. A song I recognize is playing, slow, sad, and lonely, Bob Seger recalling some long-gone main street. My father turns it up and lies beside me on the hood as we gaze at the stars. I let my mind drift back to the days when, however briefly, Mom's sadness faded and it looked like she might actually be happy. When I first got my spikes and discovered the little dirt track across from our new house. Before those cold Saturday mornings when everything fell apart.

"Pick any one you want," Dad says.

I look over at him in the dark.

"They're all yours if you want 'em." He nods upward. "Call it an early birthday present."

I gaze up.

I can't see him, but I know he's grinning. "Didn't you know the sky's a wishing well?"

Archer, Nevada
1988

All three of us are dressed up. My mother wears her best dress, a black chemise with yellow flowers and spaghetti straps. My father, clad in the thrift-store suit he dons when he leases out his old cars, is the picture of pride, while I wear a pink sundress and my favorite white sandals. We walk down the sidewalk toward the property, my father in the middle, taking us each by the hand, swinging our arms high, happier than I've seen him in a long time. I wonder if this will last, if this mysterious house, like some magic talisman, is the key to end my father's problems and if his glee is catching, might infect my mother and change her, too, dispelling the pall that has grown over her, year by year, as Dad moved us from one hopeless dream to another.

We walk past a rundown section of town, the streets strewn with trash, old buildings sagging against their foundations, not a soul around but us, as though the whole world has been left to our muse. We stand in front of what is ours, a white farmhouse with green trim, broken-out windows and a sagging stoop, a small, bent wrought-iron fence framing it all. But it is the modest yard with a patch of bare ground near the base of the steps that catches my eye. I wonder what has caused it. If it was the lounging place of an old dog or if it was once someone's vegetable garden. That spot is what I claim as mine on that first day.

I feel my father's palm on my shoulder as he bends down to me, flashing that movie star smile of his. "What do you think, Gina?"

I nod, smiling my approval.

"Like it, huh?"

My father hugs my mother to him as she dabs at her eyes with a handkerchief. "You really did it. You really bought it…" She throws her arms around him. "Oh, Robert, let's go inside."

Inside, it's a mess. Glass shards litter the black-and-white checkered kitchen floor and there are rust stains in every sink, in the toilet, in the bathtub. The attic is strewn with cobwebs and stinks of mold. A mildewed mattress stands in one corner, propped against the wall like a drunk. In another corner is a gold-rimmed picture frame with no picture, tethered to the wall and floor by spider webs. In what appears to be the living room, the ceiling fan is missing a blade and the stonework that makes up the fireplace is caked with dust. The wood floors are warped and water-stained. The basement harbors an entire community of spiders, crickets, moths, and flies, their tiny carcasses littering sills and corners. Suddenly I don't understand my mother's excitement or my father's celebratory vision.

"Like I said, she needs work," Dad says proudly. "But she's a diamond in the rough."

My mother turns to him. "I won't ask you what you paid for it."

"Next to nothing and a favor."

She doesn't ask, doesn't want to know. "We'll clean it up."

*

Our lives begin in earnest in the cleanup of that fragile house in the middle of the Nevada desert, where Dad is financing the whole thing selling insurance door-to-door and refurbishing old cars for the rental business he thinks will make him rich. He calls them his babies and has six of them now, saved from junkyards as far away as Idaho.

Making a living is tough and I want to help: "Maybe I could put up a lemonade stand." I know that Mom has been helping by taking in sewing projects for local ladies and typing projects for fifty cents a page. She once made enough to buy an entire car by typing and retyping someone's book, draft after draft. Dad calls that car Marianna in her honor.

"You're doing just fine, honey. Go to school. Get good grades. That's your job," Mom tells me. "Education is freedom," she adds, and for a moment her face slips and I see the sadness I'd hoped the new home would extinguish.

Every weekend, my parents work on the house as I play outside in the yard, my Raggedy-Ann doll on one side and my stuffed Chihuahua on the other. I sit on the patch of bare ground, a curved shard of bottle-green glass in my hand.

"Today, we're going to dig," I tell my companions. And so I dig deep, determined to find whatever treasure lies beneath. I pull up small stones and thick, hard clods of dirt, my small arms burning with the effort.

"Gina Amber Dalton, what on earth are you doing?" My mother has come around a corner of the house, her hands on her hips. I notice a big black smear on the front of her sundress.

"Look at you, you're a mess."

I giggle a little. "So are you." I point at the front of her dress and she looks down, shocked to find the stain.

"Yeah, well." There's a smile on her face as she rolls her eyes and dabs at the stain. "Grownups like to get grubby too, you know." She comes over and hugs me. "How about some lunch? I brought your favorite. Cold grilled cheese."

We eat on the front stoop, the three of us on our new porch, looking out at our new vista, at the westward hills, the whitewashed building of the Laundromat and the brick *Abelard Busby Middle School,* which dates back nearly to the turn of the century. Next to the buildings lies an old track, an oval of dirt and gravel with tufts of grass sprouting up here and there, the edge dissolving into a tangle of weeds. The fringe of tangle surrounds the track like a wreath, making it seem wild and forgotten, the small wilderness belying a pair of old metal bleachers, like skeletons, where people must once have watched heated contests, the drama of winning and losing.

"Can I go over there after I'm done?"

My mother holds her hand up, shading her eyes from the sun as she gazes at it. "Well, as long as you're careful. Be sure and look both ways crossing that street."

*

I kick up dust and rocks as I trace the quarter-mile loop, walking, then skipping, then sprinting, my sundress flying up, out-of-breath and tasting my grilled cheese sandwich after only one circuit of the track. Something about this place makes me want to claim it as mine. I've seen tracks before, vitalized by lights, crowds in the stands cheering and clapping for their favorites. As long as I can remember, Dad has taken me to high school meets, telling me: "I used to do that, way back when." He'd say this with a cock of his head, a quick nod and a prideful grin. "Could never quite break the sound barrier, though." I know now that he means the 4-minute mile, and when he says it I can always see a longing in his eyes, as though he's drifted miles away from me.

I do a few more loops, walking, plodding, skipping, playing, seeing how far I can kick a single stone. When I'm tired, I look both ways despite the fact the street is empty and return to the house where my parents have gone back to their work. My companions still sit on their perch, that sagging lower step just above the bald spot I've mangled looking for buried treasure. I return to my digging and find a tarnished button, black with age. I turn it over in my fingers, feel its smooth round contour, put it in my mouth and taste its metallic tang, along with the gritty loam of dirt. It's a treasure, so I put it in my dress pocket.

At the end of the day when we return to the tiny

apartment that's been home since we settled in Archer two years ago, we celebrate. Mom brings out her flute and plays something old. *I Love You Truly*. Dad sings. His voice is deep, velvety. I sing, too—though not as well. But it all comes together and I imagine the roof rising with our music, drifting into the wash of stars above us. You can see them from our balcony, all those points of light.

"There's nothing like starlight in the desert," Dad says. "It's so bright it's like twilight, like the sun hasn't quite made up its mind to set."

Then he flashes a knowing glance and disappears into the hall. He has a kit for such occasions, replete with magic wand, cape, and a flashlight with colored plastic to fit over the lens, along with a top hat he bought in a dime store in Reno. He moves to the balcony and begins with a juggling act: three tennis balls, then two tennis balls and an old racket he got from somewhere, then three tennis balls plus the racket...then four balls and the racket...until it's dizzying the sheer number of things he has in the air, so that I'm afraid to blink, afraid I'll break the spell and he'll drop them all.

Then, magic wand in hand, he comes back inside, shuts off the lights and turns on the flashlight, holding its colored beam under his chin for effect.

"Now," he intones, his face illuminated in ghoulish green light, "It's time for...the tricks of the ambisinister magician...and what's that mean?"

"All thumbs and two left feet," Mom and I say in unison.

He does a couple of card tricks then takes off his hat, tapping it with the wand and holding it to his ear. "Hmm," he says, "It sounds like teatime in there. What do you suppose that means?"

I shrug.

"Well, you can't have teatime by yourself now can you?" He holds out the hat to me.

I reach in and pull out a kinky-haired doll with big, imploring eyes, in an orange dress and bonnet. On her nose sits a bee, her mouth forming a surprised O as she looks at it, crossed-eyed.

Mom takes her from me, laughing. "Where on earth did you find such a thing?"

"Magic, of course." But his eyes are on me. "Like it?"

I nod as I throw my arms around him.

Later that night, I feel rich. The new doll sits with the companions who helped me dig for treasure. The button is still in my pocket, from which I pull it out every now and then, thinking of the track I'd found. Another treasure. In the living room, my parents are again making music, Dad in his dime-store hat, Mom still in the dress smeared from the day's work and the blue kerchief holding back her lovely honey-colored hair, grimy from the house at 14 Emlyn Street. It is a perfect moment.

Somewhere North of Myles Lake
1991

I think of them as I drift off to sleep, those treasures already mine.

I can settle for what I have or I can want more. One choice is safe. The other is expectation. Hope. On the safe side, even if I have nothing else, I have the stars. The land. The dead lake in the desert.

Dad hopes, wishes, dreams, but always slips back onto that plain of stars, grass, sagebrush, and alkaline water, his failures wrapped in the return to a starkly beautiful landscape and a nomadic life to which he's uniquely suited. I think of the sweep of desert grasslands, simple and broad, but not so simple when I think of details: a half-dozen towns scattered across Nevada, Oregon, and California, dreams held, then lost, the resolve to try again with something else, something new, something better, lost again, but found in some new town with some new dream, that fortune hiding behind every tree, every home, every boundary between nowhere and a makeshift future, a population, a place to belong. Life and school—or sometimes just a succession of books my mother brought home from the local library—always falling into lockstep behind the dream and the habitual Easter egg hunt our lives once were and have now again become.

*

I awaken and stare into the depths of the Universe, yellow smoke, a haze of stars—the ceiling that is not, an ironic twist on a cliché: no ceiling, yet a dead end.

"Dad?"

"Hmm?"

"You awake?"

He takes a deep breath as he turns over. "What is it, Gina?"

"Is the star to wish on?"

"What?"

"Is that what you want me to do?"

"Sure." He doesn't sound serious, his answer quick and trite.

"Will things be different?"

"I hope so." But he doesn't sound as certain.

I think about my wish. Do I get just one?

His voice gravelly from sleep: "We'll be ok, Gin. We'll make it the way we always do."

Except we never have.

"I made my wish."

I feel his gaze on me in the dark. "What'd you wish?"

"If I tell you, it won't come true." It's not the wish he thinks I've made. It's not the wish I thought I'd make. This one isn't safe, isn't an *at least*.

*

I think of our old house. Of all those nights I sat up after she left, in the room my father painted sky-blue, the lamp on by my bed. I couldn't bring myself to do anything but stare out the window, wishing she'd come home, the dim glow of starlight teasing. I'd shut off the light, letting the stars flood my room. *There's nothing like starlight in the desert.* It's true. It's palpable, like a companion. In the desert, naked as it can sometimes be, you have to find something. When the earth is barren, naturally, you look up.

I remember her sadness, the way it seemed to slowly eat her. I caught sight of it here and there, at moments when she didn't think I was looking, like moving-in day. My father was already at the house, doing some last-minute touching up. He'd painted the kitchen eggshell-white and the master bedroom the deepest forest-green you could imagine. All around were boxes, variously labeled: *Kitchen/Mom's clothes/Dad's clothes/Gina's clothes/toys/books/records/miscellaneous,* our whole lives packed up and ready to be rediscovered in this new, foreign place. The house seemed enormous, limitless. I started at the bottom and made my way to the top, exploring every nook and cranny in-between. I found dozens of dead bugs, an orange marble, and a small carving on a windowsill in the attic: *JL was here, 1976.* I wondered who JL was. I traced the letters with my fingers, the wood soft and worn.

I heard my mother come up the stairs and sensed her presence behind me though she did not speak. I turned around and watched her watching me, thinking she'd come up to tell me something.

"What?" I noticed the grief in her slate-colored eyes. "Don't you like the house?"

"Yeah, I like it." She sat on the top step. "Come here and sit by me." She put her arm around me as she kissed the top of my head. "You're going to have a good life here, a good future. You keep doing what you're doing, Gina. Keep working hard and getting good grades. Do your best every day."

I turned to look at her and saw that there were tears in her eyes. "Mom, what's wrong?"

She laughed off my question, wiping away her tears with the back of her hand. "It's nothing. It's just that you're growing up so fast…almost *ten* already." She brushed a lock of hair out of my face, tucking it behind my ear. "It's hard to believe."

I smiled. "I'm almost two numbers."

She nodded. "Practically an adult."

"But not too old for magic tricks."

"No, of course not."

"Tallyho," my father called up the stairs, almost as though on cue. "Who goes there?"

"JL," I blurted.

My mother looked at me quizzically. "Who?"

I pointed to the sill. "JL was here."

She got up and looked. "Well, sure enough. A kid, I'll bet."

"How do you know?"

She turned around and smiled. "Only kids think to do such things."

Again, I saw the sadness, and I wondered if she'd once done the same thing, boldly declaring her existence in some forgotten place.

*

Do your best every day. I haven't seen the inside of a school since we lost the house. The way things are going, my education looks like hide-and-seek in whatever small-town library I can find, scratching my initials with a dirty fingernail in a sill no one will ever see or a book binding no one will ever read.

GD was here.

*

I awaken to rain, my face damp, then realize I'm crying. I watch the night sky until a sliver of color appears in the east and the stars gradually fade. I watch until it's light enough for me to climb from my bag, slip on my spikes, and run toward dawn, the air needle-cold and the sky cobalt. It is a perfect morning, not unlike those cold, clear Saturdays on the track when I'd once had a home and a whole family. There are no neat white lines. No competitors, but for myself. Not even a coach, as my dad lies curled in his bag.

The air stings my fingers numb as I tie, not laces, but strands I think of as ribbons, as though the shoes themselves are gifts for my feet. I stand, ice in my lungs as I create my own fog, a world unto myself, preparing to run. And, from behind, I hear him awaken.

"Gina? Where are you going?"

Into the sun.

"Gina?"

I run. From the horizon, a pearly red seam appears, a birth. Another star. A real one, closer, warmer, perhaps more attainable. His voice fades and with it the night.

From the east, the day comes and swallows me. When I stop and look around, the stars are gone, replaced by blue and bright. I smile into it, turn around, sprint back, night gone, even on the western shore. These are the times I can run forever, forget all about winning the race, and live. Maybe that's also why I loved Myles Lake. It was life without expectation, without obligation. *Life without hope,* I start to think, then I realize that's not true either.

*

"Where in God's name have you been?" He is angry.

"It's beautiful, Dad."

"Don't change the subject. Why'd you run away?"

"I wasn't running away. I just wanted to see what Mom saw."

His face softens.

"She'd go toward the sun when she'd gather firewood, remember?" I think of her then, during those times between towns, when we camped rather than paid rent, and Mom would get up so early that the approaching day was compressed to a seam the color of roses. *With dawn comes hope,* she'd say.

*

The road lulls me to sleep and when I awaken, I hear the crackling of an oldies station and the patter of rain on the windshield. Dad's old wipers scrape the glass, regular as a tired heartbeat; they, like everything else, need to be replaced. My forehead, pressed against the cold glass, has started to ache, but I don't want to wake up, not completely. With my eyes still closed, I can pretend I'm on a ship instead of in a car, rocked, not by the wind, but by water, millions of tons of it, as I ride a stormy sea to…where? To England or Spain? Or to someplace warm and wet? The Philippines. Singapore. Or Tahiti? Island paradises sound nice; there'd be palm fronds the size of rafts, cobalt skies and high, puffy clouds looking solid enough to stand on. Turquoise water that magnifies everything on the bottom, even those impossible-to-reach treasures you could probably just as easily buy in a beachside shop, but are so much better to find. I'd dive down, pluck them off the bottom, hold them in my hand, and they'd glisten in the sun, different in the light. I open my eyes.

"Dad?"

"Yeah."

"Remember the shoes you gave me for my birthday? When I was 10?"

He smiles. "Of course I do."

"Where'd you get them?" It's a heart-pounding question, the kind that inspires a flutter of nerves akin to asking whether Santa Claus exists.

Archer
1988

My dad doesn't wrap my birthday presents. Instead, he puts them in his top hat and dares me to reach inside, urging me to guess at what I've caught before pulling it out. This year I pull out a new pair of shoes with spines on the bottom. I think for a moment that my father has truly spun magic, turning shoes into porcupines. His eyes, which in the right light fleetingly reflect an impossible violet, sparkle and curve upward at their corners, making half-moons, as his smile falls crookedly across his face. When he makes this expression, it always seems he's about to burst out laughing, the mirth in his eyes so intense I think he can't possibly contain it, but then he surprises me, flashing me that grin and keeping it there, waiting for me to smile with him.

I stare at the shoes, holding them up by the laces.

"Try 'em on, why don't you?" my dad says, still grinning.

"What are they?"

"They're track shoes called spikes."

He's been watching me on the track and I recall the longing that had come into his eyes as we'd watched high school meets.

"I think you've got talent, Gina," my dad says. "Courtesy of your old man, of course…" He takes a bow.

My mother watches us from the kitchen. "What I can't understand is how the heck you found a pair that *small*."

It's true. The shoes are tiny enough to slip onto my feet without so much as a corner of wasted space. They are a perfect fit.

"That's why they call me the magician," he says with bravado. "I can pull anything out of my sleeve. Or rather, my *hat*."

I giggle. It's true, too. He did it with old cars, with a whole house. A life that amazingly has kept us in the same town now for more than a year. "Can I try them out?" I ask. "At the track, I mean."

"Well, that's what they're for, my dear."

*

My father watches me from the old metal bleachers, my mother beside him. Butterflies take flight; I want to run faster than anybody's ever run—just for them. I start at one corner of the track and sprint, the cleats digging in, grinding dirt and rock. There's a ferocity in it, in that grinding, my teeth clenched as I am determined to run faster than I've ever run, that competitive longing turned passionate. At this second I understand what my father did before he gave up.

I tear around the track, my lungs burning, my legs aching, my heart pumping, thinking of the Olympic runners I'd seen on TV the time Dad found a 13-inch in someone's trash and brought it home. "Look how well it works, Marie," he'd said as the images shivered from one impossible color combination to another while Dad twisted the rabbit-ears antennae one way, then another. "I can't believe they threw it out." Not that we had it long. A month after the Olympics, it erupted in a plume of acrid smoke and Mom banished it to the cellar, never to be seen again.

Now I decide as I'm coming down the fourth quarter of the track, not really running as much as lurching to the finish, that this is what I want: to do the big things I'd seen on that small screen.

*

I come to a stop in front of the bleachers and even before I finish, I hear my mom and dad clapping.

"And she wins by a nose," my father shouts. I watch as he steps down the bleachers toward me with that wide grin and those upturned eyes. He stands in front of me, beaming as he reaches into his pocket and pulls out something shiny.

"Stand right over there." He points. "On top."

I look near the bleachers and there's a small podium with three stands, the white paint peeling, the numbers 1, 2, and 3, painted in red, faded now to pink. I step to the top rung, #1, proud as I feel myself grin, happier than I've ever been.

"And to the winner goes…" Dad places something around my neck. The cloth is faded—red, white and blue—but the medal has been newly polished.

"My 4:07 mile," my father says, nodding at the medal. "Not bad for a high school sophomore, eh?"

I'm mute as I stare at the medal, engraved with a winged foot. On the front, it says California Interscholastic Federation, Track and Field Championships. Turning it over, I see my father's carved scrawl:

Robert Caleb Dalton, May 13, 1976
Mile, 1ˢᵗ place, Petaluma, CA, 4:07

"Those were my glory days," he says, still smiling. "That was my pinnacle. That right there."

I realize I hold my father's promise in my hand and it seems fragile all of a sudden.

"Just don't forget to smell the air."

I look at him, confused.

"You'll go a lot of places," he says. "I did. I went all over California my sophomore year. I went to Petaluma, to the coast, even Los Angeles. One time, I got to go to a race in Orlando—not a good place for a high-desert boy like me. But everywhere I went smelled a little different."

I wrinkle my nose. "Really?"

"The desert smells a certain way, dry and dusty, like sage. In Orlando we nearly got fried by lightning. It smelled like thunderstorms, tinged with ozone. Near the ocean the air is heavy, wet and cool, and you catch a whiff of salt every now and then."

I giggle. "You can't smell salt."

"Sure you can. You've just never smelled it."

"We have salt in our cupboard at home and I never smell it."

"Sea salt's different."

A thrill pulses through me. "You think I'll go places?"

"If you work hard and never give up, you will."

I smile as I gaze at the medal, feeling Dad's smile upon me.

On the Road
1991

"The shoes," I repeat. "Where did you get them?"

My father's smile widens. "Magic. You and Marie didn't call me the magician for nothing."

But he knows I'm too old to be convinced he pulled them out of a hat. "I found them at a yard sale. They were absolutely perfect. When I saw them, I saw you."

I imagine it, the yard, grass matted by kids and by dogs and by life, old stuff set out, a woman with a tin hoping for people to come by, make small talk, and buy something she no longer wanted. The spikes would've belonged to a daughter who'd outgrown them. There's an irony in the fact my dream was fostered there, in someone else's yard, in a pile of things unwanted. Maybe that's what makes real magic. The unexpected things we don't count, don't consider, small wonders blooming before we know their full weight.

Then in a blitz of heartbreak, I think of Dad's medal, imagine it as a part of the earth, buried, with just a corner reflecting the sun. That's not what happened, but it's the way I think of it. A treasure lost, buried, no longer mine. "I wish I still had your medal."

I feel his hand on my shoulder. "It was just a medal, Gin."

"But it was yours—" I don't know how to put it into words. It's more a feeling, a memory, like that hard-to-describe smell—a whole world, even. "It was you."

"Not really." He looks at me. "Who you are and what you've accomplished isn't the medal. The medal's just icing."

I think about that for a minute, wondering if he actually believes that. Would we always be on the move if he did?

He mistakes my silence for misunderstanding. "You don't eat icing without a cake under it, right?"

I shake my head. *Dad*, I want to say. Ever since Mom left he sometimes talks to me like I'm the nine-year-old digging for treasures in the bare spot in front of the porch. But I stifle it. For some reason, these interactions are important to him. "But you could," I say.

"And it'd make you sick."

I giggle, playing along.

"Imagine if I made you a birthday cake out of chocolate frosting."

"That sounds good."

"You'd eat about three bites and want to puke."

I laugh. But now I want to be twelve again, not nine. "Dad?"

"Yeah."

"I want to be good."

He knows what I mean and his smile fades as he glances over at me. "Really?"

"Really."

His excitement sparks as that magical grin comes back. "Wanna go to Oregon?"

I look at him and feel myself smile. "What's in Oregon?"

"Oregon's where it all began."

I think of my little dirt one-of-a-kind track in Archer. That's the one I really want, the kind no one thinks to notice, but which becomes your secret—the one that fills your head with dreams.

"The running boom," he continues. "Back in the '70s, greats like Steve Prefontaine put Oregon on the map."

I wonder if Oregon's full of dirt tracks. "Who's Steve Prefontaine?"

Dad guffaws. "You've got to be kidding. You've never heard of Steve Prefontaine?"

"No."

"We'll go to Hayward Field. I'll show you."

"Was he as fast as you?"

He grins, glances at me. "He was much faster than me; he ran a 3:48 mile." His smile fades. "God, I wanted to run faster, would've given anything."

Astonishment floods through me. I'd never realized Dad's dreams were ever that passionate. "*Anything?*"

"Yes, anything. I watched him race once. It was an all-comers meet and he made everybody out there look like a nobody. He passed the other guys like they were standing still, never even looked at them. When he died a few months later, that's when I decided it wasn't good enough to be good; I wanted to be great, like him."

I say it before I have a chance to think: "Is that why you gave up?"

He looks at me. "That's why we're going to Oregon. I want to feel it again, that passion. I want you to feel it, too, Gina; you're worthy of it."

Pride swells through me with nerves mixed in.

"You could be really good; we could find you a coach—I mean a *real* coach…"

"But you're my coach."

"I know. But…" He takes a breath. "You're the fastest twelve-year-old this side of the Rockies. We could find someone better, someone worthy to guide your kind of talent—someone who knows what they're doing."

"You know what you're doing."

He grins, tousles my hair. "I'm glad you think so."

But the words float through my mind despite my best efforts to quash them. "What if I lose?"

"Lose?"

"I'm scared I'm going to lose."

"You will lose. Losing is a part of winning—didn't you know that?"

I make a face.

"No one wins without losing. You can't win every race and to win, you must risk losing. Even Steve didn't win every race."

"Really?"

"Really."

"Did he go to the Olympics?"

"He sure did."

Archer
1988

Ten is the age of my transition, the time I decide to put away my dolls and replace them with spikes, a track, and a dream. I feel the wind in my hair, my lungs heaving, my heart pumping. I can run over a mile now. Running has become my form of play, an elaborate game of tag, though my pursuer remains elusive.

I sprint until my legs ache, until sharp pains shoot through the arches of my feet and I can't catch my breath. Afterward, I double over, vomit, purged. I throw my head back, my arms outstretched to embrace the sky as I close my eyes and feel a warm wind across my face, riffling my hair. These are the moments I live for, just as I'm done and exhaustion takes over and there is a small measure of peace, a snippet of time when I forget why my childhood is over. And then I open my eyes, remember.

I see the sadness in my mother's eyes, now seemingly habitual and impossible to extinguish. I feel it in the pit of my stomach, the sour tang of culpability, my very existence like a stain on hers. I wonder if it is somehow my fault.

Today, my father has come to watch, but instead of clapping, there's concern in his eyes.

"You don't have to push yourself so hard."

"You did."

"Yes, but I was older."

"I want to be as good as you were."

"You will be, but give yourself time."

"Time me," I say. A dare.

I move toward the start, but my father interrupts. "Tomorrow," he says. "If you're going to do this, you might as well be rested."

*

The following day waxes golden and perfectly clear. I rise with butterflies in my gut, having not slept, regretting my hasty challenge. What if I'm not as fast as I think I am? What if I am, and he's nevertheless disappointed in me? I gulp back my doubt as I put on my shorts and green tank top, as I pull on my socks and lace up my spikes, as I tuck my father's 1st place medal into my pocket for luck.

"You ready to conquer the world?" he says, beaming, a stopwatch in his hand as I walk into the kitchen.

I take a deep breath, nod.

"Not nervous, are you?"

"A little."

"Nothing to be nervous about; just do your best."

What if my best isn't good enough?

*

My father and I are silent as we cross the street to the track. We take in the brisk air of a chilly morning, Archer like a glittering oasis, a contrast to the vast wash of desert beyond.

"Dad?" I say finally. "Did you ever try out for the Olympics?"

"The *Olympics*—oh, heavens no."

"Why not?"

He grins, mirth dancing in his eyes. "I'm glad I'm a legend in *your* mind."

"Really, Dad. Why didn't you?"

The grin fades. "Because I wasn't good enough."

"Could you have been?"

"No."

"Why not?"

"Because you're only as good as you are."

I'm not sure what he means. "Couldn't you just train really, really hard?"

"I did. And I wasn't good enough."

My biggest fear put into words. "I don't want to do this."

"What?"

"I don't want you to time me."

My father is incredulous. "Why not?"

"Because I want to be good enough."

He takes me by the shoulders. "Gina, listen. You're good enough, ok? Believe me. You run because you love to run. You're doing it for the right reason. Don't worry about your time. Run your heart out. Be proud of whatever you can do. I know I will be."

It should have been enough, Dad telling me it's ok to lose, ok not to be the best. I feel myself tear up. I have to do it, have to be the best, despite his reassurances, despite his unconditional love—because, deep down, there is a terrible realization dawning that my father's life, with its high-flying dreams, failures, weeks in the desert, and new, equally impossible dreams is not the one I want. I want to dream and not accept failure unless there's no other choice.

Again I feel his hand on my shoulder, as we face the track. "You ready?"

Nerves throb through me as I nod. I run two slow loops as a warm-up and finish right in front of the metal bleachers where my father sits, the stopwatch poised in his hand.

"Ready when you are," he says.

I take a deep breath, stretching my arms and legs. I draw a line in the dirt, my makeshift starting line, and gaze out at the desert horizon, a grayish-brown swath of ground I imagine extending forever. I push off hard, sprinting around the track, my hair flying behind me like the tail of a comet. My lungs burn after the first lap and my legs soon follow. My heart feels as though it might pound out of my chest and I see spots like dancing stars in front of my eyes. But it's worth it to win, to outrun this imaginary opponent breathing down my neck.

"*Time,*" my father calls at last, staring at the watch.

I throw my face skyward, trying to catch my breath as I fold my hands behind my head, shutting my eyes against the sun. I walk another lap, shake out my legs, and wait for my father to speak, nervousness spreading through me. I'm afraid to ask. Afraid the look on his face is not one of pride.

"I don't know if this is right," he begins tentatively.

I hold my breath. "Good or bad?"

He looks up, into my eyes, a smile spreading. "Good, *very* good. This says you did a mile in 5:33."

"Really?"

"Really."

He swings an arm around my shoulders, squeezing them, jubilance in his face. "You know, I have a plan," he says. "Next weekend, we'll go to another track just to make sure, and then…"

"Then what?" I'm excited now.

"We'll call the newspaper."

"Really?"

"Well, I don't know about you, but I don't know many ten-year-olds who can run a mile in 5:33."

"What'll happen after that?"

"The sky's the limit." Dad is unable to contain his euphoria as we walk home. "I think I'm going to start calling you my lucky Genie."

*

The next weekend, I ride with my father in his green '74 Caddie to the Abelard Busby High School track across town. The track is deluxe compared to mine, red and perfect with lanes and numbers painted on it. My feet feel small and fast in the spikes. They suspend me, slightly, from the ground, making me feel modestly winged. I stare down the track, imagine flying. It is possible. I position myself at a painted white stripe in lane one.

"You ready?" Dad asks, poised with the watch.

I nod, taking in a deep breath, calming my nerves.

"Set…"

I lean forward, my lead leg, my right, poised on the line, my left behind, ready to push off.

"*Go!*"

And I sprint, surprised at the way I'm able to propel myself forward without slipping, my spikes biting the red turf. I feel stronger today than I ever have, the run not so much a struggle. Maybe it's my newfound confidence, the realization I've got *It*, whatever *It* is. My father saw it. True gift. The capacity to do anything.

"*Time,*" he barks, immediately shoving the watch into my face as I finish, the digital numerals reading 5:27. I turn to look at him and see those dancing half-moons of his.

"You've got it, Gina; you've got what I never had."

Those are the words I've been waiting to hear. I smile up at him, realizing this is a new beginning. A means to prove to my mother and father that their one and only is a one and only.

*

That night, Dad calls the Archer Daily Herald and tells a sports columnist about my feat. I listen to the conversation from around the corner in the living room as my father talks in the kitchen.

"5:27," my dad keeps saying. "For a *ten-year-old*. You know she's the fastest kid this side of the Rockies, if not the whole nation. You gotta cover this one, Eli; she's extraordinary."

I say the word to myself. *Extraordinary*.

"Yes," he says. "Absolutely. You won't be disappointed, sir. We'll find one. And you're telling me you'll be there, right? Fantastic. Let me give you my number…"

When my dad gets off the phone, he comes into the living room beaming and claps his hands. "The Herald's interested, but we've got to find an official race."

I swallow hard, my stomach in knots. "But you've already timed me."

"That's not an official time; for them to print it in the paper, it needs to be official. You have to prove yourself, Gina." He wraps an arm around me. "But that won't be hard; you've already shown me you can out-leg anyone in this dinky little town. Now all you gotta do is show the world."

*

My father combs the newspapers for races while I train on the dirt track across the street. When he can, he drives me across town to the Abelard Busby High School. It's a good time, an exciting time. But I sense a tension between my parents that seems to metastasize to everything else. I hear them arguing one night in their bedroom.

"You've got to live in the real world, Robert," Mom snaps. "She's a child, for God's sake. You're putting too much pressure on her."

"She's doing it because she wants to."

"Maybe now. But in six months? In a year? Are you prepared for the possibility she might not want to do this forever? What if she burns out? It's what happened to you…"

"She's not a burnout. She's nothing like me. She's willing to work hard, Marianna; she's willing to go all the way. I know my Gina. This will be a lifelong passion for her, I can see it."

"No, this is just another whim for you, another distraction from reality. When are you going to stop dreaming and *wake up?*"

There's a long pause. "I'll never stop dreaming."

"Well, that's the problem."

"Why's aiming higher always been such an issue with you?"

"Because somebody's got to live down here on Earth. And Earth is tougher than heaven." I realize my mother is crying.

"Marie—"

"No, go away."

"Come on, come here."

"I don't want her to go through the same things we've gone through. Our first obligation to her has to be as *parents,* not as best friends, not as coaches…"

"Look, I already said I'd find temp work."

"That's not going to support a household, Robert. Christ."

Bruised history. Tender memories. I've heard this before in all those towns before Archer, and now it's back again, worse than ever. From behind the door, I wince, feel the heat of grief behind my eyes.

"You do what you want," my mother says at last, disgust in her voice. "But she's not going to save you. A wasted life is just that, a wasted life. You can't borrow hers and change what you've already thrown away."

*

I run to my room and hide as I pull the covers over my head. But I can still sense my father's presence when he comes to the door. "I wasn't eavesdropping," I blurt, my voice stuffy from tears.

"I told her I wanted to quit selling insurance door-to-door, so I could coach you fulltime."

I turn to look at him, a blocky silhouette in the doorway.

"What do you say?" There is excitement in his voice.

My mother's words run though my head and won't stop. "I don't know, Dad."

"What do you mean you don't know? I thought you'd be excited."

"I am, but…"

"But what?"

"What are we going to do?"

"What do you mean?"

"About…the household."

"So you *were* listening."

"Sorry."

"I have my rentals." He means the cars. "Besides, there's lots of work around here. People need their lawns mowed, their cars repaired—you know I'm a magician with a widget—they need the basics and I'm smart like that." My father comes over to my bed, sits by me. I see the sparkle of his eyes in the moonlight from my window. "You know what being street smart means?"

I shake my head.

"It means you can make something out of nothing. It means you're crafty." He smiles. "We'll make it, Gina. We always do. Your mother may not know it yet, but we're sitting on a winning lottery ticket."

"What do you mean?"

"You."

Their one and only.

"I want to see you make it. I want to see you do what I never did." He hesitates. "What I've always wanted to do."

The words come out before I can stop them. "What if I can't?"

"You can, if you want it bad enough."

"But what if something happens?"

"What do you mean?"

"What if I break my leg?"

Dad puts his hands on my shoulders. "Gina, you've got to believe in yourself. Stop worrying about what might happen. Enjoy the possibilities. That's the key. You have a right to dream; do you know how precious that is? Do you know how many people dream without any possibility that what they want will ever come true? You're so lucky that way. You can dream and there's some hope it might just happen. Enjoy that."

In the moonlight, I nod, but my mother's grief coils in my stomach, a lump of guilt.

*

I decide to take my father's words to heart, convince myself that I'll save them, that if I run fast enough, I'll pull them along with me, rescue them from whatever's giving chase. History. Old mistakes. Old hurt. Old regrets. I work like a fiend, getting up at dawn on Tuesdays and Fridays to ride with Dad across town and train an hour on the high school track, while on Mondays, Wednesdays, and Thursdays, I run the trails that trace Archer's perimeter. My dirt track languishes across the street, ignored in this new quest for glory.

"You need both speed and endurance," my father tells me. "Intervals will give you speed and long runs will build endurance. To win, you need to be faster than the competition, but you also need to be able to hang on."

But I'm barely hanging on. Our house is cold at night, when the temperature drops and we can't afford heat. We light candles when the power company shuts off our service. Mom makes peanut butter and banana sandwiches, along with whatever else isn't perishable. We make do, like Dad says. He still has his magician's flashlight and has jerry-rigged an old kaleidoscope with a magnifier so that when you shine the light through it, its intricate pattern falls across the west wall of our living room.

"You see? Who needs TV?"

But Mom isn't amused. Her anger has smoldered down to a brooding discontent. I can't help but steal quick glances at her as she sits quietly, placidly, on our ratty gingham couch, a loose-weave gray shawl pulled tight around her small shoulders, her legs tucked up beneath her dress for warmth. She looks like a child the way she's sitting, but her posture is that of an old woman. Her curly hair is pulled back beneath her blue kerchief, making her face seem angular, her eyes too dark for her pallor. When she laughs it comes in quick dismissive snorts, her eyes narrowing in what briefly looks like mirth. But there's the emerging truth behind those eyes, the haunted tragedy of a life lost. When I was younger, I had sometimes thought it was joy I saw in those little laughs. Now I know better.

Eugene, Oregon
1991

"Gina, wake up; we're here."

I open my eyes. It's still dark. There's rain on the windshield. My father points. "Do you know what that is?"

I trace his finger to the silhouettes of unremarkable buildings, shake my head.

"That's Hayward Field."

But I don't see any field. "Where?"

"The track Steve ran on—set American records on—is right in there."

But I can't see the track. It's as though it's locked away. I think of my little dirt track in the desert, right out in the open, for everyone to see and I wonder if, like gems, some tracks are worth more than others. A diamond versus fool's gold. The thought makes me sad.

"Why do they call it Hayward *Field?*" I ask, imagining a pasture of tall grass and wildflowers.

"Because it's not just a track—it's a whole stadium."

Back home, my little track had a single rack of old metal bleachers, enough for a few dozen people to cheer. Two had cheered for me. I remember that little winner's stand, a foot-and-a-half high, my first win against myself as I stood alone, my first medal, my father's. When, even so, I'd felt like a champion.

Hayward is different. Now that I can see where it is, I imagine an arena of people, thousands of them, all cheering, the roar deafening. Like it would be in the Olympics. Like it was when Steve set his records. I wonder if people cheered for Dad, when he ran in his great race, in Petaluma.

"Did people clap when you ran by?"

"If they did, I don't remember."

I feel bad because if they were cheering that loudly, he would remember. "I'd clap for you."

He puts his arm around me. "I know you would." He nods toward the darkened buildings. "Let's get out and take a look around."

*

The air smells like wet asphalt and loam, a fall smell. We cross the street to a fence, hop it. On top, he reaches down, pulling me up by that strong arm of his as though I'm nothing. I realize we're sharing a secret.

"There it is," he says.

I look down on an enormous stadium, big enough to hold thousands. But the track itself is nothing special; it looks like the one at the Abelard Busby High School. "It's just a track," I say.

"It sure is." Then my father does something surprising. He kicks off his shoes, hops down the stairs, and runs barefoot. It occurs to me that for all of his stories, I've never seen him run. But he runs for me now, lithe and graceful as though he's been doing it all along, his stride perfect, his dark hair flying. He runs despite his bare feet, despite the rain, now pouring. I clap for him. Each lap. Until it stings and my hands turn hot. I wonder if what he needs is to hear the roar of the crowd, but I can't possibly clap loud enough.

He keeps running, lap after lap, until I notice a limp, subtle at first, then not so subtle.

"Dad!" But he doesn't seem to hear. "Dad, I'm clapping!" No wonder he doesn't remember the cheers; they didn't matter to him then and they don't matter now.

"Dad!"

He doesn't slow down. How many laps has he run? I've lost count. "Dad, can we go now?"

Another lap.

"Dad, I'm cold." I hug myself. "It's *freezing.*"

Another lap.

"Dad, I'm hungry."

Another.

"I'm tired, Dad."

Another.

I sit, my butt wet, pouting so that I feel fat raindrops on my lip. I open my mouth, letting them fill me, pop me, so that I'll turn into a deflated balloon. Then he'll be sorry. Because that's how I feel. Deflated.

When he limps up the stairs, he grins, holding up the bottom of a foot so that I see the blood.

"Gross."

He smiles. "This is *Hayward Field.*"

I gaze out into the dark, into that void of rain, gloom, and my father's blood, wanting to cry. How could this possibly be anyone's dream? "I want to go home." Myles Lake flashes through my mind, along with my father's promise that I'd always have it.

But I've got this instead.

"I haven't run like that since high school," he says, wrapping an arm around me, still breathless. "Not bad for an old man."

"I'm cold."

"I know. Tonight we're staying in a motel."

I should be excited. But my father's celebration comes as a rundown room with pea-green carpeting and '70s-style yellow tile. The walls are fake-wood paneling and stink of cigarette smoke. The beds have coin slots next to them so that 25 cents will make them vibrate. I only have one quarter, but I try it and am disappointed to find that all it does is make me sick.

Dad sits on the edge of the chipped tub, white with black underneath, and runs warm water over his bloodied feet, turning the water pink. *Rosewater,* I think, remembering the times Mom used it. *Her bid on beauty, silky skin bequeathed by pink petals.*

"I'm bored," I say, tracing the chipped place, lemon-shaped.

"Boredom is a state of mind." He winks, trying to con me with that movie star grin.

"It's not a state of mind." I fold my arms over my chest, defiant. "It's real. And it really sucks."

"I'm sorry you feel that way. I would've thought that in a place like this you'd be anything but bored."

I look around. "It's ugly."

"I don't mean the room. I mean Eugene. It's a running mecca, Gin. It's where all of your dreams will come true—if you work hard enough."

Always that caveat. If I work hard enough...What's hard enough? I worked hard in Archer and it wasn't enough. "What's a mecca?"

"It's where everything starts."

But this feels more like an end. "I miss Mom." And my track, but I don't say that part. I wonder what Dad's feet would look like if he'd run on my dirt track barefoot. Worse. The thought gives me a strange satisfaction.

"I know you miss home, sweetie—and the way things used to be—but all we've got is this new start. We might as well make the most of it."

"But Mom won't know where we are." I feel my face dissolve into tears.

Dad puts his hand on my shoulder. "Tell you what; you write that letter and I'll get it to her, ok?"

As I gaze into his violet eyes, I believe him, even though he has no idea where she is. He's always been like that. You want to believe him, no matter what. Even when you know he's wrong. Even when you know that what he wants is impossible.

Dear Mom—

We're in Eugene, Oregon. Do you know where that is? Dad says it's a place where everything starts. Have you ever heard of Steve

Prefontaine? I wish you were here. I miss you. Maybe you could ride a train to Eugene. I wish you would. I'd wait for you at the station. And things would be ok again.

   Love,

   Gina

I have so much to say, but I don't know how to say it, and when I try, my tears make the ink run.

I hand it to Dad, folded over until the paper's just a thick, creased square. "Do you have any tape?" Even the sheer number of folds can't make it secret enough.

"I think it's fine the way it is," he says.

Hayward Field flashes through my mind. I forgot to tell Mom about it. I take a deep breath. "I guess it's ready."

Dad smiles at the thick square, putting it in his pocket. "Looks like it is."

*

I never do see him mail the letter, but I choose to believe, the way I once believed that letters to the North Pole actually made it to Santa Claus. Dad will find a way. I imagine Mom reading it, catching the next train, waiting for me at the station, standing there alone, turning and spotting me, the smile spreading across her face as she recognizes me (even though it's been two years and I've grown), her arms reaching to embrace me. In my daydream, she looks the same, with that pale, freckled skin, those generous eyes, cornflower blue, and that wheat-colored curly hair held back in a paisley kerchief. Though I wonder about her spirit, if she's changed in some celestial way, if wherever she is, she's still my mother.

Archer
1988

We leave for the race early, during the twilight. As I gaze out the window from the backseat of my father's Cadillac, I see the desert, still asleep, the dark silhouettes of hillsides cast against the pink hue of a still-distant dawn. The beams of Dad's headlights cut a bright swath through the gloom. I feel an excitement pulse through me; I've never been to Lodema. *Don't forget to smell the air...* I wonder if it's all that different from Archer.

When we arrive, I notice other runners milling about in sweats and sneakers – *sneakers?* I tug on my dad's sleeve. "Why aren't they wearing spikes?"

"Spikes are track shoes," my father says.

"Yeah, but aren't you supposed to wear track shoes when you run?"

"Not always. This is a road race; it's different than running on a track."

I feel something akin to betrayal. I look into my father's eyes, glaring. But he's still smiling at me with those half-moons, oblivious. "What am I going to do?" I snap.

The smile falls off his face. "What do you mean?"

"I can't run a road race in track shoes."

"Sure you can."

"But they're *track* shoes. That's what you said."

The smile returns as he puts his hands on my shoulders. "Think of it this way: you can still grill steaks in an oven, right? You can still pour vodka into a wine glass."

I knit my brow. "This is different."

"Gina, listen. It's not different. You're just fixated on this because you're nervous. You've run on trails in those shoes with the spikes out, right?" He holds up the tiny wrench he's used to remove the spikes. "There's no reason to think you can't do it on the road."

I shake my head, unconvinced. "Roads are *hard.*"

"But you're harder." He says it with a thumbs-up. "You're one tough cookie, alright."

*

My father takes my hand and walks with me to the starting line. "You'll do just fine."

But I can't get over my anger. And my disappointment; the air smells no different here than it does in Archer. This little town might as well be Archer's twin, with a mini-mart and a gas station and a Laundromat.

A thin, wiry man stands up on the trophy podium with a megaphone in his hand. "Line up folks," he barks through it, his poorly amplified words crackling and screeching. "Race starts in five minutes."

Adrenaline floods through me. From the sidelines, Dad makes a thumbs-up sign with each hand. I take a deep breath trying to quell my nerves, but it seems to do no good. Already, I feel I've lost the race, and I can't explain why my confidence has slipped away. I try to think of all my practices, all of those hard sessions on the track, my legs certain and swift beneath me, but those feelings of invincibility have vanished. Why do my legs feel like lead when I haven't even started?

I strain to see the newspaper man my father has invited. But I don't know what he looks like, and I try to imagine how a reporter might be dressed, how he'd part his hair and what kind of shoes he'd wear. I think of a man in a suit and a bowtie, a gray hat perched crookedly on his head and men's dress shoes on his feet. I imagine a man with black wire-rim glasses and an intellectual nature who talks the way men in old movies talk. I can imagine him clear as day, pacing back and forth in front of the bystanders, straining to get a good shot of me with his flashbulb. But despite the fact I see him clearly in my mind, I can't get my eye on him as I scan the crowd. Disappointment floods through me. I wanted this to be the Big Race. I wanted to prove myself here, to get my picture in the Archer Daily Herald.

"Runners on your mark," the wiry man barks through the megaphone.

Scattered conversations fall silent and there's a quiet shuffling, a repositioning.

"Get set..."

I lean forward, right leg poised, left leg behind, ready to push off.

The starter's pistol sounds with a loud *Pop,* and off we go, at first jouncing and jostling against each other, jockeying for position. But I'm hemmed in, big bodies on all sides. I can't go out hard the way I told my father I would. And the pavement is cruel beneath my feet, unforgiving. Without the spikes, and on the hard surface, I can't dig in the way I'm used to at the track or on the trail, and each footfall seems to rattle my bones.

A mile out, I'm still hemmed in and I feel something in my shin. It's slight at first, a minor throb, but with each step it grows until it's the size of a giant. I keep running, altering my gait, hoping that will ease the pain, but instead it gets worse until I have to slow my pace. Until I have to stop and walk. It feels like defeat; it *is* defeat. Absolute and total failure. My world blurs as tears well up in my eyes. I think of all those loops around the track. All for naught. I wonder how my father will react. If he'll be disappointed in me. If he'll make me run more intervals or if, instead, he'll tell me to quit, like he did, not wanting ever to give me the opportunity to embarrass him this way again. Right now I want to quit, would welcome my father's resignation to my mediocrity.

*

As I come over the hill just before the finish line, I see Dad waiting by himself, his hands gripping the rope separating the bystanders from the athletes, concern and confusion on his face as each runner whizzes by, ahead of me. He catches sight of me as I grit my teeth through the pain and sprint toward the finish. Quick as light, he ducks under the rope and runs toward me, knowing from my face that something is wrong. I lower my head, driving forward, not wanting to see that look of disappointment in his eyes as I push, desperate to reach the line.

"Gina," I hear him shout.

But I ignore him, driving hard through the line, catching sight of my time on the giant digital clock: 37:48. Twelve minutes per mile. Less than half the speed I'm used to running on the track. I stop, walking to the end of the chute, my face to the sky and my eyes shut against the sun as I suck at the dry desert air.

"I'm sorry, Dad," I sob as he approaches me. I feel his arms around me then, lifting me up. I tighten my grip around his neck, relief flooding through me as he flashes that crooked grin and those violet half-moons. I failed miserably, but not so miserably he's given up. We've simply fallen back to the desert, another dream yet to come.

"Your first battle scar," he says. "Where's it hurt?"

I point to the front of my leg.

"Nothing like being kicked in the shin by a highway." He hoists me onto his shoulders and walks with me toward the crowd. I'm still glancing around, on the lookout for the reporter I know I'll never find. I'm relieved the way I was the moment I felt my father's arms around me. For all my eagerness to stand out, I'm afraid of that moment of truth, afraid of trying to prove myself only to fail. I can't bring myself to risk what I already have, that enigmatic thing my father described. The dream. The right to believe in something impossible. That belief is so fragile, so easily crushed. I tell myself that this race wasn't lost by a lack of talent or fortitude, but because my leg hurt. And in some strange way, I'm grateful for the pain.

Eugene
1992

It's winter and we've made ourselves a shelter under a bridge, not far off a deer trail Dad says Prefontaine used to run every Sunday on his 15-milers. I imagine him, a man like my father, only a ghost, gliding past us every dawn, never looking right nor left, sure of his way, never wondering if he is lost.

I hold my coat around me for warmth as Dad makes a fire. "Why don't you run?" I ask.

"It's a treat for me, so I save it."

"*Save it?* For what?"

"For when it matters."

I think of Hayward Field. It must've mattered a lot. "Dad?"

"Yeah."

"What if that happens to me?"

He knits his brow. "What?"

"What if I get tired of it?"

"Remember yourself. You've got it. I didn't have it and I certainly don't have it now. For me, it was just a hobby. But you've got it, Gin—pure gift—it can give you everything you've ever wanted." There's a grief in my father's gaze, something unspoken, a secret perhaps, and it occurs to me that he's never forgiven himself for not being good enough.

"Your gift will drive you. When you realize it can get you out of this…" He makes a gesture upward, into those dripping crevices, a road for everyone else, for us, a roof.

*

Spring comes. My feet have grown and I don't have much in the way of shoes but for some sneakers, too small, so that with each step, I hammer my toes against the canvas. I follow the deer trail to a larger path, running loops across the river, stopping on the bridge to look, then on again, back into the woods, the smell of loam, around to the grasslands and a small pond. I'll run all day if I have to.

But I can't. On the fifth lap, I notice the blood, each toe illuminated in red through the white canvas. I slip them off. I'll do what my father did. I'll run barefoot and I'll waste my pain on this unknown trail, now left to the deer. It's not Hayward Field, but it's mine. Like that dirt track. The dew smears the blood and blades of grass, like slender paintbrushes, leave thin red lines across the tops of my feet. I wonder if Steve knew this, too, the naked part of running, the intimate part that the crowds never see. He must have known it and loved it. It was the part of Dad that never took, the part that burned out. All he had were the crowds and the crowds were never enough.

I think of Myles Lake and that long-ago button. I collect this too, so that I'll have it even when the lights are bright and people cheer.

*

When I feel my father's gentle nudge, I think we're on the move again. I don't want that anymore. I like my trail along the river. I like the duck pond and the grass field west of us. I like knowing where I'm going just like that ghost I imagine sprinting past us every morning. I like the new landscape of my life, new associations as I round the bend and there's that huge pine, leaning over water swathed in mist, as though it may just topple in. I love the gray stump on the west side of the duck pond, bleached by the sun. I love the hum of distant traffic, blunted by the twitter of robins.

He shakes me harder, and I shrug his hand off. "Go away."

"I've got something for you." I turn over and I notice immediately the sparkle in his eye. "Call it an early birthday present."

Like a hatful of stars, that impossible wishing well, I suddenly think. I sit up. It's a cool morning. I gather my sleeping bag around my shoulders for warmth.

"We're going to celebrate your birthday a little bit early this year."

"What difference does it make?"

"What are you talking about? It's for your *birthday.*"

"So?"

"So, it's a day for celebration."

I think of the story Mom once told about how I came to be in the backseat of my father's Caddie on the edge of the desert, back when the Caddie was young. Funny how lonely that story is. Not much has changed. "We gonna go dumpster diving through the party packages at Chuck-E-Cheese?"

He sits back. "Could you not be a smartass?"

I sit forward. "I wipe my butt with sumac. What do you think?"

"We can make it a good day." He takes a breath and claps his hands. "You'll love it, I promise."

Just like that alkaline lake.

"He works in Portland; all we gotta do is get there."

*

We bathe in the river, dirt and stink swirling away in eddies. At least for a while, we'll be clean. Dad has an old pumice stone I use to scrub the dirt from all of those places that have calloused under my ethereal dream, the thick skin on my heels and the balls of my feet. I dig the grit out from under my nails and wash my face, becoming me again a little at a time. The cold is shocking on my scalp as I lean back into the water, washing my hair, matted and filthy. I open the plastic camp container of lava soap, lay my hair on a rock, and rub the gritty bar over it. I think of the pioneer women I read about last week in the library, who used to scrub laundry on a washboard and wonder if they got tired, if they got discouraged.

I flip onto my back to rinse, gazing into the blue and the occasional bright white cloud, looking closer to find all of those shadows, white and gray, three-dimensions, an ivory world above. It's a place I'm not used to seeing, yet here I am.

*

Dad managed to buy me some thrift-store shoes without too much wear on them, and some clothing that didn't make me stand out too badly on the afternoons and evenings I spend in the library. He's been in one of his down cycles, not working much, no money for gas, so instead, we park the car and hitchhike, Dad's "present" a trip in the back of a brown '79 Chevy pickup, the sun on our backs and the wind in our faces. We play with it for a while, popping our heads up over the cab as we let the wind blow our hair back and contort our cheeks. Sixty-five miles an hour is an interesting look. We hit patches of warmer and cooler eddies in this speed-generated tempest, as though summer, at this speed, passes in bits and pieces, seconds instead of seasons.

We laugh, but we can't hear it. Back here, it is deafening. We slump into the bed, dodging the wind, and watch as the landscape of shrubs and litter slips behind us, eaten up by distance. This is one of those daring adventures we'll remember forever. It reminds me of the time Dad said, *remember to smell the air.* I feel myself grin. This is smelling the air times ten thousand.

Mom flashes through my mind. What would she think? Before I was born, she once hopped a freight train to Portland. I didn't think to ask Dad why. What was it like for her? Did she laugh as hard as we have? Was she on her way to a dream?

*

Luke Havelock sits across from us in a leather chair, skeptical. The first thing I notice is his chewing gum, turning over and over like a shirt in a dryer. It strikes me as impatient, his chewing, fast and nervous as I watch the motion in his temples. He's a 50ish handsome man, tall and lithe, like the athletes he coaches, and completely bald. He reminds me of Mr. Clean with a goatee. An older version of Dad, perhaps—minus the dancing eyes, the hair, and the smile. White shirt and tie. Dressed up for the people who'll do him proud. This program is known for its recruitment of younger runners, middle school and high school prospects who show true potential. Luke Havelock was himself an Olympian and he's always got his eyes peeled for more, Dad says.

Nervous, I finger the new nail clippers Dad bought for me at the dollar store, a practical gift; I can't shower every day, but I can trim my nails, can dig the grit out from under them.

"What you're saying, Mr. Dalton, is that your daughter is an American record holder…" Luke glances at me. "And nobody knows it but you."

There is something in the coach's brown eyes. Not quite mirth, not quite anger. A hybrid. *Mr. Dalton.* It's strange to hear Dad called that when I know who he really is. The man in the Stetson and cowboy boots who cracks silly jokes. The dreamer.

"You just watch her run, Mr. Havelock. I can guarantee you're not wasting your time."

Luke stands. "I don't have time for this today." He looks at me. "I'm sure you're a great kid. Keep running." He ushers us out into the sunshine overlooking the track.

"Wait." Dad puts his hand on the coach's arm. "Please just watch her."

No, Dad, no. Not today. I didn't sleep well last night. I haven't had breakfast. My knee hurts. I don't feel good. What happens when I go out there and it doesn't happen? What happens if I'm not myself? Or worse, I am?

"I don't have time today, Mr. Dalton."

Dad grabs my sleeve and pulls me down the steps. "Run, Gina. *Run.*" He shoves me onto the track and I hear him calling after me as I bolt. *"Run."* Adrenaline floods through me. It's time to show Coach Luke Havelock what I've got. The rest of my life may depend on it.

I run as hard as I can for as long as I can. I don't count laps, don't take splits. I don't have any goal in mind. I'm not trying just to get to a mile or a 5k. I'll keep running until someone tells me to stop, even if that takes all day, even if I fall down first. Lap after lap, I sprint, talking myself to the next painted white stripe. *All I've got to do is one more quarter, just one more quarter…* I tell myself that at least a dozen times. One hundred meters is just one hundred meters. Two hundred is just two hundred. Really, what's another mile?

I run until someone's voice cuts the air, not my father's. I fall to my knees, puke, orange bile on the blue track. A man's shadow colors it.

"You've got a hell of lot of guts, I'll give you that."

I look up into his face, hard to make out against the sun.

"Keep working at it. It'll be interesting to see where you're at in a year."

"Huh?" I swallow, my throat on fire, tears in my eyes from the sharp tang of bile.

"You're not ready yet, kiddo. We'll take a look in a year, though, ok?"

I stand, wobbly, my head throbbing, heat in my face. "I'm not good enough?"

Where there was a mixture of mirth and anger, I see pity or something akin to it. "You've got talent, sweetheart, no question about it, but it's undeveloped. This is a really competitive program."

I need him to give me something, anything. "Do you think I'll make it next year?"

"I think if you work hard at it, and I mean really hard, you've got a shot."

"Really?"

"We'll see, won't we?"

*

I sulk as Dad and I walk toward Interstate-5.

"You're awfully quiet," he begins.

"I didn't make it; didn't you hear?"

"You've got next year."

I snort.

He stops me, putting a hand on my shoulder. "Look at me, Gina."

I turn, gaze up into his face. He is smiling. "You've got a whole year to prove him wrong. So do it."

"Yeah," I mumble. "I will."

WISHING ON MY FATHER'S STAR 69

"So you're a little out-of-shape right now. That's understandable; you haven't really been training all that hard. Now you're rested and ready to go again. If you'd run today the way you used to, you would've been in. And if you did it once, you can do it again. All we've got to do is get you back in shape." He thinks for a minute. "Altitude training would be just the thing." He holds up a finger, and I can see him mentally shifting gears, the optimist rising again from defeat. "Northeastern California. Great for altitude training."

"What's altitude training?"

"Oxygen is thinner at higher altitudes, which forces your body to become more efficient. Running'll feel tougher at first, but you'll adapt. If you spend any length of time at altitude, your body makes more red blood cells, which carry oxygen to your muscles. Then when you race at lower altitudes, running feels effortless. More oxygen means more energy and less fatigue."

"Oh."

He claps his hands. "Hot dog. A new adventure. Let's do it. It's gorgeous country, high desert. My favorite."

"Do you think this will work?"

"I sure do. We've got a year; let's make the most of it."

Archer
1988

The first time I lay eyes on Linn Busby, he's a gawky, knobby-kneed kid known only for being the mayor's son. At 12, he's two years older than me. I watch him on my dirt track, outraged he's invaded my turf.

I approach him one afternoon as he does mile repeats, whipping through them with the barest sign of fatigue.

"I'm afraid you're trespassing," I say, my arms folded over my chest.

He stops. "What?"

"You're trespassing. Do you know what *trespassing* means?"

"You mean you *live* here?" He scoffs. "So you sleep out here with the mice and dog turds?"

I ignore his dig. "This is *my* track."

"Do you know who I am?"

"An ugly boy with zits?"

He frowns, snorts. "I'm *Arthur Busby's* son."

I pretend not to know. I won't give him anything. "Who's that?"

"Only the most powerful man in town."

"Yeah, right."

"Yeah, *really*. And if he finds out how you're treating me, he'll run you out of town."

"Ooh, I'm *shaking*."

"Shut up, you little pansy."

"I'm not a pansy."

He folds his arms, narrowing his gaze on me. "Prove it."

"How?"

"Line up with me. We'll see who's the pansy and who's not."

I hear my father's voice in my head. *Toe behind the white line.* Only there's no white line so I draw one in the dirt with my foot.

"What the heck's *that?*"

"The starting line, stupid."

"Only a pansy would think an inch would make that much of a difference."

"That's a bunch of malarkey. I've seen people in the Olympics win by like a *millionth* of an inch."

"That's crap if I ever heard it. Just you watch; I'll beat you by a mile."

So Linn Busby and I go head-to-head, toe-to-toe.

"On three," he says.

"Wait just a cotton-picking minute. Why should you get to do the count-down?"

"Because I'm older than you."

"So?"

"So I got dibs. On three…"

At three, we push off, determination set in our grimaces, resolve clenched in our fists as our cleats bite the dirt and the dust floats up, conquered, behind us. We fly around the track, our arms and legs in furious trajectories, eyes squeezed in concentration, but Linn gains more and more ground with each stride, leaving me embarrassingly far behind. The 5k race in Lodema flashes through my mind: *not again.* I slow down and stop after only one lap, walking breathlessly, my hands on my hips and my head back. Linn whips around me four more times before stopping and jogging beside me, a smirk on his pocked face.

"Told you I'd beat you by a mile," he says. I sense his smirk, a snicker on his lips.

"That wasn't a mile," I snap.

"Each lap's a quarter-mile. Four times around. Five, counting the one I baby-stepped with you."

I glare at him and stick out my tongue.

"That all you got?"

"What do you mean?"

"All you got is an ugly face?" He sneers and jogs away, leaving me alone with my failure.

*

That night, I dream about Linn, going over and over in my mind what I could've done differently. I ran as fast as I could, so how on earth could I possibly run faster? I'm afraid to tell my father how badly I lost, but feel the paradoxical pull to confide, to let him convince me I'm faster than I think, that I could've beaten Linn Busby if I'd really wanted to.

I see Linn again the next morning, a Sunday. He's doing 400s with 200-meter recoveries. I watch for a while the powerful form, the effortlessly graceful stride, his gray-sand colored eyes fixed on the horizon, at that place earth meets sky and wrinkled air distorts the line separating wind from the dust-blown scatter of desert. I feel something hot and insidious flowing through me, jealousy. I cross my arms, skeptical as I watch him.

"Bet you can't do two in a row," I bark.

Linn stops, smiling as though suddenly realizing my presence, though I suspect he's been showing off, knowing all along I was there. "It's not good to bet when the odds are against you," he says, walking up to me, only slightly winded. "What you got?"

"Got?"

"To bet."

"I'm not betting anything."

"You can't bet unless you got something to bet."

"I'm betting my word."

Linn shakes his head. "Not good enough."

"It's all I got."

"You have to bet *something*."

I pull the button out of my pocket and hold it in my open palm.

"What the heck's that?"

"My lucky charm."

He shoots me a skeptical gaze. "Don't try to hoodwink me."

I make a face. "Hoodwink?"

"Yeah. It means dupe, like, trick." He smiles. "You want to see *my* lucky charm?"

"Not really."

"Well, it's a heck of a lot better than that." He nods at the button. "Mine's a real trophy."

I imagine it, a trophy cup the size of my mother's birdbath made of solid gold.

He stands tall, his bony chest thrust out. "I won it."

I scrunch up my face. "I'll bet you cheated to get it, too."

He narrows his gaze on me. "Oh yeah?"

And then he does something incredible. He doesn't do just one fast lap or even two in a row, but *four,* whipping around the track with breakneck speed, his lanky form like a pinwheel caught in a hurricane. And when he finally trots to a stop, he's only slightly winded, proudly smiling as he walks up, a stopwatch in his palm.

"So hand over that picayune charm of yours."

"What? *No.*"

"You made the bet." He shows me a stopwatch reading *4:47.* "You lost."

"How do I know you didn't cheat?"

"You saw me." He smiles, confident. "You can't deny what you saw with your own eyes."

He has a point. I sullenly hand over the button, both awestruck and discouraged.

"Don't worry; I'll give you a chance to win it back."

I look up at him, trying to read the derision in his eyes. "How?"

"By placing another bet. You win, you get your measly button back. I win…You got anything else?"

"Nothing you'd want."

He points at my other pocket, the one bulging with my father's 1ˢᵗ place medal. "What's that?"

I shake my head so hard my neck pops. "I'm not betting."

"Show me what you got."

"No."

He rolls his eyes. "For God sake, I'm not gonna run off with it; just show me what you got."

Reluctantly, I pull my father's medal out of my pocket and Linn snatches it, reading aloud Dad's carved scrawl:

Robert Caleb Dalton, May 13, 1976
Mile, 1ˢᵗ place, Petaluma, CA, 4:07

He looks at me with a mordant glint in his eye. "Think I can beat that?"

I want to say no but I can't. I can't risk making another reckless mistake, a bet that could cost me my father's medal.

"Cat got your tongue?"

"No."

"Then answer me."

I shrug.

"Convinced I'm the best that's ever lived, huh? I knew it."

"I seriously doubt that."

"That a bet?"

"No." I grab for the medal, but Linn holds it up, out of reach.

"I think maybe it is."

"No, it's not. *Give it back.*"

"Not until you give me an answer."

I have to be loyal to my father. "Ok. I don't think you can beat 4:07."

Linn smiles wryly. "You win, you get your button back. I win, I make this first-place medal a second place at the bottom of my junk drawer."

"No. I'm not betting it."

"You already did."

"No, I didn't."

"Did too."

"Did not." I jump, futilely grasping at Linn's outstretched arm. "Come on; give it *back*. You can keep the button."

Linn's blond brows furrow as an irreverent grin forms on his lips. "Why would I want to?" He throws it over his shoulder as he pockets my father's medal and strides away. "California Interscholastic Federation," he calls over his shoulder. "That's high school; I've got *years* to win this bet."

*

I dig through the grass long after dusk, feeling for what I cannot see. I imagine my button's smooth edges, worn soft like the round contours of ocean pebbles. I see it clearly, the black tarnish, hairline streaks of gold through the ebony of age. And I want it back more than I've ever wanted anything. I dig through the grass as though my life depends on finding it, as though getting the button back will somehow negate the tragedy of losing my father's very pride.

"Gina?"

The sound of my name jolts me, sending my heart into my throat. I recognize Dad coming toward me in the dim. I can't face him, can't bring myself to admit what I've lost.

"What on God's green earth are you doing?"

"I lost my button," I sob, despair and regret flowing through me. I want to confess. I want desperately to be forgiven.

"Oh for heaven's sake, we'll get you a new button."

But I can't explain it, can't bring myself to tell him the heartbreaking truth. "It won't be the same," I bawl.

He picks me up, hoisting me effortlessly onto his shoulders as though he's the strongest man in the world, Sampson perhaps. "You'll catch your death out here."

"I don't care."

"You will about the time little green polka-dotted bugs start crawling in and out between your toes doing the mamba."

I laugh despite my sadness.

"I promise we'll look for it in the morning, ok?"

"What if it's gone by then?"

"It won't be."

"But how do you know?"

"It's a treasure, remember?"

"So?"

"Treasure's not meant to be easily found."

I smile in the dark. I want so much to believe him.

"Except by those who are experts at finding buried treasure, that is." My father pats my knee as he carries me home on his shoulders.

On the Road Again
1992

There's something about Dad's willingness to leave Hayward Field (and spend a week at Trusty's Food Mart pumping gas to pay for it) that inspires me. I choose to believe it's his faith in me that takes us back to the desert, that turns the mysterious place he says locals call the devil's playground into my new hope.

"What do you think?" he asks as we drive south on route 17.

I gaze out at an aggressive landscape. There are rugged red and black rocks, scraggly trees poking out from between them like the twisted, gristly hairs on a giant's face. It's an unsettled yet beautiful world.

"You know where all of those rocks came from?"

I shake my head.

"The belly of the world. All of that was once magma. You know what magma is?"

I roll my eyes. "It's not like I don't know anything about earth science, Dad." Even though I'd not seen the inside of a school since Archer, Eugene had good libraries. *Go to school. Get good grades. That's your job.* I tried, Mom. "So this stuff's all lava?"

He chuckles. "You're a smart one, alright." He glances out the window as he drives. "Millions of years ago, these were rivers of red-hot flowing rock. Hard to believe, isn't it?"

I huff, wishing his excitement were catching. "Uh-huh."

"This is high-altitude country. We're at 4500 feet here. It's not tremendous, but it's enough of a lift that it'll help you at sea level."

"Like Myles Lake, right?" Why couldn't we just go back there? Then it would be mine again, like the lost button, the medal, the spikes I've long outgrown, and everything else. But there's no point saying it. Dad is off on a new dream, and Myles Lake is in the past. "Are we going to live here?" I ask instead.

He thinks for a minute. "Maybe."

*

Before he'd quit at Trusty's, Dad had saved enough money to buy a tent. A step up, our own private space. Under the bridge, we had to share our room with other nameless/faceless people, dirt-smeared and stinking. Some were silent. Others talked to themselves or screamed at the air. Sometimes they screamed at us. Dad would tell me not to look, that to do so could be like staring into the eyes of a rabid dog.

The tent, at least, is ours. But it's small. I wake up with the smell of waterproofed nylon in my nose, Dad's back crushed up against mine. Our home, a quarter-millimeter border to another country.

*

Our first night, somewhere not far across the California border, we camp at the base of a ridge that reminds me of giant vertebrae. I imagine the hump of a dinosaur, many times the size of what science says dinosaurs were, an ancient, giant death. A scar healed over by lichen, grass, sagebrush, and junipers. Something ordinary now.

As late afternoon turns into evening and we find ourselves in the ridge's shadow, Dad builds a fire. "Look out there," he points to hills still capped with snow. "It makes me feel like I could go anywhere. All this open space…" He takes a breath. "It makes me feel *free*."

"You think Mom's out there somewhere?"

He sighs. "Somewhere."

*

We eat in silence. Roasted hot dogs and marshmallows on the shaved ends of willow sticks, served with whipped cream from a can Dad had miraculously found somewhere. Fun food. Camp food. An old childhood favorite, sugar and fat caught in the smell of wood smoke. Only now it is our everyday. Funny how favorites can bury themselves under routine.

As twilight settles, the sounds of crickets erupt. Above, I see the pastel glow of a crescent moon and a pinpoint of light from Venus. *Ours,* I think. Like Myles Lake, a new gift to unwrap and explore.

"Time for bed," Dad says finally. "We have a big day ahead; we're going into Leeper tomorrow."

"But it's not even fully dark yet."

He holds up a finger. "Ah…camp rules, remember?"

"Camp rules?"

"When the sun goes down, so do we."

"That doesn't make sense."

"Why not?"

I catch his gaze. "There are no rules out here."

He grins. "There are always rules."

I think of the story Mom once told, when Dad was a boy and his father spent his days passed-out on the couch. "You don't live by rules," I snort.

"Sure I do."

"No you don't."

"Everybody does, Gina."

I scowl at him. "Since when?"

"They may seem invisible, but they're there."

I think of Dad's dad and wonder if that's what he means. When some rules die, others are born. Dad wrote his own back then, when he got himself up and to school, no one telling him what to do. But I don't have the guts to bring it up. "Like when Mom's family thought she was going to Juilliard," I say instead.

His expression changes. "How'd you know about that?"

"She told me. Everybody expected her to go. Is that what you mean?"

He takes a breath. "Yeah. Kind of."

The rules we write are emotional topographies, I realize. Things roll downhill. Like the autumn day Dad gave up on another shot at glory at the California Cross Country Championships and drove away in that Caddie—the same one now parked 20 feet from us—with Mom. It's a kind of momentum. An emotional physics. A domino string or a lit fuse. Once it gets started, it doesn't stop. "I think I understand," I say at last.

*

I dream that night about the heart-stopping moment it occurred to me that love wasn't a given. I'd asked my mother: "Do you still love Dad?"

She caught my gaze. "Love's hard to define. You can love someone and not like them."

My stomach dropped. "You mean you don't like Dad?"

She pursed her lips as though tasting something sour. "Sometimes I do and sometimes I don't."

"But I always like him."

"Of course you do; he's your dad."

"Yeah, but he's *Dad* to you, too. *You* call him *Dad.*"

"It's different, Gina."

"How's it different? Dad's just Dad."

She smiled, but it was a sad smile. "When I was younger, I'd have told you it's all about love. But it isn't always. There are things people do out of desperation. When you come to know that, something breaks and love is never the same."

My mind scrambled. What did she mean? "What do people do out of desperation?"

"They stay together."

I thought about that for a minute.

And as though reading my mind, she said: "Love takes time. Sometimes decades."

The word was grand. "What are decades?"

"Lifetimes." She said the word on a sigh, as though it was heavy. Lifetimes were long.

"I knew your dad from the time he was a little boy. He came from a rough neighborhood. His father drank. Your dad—Robby as he was known back then—still came to school, day after day, no matter what, even when his father was passed out every morning or had disappeared altogether. I admired that because I came from a family that expected certain things."

She took a deep breath, seeming to drift away. "He was one of the popular boys in school, an athlete. Cocky and loud. But I still remembered the vulnerable little kid I'd been friends with." She gazed out the window. "He came from a rough neighborhood, but he'd walk to school all the way from his house, almost six miles away. I envied that because I had a mother who got me up at 5 every morning to practice piano before school and drove me to violin practice afterward. The evenings were all about practicing what I'd learned in the morning. My whole life was planned out. There was never any doubt about what I'd do."

She returned her gaze to me. "I knew that given the chance, I'd bolt. Throw off all those expectations and disappear. If I got the flu, well that was just fine with me. Better yet, I wanted something more serious: measles, mumps, chicken pox, maybe polio so that I wouldn't have to play piano anymore, or mononucleosis so I could do nothing but spend six months in bed. I was so tired. But Robert. Here he was, trekking twelve miles every day just so he could get in on *A Wrinkle in Time* or *Call of the Wild*. I couldn't believe how determined he was."

She put her arm around me. "He was a lot like you, Gina. Driven. Smart and talented—and desperate to use it." Again, she drifted away from me. "I talked my mother into driving him to and from school and that's how it started, our friendship. I loved him so much back then. We were best friends. We caught grasshoppers and climbed trees in the summertime and made snowmen and ice-skated on a backyard pond in the winter. Mom even invited him over around the holidays to treat him to eggnog and spiced pumpkin pie, things your dad wasn't used to having.

"And then, one day…" She shrugged. "He grew up. He became one of the guys. He turned into a jock. He aimed to make his father proud because for some strange reason he was convinced that if he ran fast enough, his father would stop being a drunk. I never understood it, never got how he could erase someone else's mistakes merely by running faster than everyone else, but he was convinced of it, knew it in his heart. So all he did was run, and he approached it with the same determination I'd seen when he'd walked twelve miles every day just to be a normal kid. And it paid off. He was a regional track and cross-country star, on his way to a national championship. And not just that—he was Student Body President and had dreams of getting into politics. He was athletic *and* smart."

The words came before I could stop them. "What happened?"

"He hit a wall. It came to a head at the state high school cross-country championship in 1977. It was fall, a beautiful day, sunshine and all these colorful leaves on the ground. I was in the stands and there was Dad, who was by then a junior in high school, all by himself, still dressed in his street clothes, watching everyone else. I knew right then something was wrong. He'd had a stellar year in 1976, as a sophomore, but since then he'd been struggling.

"I walked down to him and the first thing he did was look up at me with tears in his eyes and say he couldn't do it. There was no way he could run any faster. It was the championship race, and he knew in his gut he couldn't do what everybody expected him to do. I told him he didn't need to, that I knew who he was and loved him anyway. I remember wanting him just to snap out of it and go back to being the little boy who loved climbing trees and catching grasshoppers. I didn't want him to be like me, hopelessly tied down to obligation and expectation. That was something I'd grown used to, but Robert Dalton was different; he was free." She smiled, and for a moment the sadness vanished and I could imagine her as the girl who'd fallen in love.

"I'd always seen him as Peter Pan, as someone who didn't have to worry about everyday things. He'd been on his own so long, free to do as he wanted even as a grade school kid, no one telling him to brush his teeth, no one making sure his homework got done, no one there to punish him for eating cookies before supper. I envied him, I really did. He gave me hope. He made me believe that there was a life beyond the expectation of a family name and a prestigious school. I was on my way to Juilliard and Robert, because of his prowess as a runner, had his pick of any school in the country. He could've gone to Harvard or Yale. But it didn't make him happy."

She took a breath, as though the story had worn her out. "He didn't race that day. Instead, he went back to the locker room, got his gym bag, and walked with me to the parking lot. He'd bought a car; I remember being impressed by that." She smiled. "It was that 1974 Cadillac he still loves, and that night, we slept in it at the side of the road. The stars were brighter than I'd ever seen them and I knew I'd never go home again. We were two kids with the whole town's expectations on our shoulders and we were shucking it all for the unknown. It was the happiest night of my life." My mother brushed a lock of hair out of my face and tucked it behind my ear. "I got you that night."

But the sadness was still there, and I couldn't help but wonder. If I hadn't come along nine months later, would her destiny have led her to Juilliard, or the symphony, or something else far removed from the succession of desert towns and campsites she'd known ever since? Dad loved the stars, sagebrush, and vanishing-point vistas for their own beauties. But did she? She could have been anywhere, doing anything. Was she here because I'd given her no choice?

Archer
1988

I walk across the street to school, my head down as I trudge up the concrete steps. I see Linn at his locker, suddenly not so formidable, but small, like me.

"Hey, Linn the Pin," Joshua Fane says as he shoves Linn into his locker. I see books and papers go flying. "This nincompoop doesn't even wear a jockstrap," Joshua bellows to everyone and no one in particular. "He's not even an A-cup."

Loud guffaws erupt up and down the hall as Linn bends to pick up his books, red-faced.

I watch this spectacle in horror. I don't even want to breathe for fear of being noticed.

"I can't believe your father's the frigging *mayor*," Joshua continues. "I'll bet he hides you in the closet."

Linn shoves Joshua hard, furious tears in his eyes. "Why don't you go fuck yourself?"

"Ooh, I'm gonna tell Ms. Philips you said the F-word."

Linn is sobbing. "Go ahead."

"Come on, cry harder, butt-munch. Boo-hoo-hoo, boo-hoo…"

Linn turns and runs down the hall, away from the taunts and derisive laughter. I walk in the direction he fled, down the stairs, through the huge double doors leading into the isolated hall flanking the gym and locker room. Something about his smallness reminds me of my own and, paradoxically, makes me feel stronger. Even though he took my button and medal, I want to save him the way I'd save a turtle in the road.

I hear quiet sobbing and realize it's coming from the broom closet. Opening it, I find Linn, red-faced and tear-streaked, his knees pulled up to his chest and his arms wrapped tightly around himself. I stare at him, unable to speak.

"Go away," he shouts.

As he shifts to get away from me, I notice the large dark splotch on his slacks, impossible to hide, the pungent stink of urine drifting heavily on the air. He covers it self-consciously with his palms.

"I hate you," he spits. *"Leave me alone."*

I turn and run out of the school's giant double doors, across the street to my house where my father still sits at the kitchen table reading the paper. Dad jumps out of his chair, the paper suddenly on the floor.

"Gina, what's wrong?"

"This kid…" I bawl, gasping for breath. "In trouble…" I point toward the school. "I don't know what to do…" My mind is whirring faster than I can keep track. My confession tumbles out in a terrible, high-pitched, grief-stricken sputter:

"He has your medal. He took the medal. We were running on the track and I tried not to let him but he grabbed it and I tried to get it back but he won't give it back and I don't know what to do I'm sorry, Dad, I'm sorry…" I take a breath.

I notice a subtle smile tugging at the corners of my father's mouth as he takes me in his arms. "Let's not worry about the medal right now." The smile fades. "Where's this kid and why's he in trouble?"

"He's in the closet and I don't know why he's in trouble. I think it's because he said the F-word."

My father's smile returns as he takes me by the shoulders. "Show me."

*

We walk to the school, through the double doors, the familiar passages now seeming foreign. The halls are empty. The bell signaling the end of first period will ring in fifteen minutes, plenty of time for my father and me to find Linn. I lead my dad down the stairs to where the door to the broom closet stands wide open. I feel myself gasp.

"He was here when I left," I say.

Dad glances around quickly. "What'd you say his name was?"

"Linn."

My father speaks in a quiet, gentle voice. "Linn? I'm Gina's dad. She thought you could use a hand."

It's then I see him, peering out from behind the door to the gym. Next to my dad, he is just a fearful child and this makes me feel strong, stronger than Linn. Bigger, even. The boy who beat me on the track is now at my mercy and at my father's.

Dad sees him and approaches, extending his hand, an easy smile gracing his face as his eyes form those violet half-moons. "Robert Dalton."

Linn takes his hand, mumbling, "Linn Busby," though he does not come out from behind the door, ashamed of his show of fear.

I notice the immediate surprise on my father's face. *"Busby?"*

Linn looks down, his face reddening.

"You're Arthur Busby's boy."

"Yeah," Linn says quietly.

"Well, come on out of there."

"I can't."

"Why not?"

"I…just…" Linn looks at me, his face red, scared.

"I spilled water on him," I interject. "He's worried everybody'll think he peed his pants."

I watch as the fear evaporates from Linn's face. For a second, we are friends, though I know it won't last. I once used a stick to move a baby rattlesnake out of the road on one of my long Saturday runs because I didn't want it to get squashed by a car. But I had no illusions that it would do the same for me.

"Well, no one here's going to think anything of it," my father says. "Come on out."

Gingerly, Linn steps out, keeping his palms over the stain.

"Let's get you back to the house," Dad says. "We'll call your father and— "

"No," Linn blurts, terrified.

Trouble comes into my dad's face and his voice gets very quiet. "Why not?"

"He's…not to be bothered."

"Surely, he'll understand—"

"No. Please," Linn's voice has turned imploring and his face is pinched. "He won't understand."

My father nods. "Ok. At least come back to the house. Marie'll get you fixed up good as new."

*

Linn wears one of Dad's oversized work shirts and swims in a pair of his running shorts, his skinny legs sticking out like straws beneath the giant bells of nylon as we wait for the wash cycle to run its course. Mom has fixed peanut-butter-and-jelly sandwiches, and the four of us eat in relative silence.

"Gina tells me you're quite a runner," my father tries. I know he must be recalling the stammering confession I made earlier regarding me and Linn on the track.

The boy stops mid-bite, glancing at me, unsure of what to say.

"Gina trains every day."

"I know," Linn says glumly, returning to his sandwich.

"You guys should train together. Wouldn't that be fun?"

No, Dad, No, I want to shout, throwing him the evilest glare I can muster. I saved him, but he's like that baby snake that would never really be my friend. And I can't let out my secret, that, really, I'm not as good as Dad thinks, not compared to Linn. I lost the medal; I can't possibly live with my father's long-sought hope, also lost.

"I take Gina to the high school track on weekends. You're welcome to come along."

I can't hold my angst in any longer. *"Dad…"*

"Gina Amber Dalton, what have I told you about talking out of turn?" My mother's voice is harsh.

I look down into my plate.

"Come with me right now," she says, getting up.

I follow her into my bedroom.

"Now that was very, very rude of you," she snaps, her arms crossed over her chest, over the floral print dress she's wearing. Her face is pinched in anger, in hurt for the boy at our table. "I want you to march out there right now and tell your friend you want him to join you on the track."

"But *Mom*—"

"I mean it."

I try to think of a word my mother would use. "He's…*snotty.*"

But instead she raises a skeptical eyebrow.

"Really, he is."

"I think you're being a little snotty."

I hang my head, fury pulsing through me. If only she knew how cruelly Linn has treated me, how picked on I am and how utterly miserable. I can't reveal the secret that will make my father lose faith in me: I can't beat Linn on the track—I'd need rockets on my feet, and even then… The little wings my spikes grant are too small. Will always be too small. "I hate him."

She leans down to me, her face level with mine. "Now you listen up. You never, ever say that—about anybody."

"But it's true."

"It's *not* true." She stands up and takes me by the shoulders. "You go out there and make his day." And before I can protest, she has me by the arm and is hauling me out into the kitchen.

"Gina has something to say," she begins, looking at Linn.

I stand with my head down, crimson embarrassment in my face. I might as well be standing here naked.

"Go ahead, Gina. Linn's waiting," Mom pushes.

"You can come with us to the track if you want." I mumble the words, purposely garbling them so that maybe he'll misunderstand.

"Speak up." My mother is still standing with her arms crossed.

"You can come with us to the track if you want," I say, speaking up—only I shout it, cupping my palms over my mouth to emphasize the fact I'm doing exactly what my mother asked. That's when Linn starts giggling uncontrollably and Mom's face gets very red.

"Go to your room," she says.

On the Road
1992

The next morning, I sit sullenly as we bump along on a highway full of potholes. I gaze out at a strange landscape, flat but for a few snow-capped peaks on the horizon. Despite the fact it's desert, it's nothing like home.

It's a hot Saturday, a day for play under the sun. But there's nowhere to play. I feel a pall fall over me. There are no havens here. No cozy houses. No dirt tracks. No Mom despite the fact I look for her under every lonely tree I see. I want to tell Dad: to hell with altitude training. To hell with Luke Havelock and his world-class team and your world-class dream; I want to go home.

But I don't know how to tell him. "This road sucks," I say instead.

"It's better than gravel."

"How far are we going?"

"About 30 miles."

"On *this?*"

"If you think this is the hard part, just wait."

*

The temp agency is nothing more than a cement building that had once been a gas station. An old Shell sign is painted over in pale blue letters: Right To Work Temp Agency: serving greater Leeper for 15 proud years.

What town could possibly be proud of its unemployment status? There isn't much to Leeper. It's a cow town with large ranches on its periphery, a small strip-mall, an A&W, a Collie's Hometown Buffet, and a Lamb's Super Grocer. Its best feature is its sky, like a giant bay above us.

"At least it has a grocery store," I say.

"It's not a bad place," Dad says, nodding as he looks around, grinning into the sun as we get out of the Caddie. "I could settle in here if I had to."

"Let's hope we don't have to," I mumble.

*

The smell of old linoleum fills my nose as we walk in. It's a dismal place with its spare windows, buzzing fluorescent lights, and cement walls. The carpet's gray and thin and fraying where it ends and cracked cement begins. A woman with butterfly glasses, dyed red hair, and bright red lipstick sits at the front, knitting her brow over a list of names.

She glances at us over her glasses as we approach. "Can I help you?"

"We're new in town," Dad says. "Just looking to keep body and soul together at this point." He nods at me. "My daughter and I are both looking for work."

She pulls out a sheet and follows listings with a long painted fingernail. "We got construction and factory work right now."

"We'll take it."

She smiles. "I'll need to see some ID and Social Security cards to get you started."

Something in my father's face falters. "We have our IDs." He thrusts his out to her and nods at me to show mine, a lie with a 16th birthday that's still more than two years away. Something he'd gotten in Eugene, somehow, to keep the truant officers away. One of those things it's best not to ask about, which might have cost him a lot more time pumping gas at Trusty's than anything else he's done since leaving Archer. I've never been able to decide whether that makes me feel wanted...or dirty. At Trusty's, they hadn't asked. The manager had simply paid Dad cash, no questions asked. He'd been desperate for an employee, and Dad had been desperate for work. There have even been times when gas stations have let Dad work just for the chance to put gas in the tank. A fraction of minimum wage for half a day, just to get the chance to drive another couple hundred miles, with no paperwork, no records, nothing but gas in the tank and maybe some stale Hot Pockets or whatever else they're about to throw out.

But it's not going to work today. "I'll need to see your Social Security cards as well," Ms. butterfly glasses says.

Dad looks around, then speaks more quietly: "Look. We've fallen on some really hard times. We don't even have a physical address right now. We've lost our Social Security cards and it's going to take weeks to get them. We need money now."

"I can't help you without those cards, sir. I'm sorry."

My father is imploring. "Please."

"It's the law, sir."

*

The money Dad used to get us here from Oregon is gone, our last pennies put into the Caddie's gas tank 100 miles ago. He *could* have pumped gas a few days longer, giving us a few more dollars, a few more days' grace. But as always, his excitement over this new dream eclipsed any such practicality. The moment he thought he had enough, we were on the road, the money—or lack of money—again fitting neatly around the contours of his whim, with zero room to spare.

But there's a dumpster behind Lamb's Super Grocer where we find unopened loaves of bread, day-old pastries, and expired canned goods. And like those nail clippers Dad bought before my visit to Luke Havelock's office, a $2.99 can opener proves to be a practical purchase once we have the means. Though it's hard to relinquish the $2.99 after two days' worth of can and bottle collection along the side of the road. Some have been there so long that their colors are bleached, the bold red-and-blue of Pepsi baby-blanket hued. Others are wrapped in weeds, having grown into the ground until the pale green of a Mt. Dew can barely be found, glinting through the threads of dry, brown grass.

After buying the can opener, we start from zero again, searching for aluminum and glass cents in the grass like gems. But they don't feel like gems. Instead, they feel worthless. Like I'll be doing this forever and it still won't amount to anything.

"Are we almost done?" I snap, a few days later.

"We're done when we can eat."

"When will that be?"

"When we've got more than 65 cents in our pockets."

What could 65 cents buy? A few gumballs, or one of those toys you could get in a plastic bubble out of the vending machine at Lamb's as you walk out through the sliding glass doors, like an aperitif after you've shopped for real things. But we can't buy real things. Even the gumball seems impossible.

I sit down on the baked ground, tears blurring it until it's mud.

My father is impatient. "What is it, Gina?"

"I can't do this."

"Do what?"

"Live this way." I look up into his face. "I want a home, Dad. I want real food."

His voice is hard. "Real food keeps you alive. What you want is gourmet."

"It's garbage, Dad."

"It's what people consider garbage. There's a difference between perception and reality."

"It's in the dumpster. That's the reality; it's garbage." Then I think of the rumbling, the thundering hunger, angry, spiked, and stabbing, stomach acid like the steel of a dagger. Those are the times when I weaken, when I decide I don't care who has taken a bite of my sandwich.

"You're not starving to death," Dad says.

"So?"

"So that's enough."

*

I don't agree. I don't agree that not dying should be enough to live on. I train harder than I ever have. I run up the ridge and down again, training my strength on steep volcanic rocks that tear my shoes and gash my legs when I trip. I jump over sagebrush, bounding over the scratchy branches and gnarled wood that sometimes leaves me with slivers. I sprint on the dirt road leading to our always-changing camps, dusty tracks that extend from horizon to horizon but never fail to lead away from here. I run twice a day, reminding myself as the sun comes up and as it sinks that there is more to life than this. I run because however beautiful this place is, it's not Myles Lake and can never, ever be "enough." I never once think of the day I ran into the dawn, simply for the joy of it. There is sometimes pleasure in the running here, but there is also purpose. My father's purpose or my mother's, I'm not sure, but this is not Myles Lake and I do not intend to remain here forever.

I run to the pine forest and back. To the lake and back. To the ridge and back, and I chart my summer in my routes around this, my home, the shape of my life an endless loop I hope will end in a place other than where it began. In each direction are landmarks I will never reach, snow-capped peaks in the distance reminding me that there is always something farther away, something untouchable. The unreachables keep despair at bay because in the back of my mind is the maybe.

Archer
1989

Every Saturday morning, my father gets me up at dawn while his Cadillac idles roughly in the driveway, blowing hot clouds of carbon monoxide into the frigid air. I put on my singlet and shorts, a fleece pullover, and my sweats, finally lacing up my shoes when we're ready to face a cold, dark morning. We pick up Linn on the north side of town, the wealthy side, and when we arrive at his house, the light upstairs in the old Victorian is always on behind lace curtains. I make out the silhouette of a man hard at work, the mayor attending to his citizenry while most of the world still sleeps.

"You ready for a hard workout?" Dad pipes up, gazing into the rearview mirror at the sullen boy.

All Linn ever does is shrug.

We ride in silence, arriving at the track just as the eastern horizon begins to glow. On the line, my father changes from gregarious dad into coach, a stopwatch in hand.

"Today we're doing something a little different. Mile repeats. They're tough but they'll build both your speed and stamina."

I see a trace of the old smirk on Linn's face. He's good at these.

Dad glances at his watch. "Ok. Do your warm-up and be back on the line at 0600."

When it's time, we put our toes on the line and lean forward, two silhouettes in the twilight, still but for the breath billowing out in hot, white clouds. We wait for the sound of my father's whistle. When he blows it, we bolt, sprinting hard down the straight, way too fast.

"Remember, these are *mile* repeats," Dad shouts after us.

But that doesn't matter. Linn and I are alone in the world, vying for dominance. A king and a queen in a fiefdom of numbers and precious metals. Gold. Or silver. I think of my father's medal and realize it's worth more than gold, unquantifiable. The sprint around the track suddenly represents a bid to win it back. But Linn is leading with an impressive stride, nimble and graceful despite the gawkiness that takes over the minute he steps off the track. Jealousy surges through me; I am no longer my father's only hope.

Linn finishes strong, barely breathing hard. But my stride's been reduced to an uneven lurch as I struggle for air, wheezing and coughing as I cross the line. How I dream I might run like Linn someday, effortlessly invincible. I imagine what it must be like, sprinting yet feeling nothing, as though in a dream. A mind detached from the body. Dad lifting me into his arms as *the winner*. Linn, conceding his failure, handing back my father's medal. But it's an impossible wish. Deep down, I know I'll never outrun Linn Busby.

I burst into tears.

"Gina, what is it?" I sense a note of impatience in my dad's voice.

"I don't feel good."

"Well, you went out too fast. What do you expect?"

I shoot a menacing glare in Linn's direction. "It wasn't too fast. *He* did it."

"He's older than you are. And he's a boy."

"So?"

"Boys are faster than girls."

The words send me reeling. How could my father be so biased? How could he like Linn more? Think him capable and me not? Pin his greatest hopes on a cruel boy I can't even stand? A boy I can't *beat*.

"You're lying," I shout. *"I'm* faster. I'm better."

"Gina Amber—"

"No, I'm better." I burst into sobs, my dreams vanishing. "I thought you said *I* could be the best, not him. He's just a mean boy with a mean dad and he's stupid and ugly and everybody laughs at him because he looks like a giraffe with zits."

The world stops as my father grabs me by the arm, dragging me off the track. I see Linn standing at the edge, defeated suddenly, his face red and pinched in fury. Not a winner at all, but an unwanted guest, a social burr, a pariah.

At the car, Dad shoves me into the front seat and gets in the driver's side, slamming the door harder than usual. We sit there a few excruciating seconds, silent, the morning around us still and quiet and cold. Finally, he speaks:

"I've never been so disappointed in my life."

His words make a terrible heat rise into my face and I feel a sense of shame I've never felt before.

"Look at me."

Terrified, I look up into his face, into those eyes the color of violets.

"I didn't raise you to be a loser."

"I tried to win—"

"I'm not talking about winning. I'm talking about what you said back there. I'm talking about how you treat other people."

I look down, defeated, despairing.

"It's never ok to say things you can't take back, Gina. You will never win if you act that way. I mean it. You act like that and you'll always lose. And you lost today. Big time."

I can't control my tears, now rolling liberally down my face, falling onto my hands like rain.

"I think you need to stop running for a while."

I look up, imploring, desperate for forgiveness. "No. *Please*, I'm sorry."

"No, Gina. This is a hard lesson. If you want to win, you have to act like a winner and I don't see a winner sitting where you're sitting. You need to think about what it means to win and I'm not talking about fast times or medals. I'm taking you home."

I'm crying, begging. "No, Dad. I'm sorry."

But he's already started the engine. "I'm going to get Linn. You wait here and we'll be right back." His voice is somber, containing none of the mirth it's usually brimming with.

"I'll tell him I'm sorry," I try, desperate to win his absolution.

But he shakes his head. "Not good enough."

*

He takes a long time and I wonder if he's abandoned me, having totally given up on a daughter who has disappointed him so deeply. I imagine him and Linn finishing the workout, the camaraderie between them, my father like a second dad to a boy whose own father couldn't care less, and I fear in a sudden hopeless rush that I'm being replaced. I'm no longer my dad's gem, no longer the best of the best in his eyes, no longer perfect.

By the time they come back, I've buried my head, refusing to be a part of the world. I feel the displacement of cool air as my father gets in beside me and the subtle rock of the car as Linn climbs into the backseat. I feel the car lurch and rev, the hum of pavement under tires, the swish of other cars as they pass us, the lull of movement. We come to a stop and I hear one of the backdoors open and close. Nothing else. I wonder how they spoke, if my father reassured Linn like he once reassured me.

Again, we drive. This time, I feel conspicuous. With Linn gone, my father will surely speak to me. But I'm surprised when the silence continues, as though I'm invisible, as though I've truly wished myself away, vanished from the world. We drive for a while, further than what should've gotten us home. After what seems like an eternity, I feel the car slow, the right front tire going over a small abutment, the transition from pavement to gravel, the shift from *drive* to *park*.

That's when I feel it, the palm on my shoulder. And I can't contain my grief, the sobs escaping like a succession of violent storms. I want his forgiveness so badly, his strong arm around me, that familiar pull of mirth between us. I let him hold me, my tears staining his shirt, content for a while just to be his again. I relish getting something back I thought I'd lost forever, relief flooding through me the way it does after a nightmare.

I look up as he wipes away my tears and see that he is smiling. He nods toward the window.

"Look out there."

And as I do, I realize we're at Myles Lake.

"I want you to think of this place every time you get angry or sad," he says.

"Why?"

"Because the land will always be here." He looks over at me. "No matter what else happens, win or lose, happy or sad, it's here. If it's beautiful to you, then you're among the luckiest people in the world."

I feel my brow knit. I don't understand. What's this got to do with winning or losing? With me or Linn? With good and bad people?

"It's easy to get caught up in things, to get hung-up on life. I know you wanted to win today. I know how badly you want to beat Linn."

I look down, feeling my face color.

"You're always going to feel this way, Gina. There's always going to be someone faster than you or smarter than you or more accomplished than you. You're going to feel bad sometimes. You're going to lose sometimes. You do your best. You wish your competitor well. You're gracious when you lose but it doesn't mean it won't hurt. I'm giving this to you…" My father nods toward the lake. "It's yours when you need it. When you lose. When you're hurt."

I think I understand. I look out at the vista, the early morning palette of mute colors, salt water and sunshine. *Mine.*

"Next time Linn beats you on the track, and he will, you think of this place."

"I thought you said I had to stop running."

"Only for a while. I think it's important that you take a step back. That's needed every now and then to get perspective." He gazes at the horizon. "This'll help."

But my hurt feelings return to me in a rush. "Why do you like him so much?"

A smile graces Dad's face. "He's a good kid."

"He's a *jerk.*"

"Sometimes."

"All the time."

He squeezes my shoulder. "He's gifted, like you. And he's faster, not because he's better than you or more deserving than you. But because he's talented—and he's older. You'll never be the fastest, Gina."

"I don't believe that."

He shrugs. "Then don't believe it."

I'm surprised by my father's dismissive statement. I look up at him and he's inexplicably smiling, those half-moons dancing. "Part of sport is having impossible dreams," he adds. "Don't believe it if you don't want to believe it."

I feel determination flood through me, an unsettling mix of hope and anger. "You think I can beat him?" I want to hear it from my father's lips, his undaunted belief in me.

But instead he takes a deep breath, shakes his head. "No."

I feel my hope slip away, the anger taking over. *"No?"*

"Believe in yourself, Gina. If you think you can beat him, you can try. What I think won't determine what your best is."

But it's not good enough. Again, I feel frustration and hurt over my dad's seeming inconsistency. What does it all mean? *You'll never be the best but you can try? Have impossible dreams, but there'll always be someone faster, smarter, better?*

"I thought you wanted me to be the best," I say, looking down, tears clouding my vision. "Why don't you still believe it?"

"I want you to try your best. But keep it all in perspective. Look at me." He puts a finger under my chin, bringing my face up so that I can meet his gaze. "I have a secret. I was once where you are right now and I was on top of the world. You know what happened?"

I hold my breath, recalling my mother's story of his walk-away day at the California State Cross Country Championships.

"I threw it all away."

I swallow hard, the impulse to finish his sentence flowing through me like a river: *And then you got me...*

"I was pigheaded. I didn't know how to handle the inevitable disappointment of losing. I thought I'd be the best. I thought I'd go to the Olympics and be a professional athlete. I thought I'd run the perfect mile and be the next Roger Bannister."

I wait, knowing the little secret tucked between the grander pronouncements, in those quiet hours of the night, after they'd both given up and walked away, me appearing in that smallness somehow, like a tiny prism throwing color across a whole room.

"4:07 wasn't good enough for that, and I couldn't imagine running any faster. So I gave it up and tried something else." *And something else, and something else, and something else*, I think. But a sadness has come into my dad's face.

The Devil's Playground
1992

One evening, below the massive ridge where we've camped undisturbed for three months, I run loops around our campsite. Time to practice greatness. I think of Luke and those intense brown eyes on the lookout for a champion. An emerald in the grass. Me, I hope.

Beyond the ridge's shadow is sagebrush and sun. Time to explore something new. I take off, cross-country, trading the grit and gravel of the road for the obstacle course of waist-high wilderness. I run east, toward a mesa, blue-gray on the horizon. It's unattainable, but I pretend it isn't. I could run forever toward it, that dove-colored smear. A prize in the sky, like that Olympic gold I imagine. Then I see someone who knows this place better than I do. A doe, eyes shining in the sun. She is skittish as she dances away from me, leaping over sagebrush, graceful in her escape. I chase her. Toward an imaginary finish line, that mesa perhaps. Like her, I bound over sagebrush, trying to be as graceful, convinced that if I could run like her, I'd have no problem getting into Luke Havelock's program.

Then she is gone, vanished in an instant. I stop, a knot in my throat, my heart knocking wildly against my ribs. Something is wrong. I hear her. A bleat. A cry. Ear-splitting and hair-raising. I pick my way through the sagebrush, goose bumps on my arms despite the heat.

Then I see it. The opening that swallowed her. A cave like a mouth, hidden by sagebrush. She has fallen at least twenty feet and the grace I saw moments before now lies ruined beneath me. But the fall wasn't merciful; she is still alive.

My shout is reflexive. *"DAD!"*

I'm crying by the time I reach him, my words wracked by grief and fear. "Dad…there's… hurry…there's this…I was running and I saw this…deer…and she…I chased her…I didn't mean to…she fell…"

He grabs my shoulders. "Gina, slow down. What's going on?"

I point. "Please…please come…I don't know what to do…I can't reach her."

*

I show him. But I can't look at her. Like a coward, I stand away from the edge, cover my eyes with one hand and point with the other. I can't stop crying.

"We'll help her," Dad says.

"How?"

We run back to camp. I watch as Dad pulls out a canvas bag from the trunk of our Caddie, reaches into a pocket and withdraws something shining and stunning, loads it with bullets and walks back toward the mesa we'd been chasing.

"Dad, what are you doing?" My heart hammers as a spike of lactic acid courses through my legs, adrenaline white-hot, mouth like cotton. I'm sweating even though I'm suddenly cold.

"We're helping her."

"We can't *kill* her." My voice is not my own. It's high-pitched. Scared.

He looks at me, puts a hand on my arm. "Gina, listen; we can't get her out. She's suffering. The only option is to set her free."

"But that's not setting her free." My words dissolve into sobs.

"You'll understand someday."

"No I won't." I let him go, watching as he continues through the sagebrush to that place worthy of nightmares. I cover my ears, but it's not enough. I hear the shot through the chaotic pulse of my own heart, a memory I know I'll never shed.

*

We're on the road again. I wake up to rain on the windshield and the scents of gas and wet pavement. I rub my eyes and see a Chevron sign looming above me. He's about to fill the tank, again dumping every cent we have into it. I sit up. "Where are we?" When he'd awoken me to break camp hours before sunrise, all he'd said was that it was time to move on.

"We're headed to Portland."

I'm suddenly wide-awake. "*What?*"

Dad smiles. "Where it all begins."

"I thought that was Eugene."

"Remember Luke?"

My heart lurches.

"We're gonna show him this time."

"But I'm not ready." I sit up straighter, suddenly angry. "How could you do this? I never said I was ready. You said we had a *year.*"

"Life is short, Gina; you've got to grab it while you can."

"But, Dad, I can't—"

"That whole thing yesterday made me think." He looks over at me. "That could've been you."

"Huh?"

"That doe might have saved your life."

*

The coach stands with his arms crossed, unimpressed in the rain. My legs feel like lead and my throat is on fire. I can't do this. Not today. Not with him watching. My father is, once again, the reticent man with the hat in his hands. And who am I? A nobody trying to be good. Not great, just good enough.

I imagine a nameless, faceless nemesis in the swath of gray ahead, in the rain, gloom, and the painted white lines of a mediocre destiny. I'll do my best and hope it is enough. I take a breath, hit *mode* on my watch—a gift from a time before 'luxury' had become synonymous with simple things like a chance to wash my hair—and wait for the chrono to come up 00:00. A clean slate. A blank page. There is no greater excitement (or angst) for a runner than 00:00 on a clock, the possibilities limitless.

"On your mark," Luke says. I imagine them around me, all those champions I used to see on TV, the ones in my head as I ran my first race around that dirt track with two people cheering. "Set." I lean forward, poised. "Go." I hit *start* on my watch and go out hard. I don't look at them, pretending that I'm by myself, running for all of those phantoms in my head. I'm running for Dad, and for Mom.

I fly around the bend, down the straight, around another bend, down another straight and do that for seemingly countless laps. I don't dare look at my watch. Because the splits don't matter. I'm running as fast as I can. There is nothing in me that will push me farther, faster, not even a lousy time. This is it. My potential. My capacity. My best. The thought terrifies me.

I'm hurting, but that doesn't matter, either. Nothing matters except my legs, turning over and over, my feet, one in front of the other, my heart, pumping hard and fast, the swish of blood in my ears, my lungs, taking in air, breathless, but not so breathless I can't feel the strength in my body. I'm fit. Not great. Not as fast as Dad. Or as Prefontaine, but good enough to be proud of this body I've created through my twilight adventures in the tired ruts of abandoned desert roads.

And that's when it hits me. The intimacy of it. That nakedness, the scratches from sagebrush on my thigh, weed seeds in my socks rubbing my ankles raw, the cold air stinging my hands and making my eyes water, the color of the sky and the shadows, the silence of the hour, a time of day most people never really know. Me at my best. Not a medal, but all of those other common forgotten things as veritable and weighty as gold in my palm. I think of them now as I run and as Luke watches.

"Time," he yells at last. He looks at his watch, nods, an eyebrow arched. "Not bad. You've definitely got potential."

Potential. It's a step up. A rung up the ladder from *guts.* As I stand in the rain, I feel a sense of pride I haven't felt in a long time. I've got potential. It's better than nothing.

Archer
1989

"Up and at 'em," my father says, poking his head through my bedroom door, already clad in a coach's attire, sweats and tennis shoes with two stopwatches dangling like pendulums around his neck, a bright smile on his face. "Glad to be back on track? Pardon the pun…"

My enforced layoff ended three weeks ago, and I should be enthusiastic, but I'm not. "Can I skip it this morning?"

"What?"

"I can't do it today."

"You don't look sick to me."

"You've got Linn. I don't know why you need me."

His smile fades. "Don't tell me this is still some kind of competition between you two."

"No, Dad. It's just that…" I grit my teeth and finally say what I've been meaning to say for months: "I don't like him."

My father sits next to me on the bed. "You know, when I was a youngster it would've been nice to have had someone I could've gone to about my doubts. We all have them. I don't think Linn has anyone he can go to, confide in."

"So? Why's it your job?"

"He's talented. And I'm the only one who seems to see it."

"So if he wasn't talented, you wouldn't care?"

He hesitates. "He's got too much potential to risk wasting it, let's just put it that way. He needs some direction."

"He reminds you of you."

My father sits back, a subtle, surprised smile on his lips. "Maybe."

Something about that gives me the courage to ask: "When are you going to get your medal back?" My heart hammers. His answer will tell me whether Linn has taken my place.

Then the heart-stopping moment: "I think Linn should keep it."

The lump in my throat explodes like a cloudburst. I don't want to cry in front of him, but I can't help it. I feel his palm on my shoulder. "If he's that determined to keep it, he needs it more than we do."

"*I* need it," I shout. "You gave it to *me*." I turn over in bed, away from my father. I feel the bed relinquish his weight as he gets up and I realize that he is once again disappointed in me and my unwillingness to accept Linn as an extended part of our family. I turn over toward the door after he leaves, staring after him, tears in my eyes. *Why can't I be good enough for you?*

But to be good enough, I have to run, so I get up, put on my tights and my favorite hooded sweatshirt.

My father's sitting at the kitchen table, sipping coffee and reading the paper.

"I've changed my mind," I announce.

*

We pull up in front of Linn's, and he's already waiting on the wraparound porch, bundled up, his long legs in sweatpants, a stocking cap on his head, looking utterly ridiculous. It's war, I tell myself.

"You ready to set the track on fire?" my dad pipes up as he gets in.

Linn nods sullenly.

"This cold weather shouldn't last; we'll be getting into spring before you know it."

Silence.

"We've got hoar frost on the trees, believe it or not."

I want to bark, *stop trying so hard. Stop talking about things that don't matter. Stop trying to be his father...*

"What's got you in a tizzy?"

Finally, I think. *It's about time Dad called him out.* But I suddenly realize my father's looking over at me.

"So is sitting with my arms crossed a crime?" I snap.

"It is now. What's the problem?"

"Nothing."

"We can't start the morning off this way. You've got to train in a positive state of mind if you're going to get everything you can out of the workout."

"You've got to be kidding; you're griping at *me?* What about him?" I shove a thumb over my shoulder. "He's the one sulking."

"Gina Amber Dalton; you mind your tongue."

I shake my head, disbelieving.

*

On the track, I refuse to speak to Linn despite my father's admonishments for me to straighten up. I watch as he strides effortlessly down the track ahead of me, agile as I lurch across the line, breathless. I'm too far behind to ever catch up. Going on eleven, I'm already a wash-up. After the workout, we drop Linn off wordlessly.

I watch as he goes up the steps, through the front door, not once looking back. "Why do you care?" I ask Dad resentfully. *"He* doesn't even care."

"He's thirteen."

"So?"

"He's young. He'll care someday." There's a sadness in my father's face as he stares after Linn.

"Mom told me the story," I begin, realizing I promised her I'd never tell.

He looks over at me. "What story?"

"About you and her." I look down. "About the night you stopped running." I want to say *about how you traded your dream for me, how, were it not for your failure, I wouldn't even be here.*

I feel his eyes on me. "Is that a fact?"

I can't look at him, but I nod.

"There's a lot you don't understand, Gina. You've never had to win a parent's love."

I look up at him.

"I'm not trying to single you out for criticism in front of Linn, but you've got to understand that you're an example for him. I'm proud of you. And if truth be told, I like showing you off. You're smart and you're funny—and you're someone to emulate. You know what *emulate* means?"

I shake my head.

"It means to follow one's example. I want Linn to follow your example. I want him to work hard, to be enthusiastic, and to look forward to a decent future. You're all those things and more—when you want to be. The problem is, you haven't been yourself."

I feel my eyes well up.

He puts a finger under my chin. "I'll tell you the truth; I don't have much faith in Linn, I really don't. You can have all the talent in the world and it does you no good if you throw it all away on cynicism and anger. Attitude is everything; I know that from firsthand experience. There's such a thing as apathy, as really not caring. I don't know what your mother told you, but I didn't quit because I didn't care. If anything, I cared too much. I don't know if Linn's capable of being helped or not. But the one thing I *do* know is that I have more faith in you. So be that person I have all the faith in the world in. That's who I want to show to Linn."

First Race
Portland, Oregon
1992

I breathe evenly as I do my warm-up, striding up and down a length of the track, sweat making my jersey stick to my back. I welcome the breeze, cool on my temples. I close my eyes against the sun, queasiness swelling through me. This is it. I have to make good. Luke is watching, and how I place will determine whether he agrees to coach me. We'll start and finish the 5000m course on the track, following a trail toward the water tower before dipping down along the back of the municipal pool and coming out on a sidewalk, making a giant loop through the school grounds and a park, finishing back at the high school.

My race is first. It's a pre-season meet—a mix of high school girls, middle schoolers, and people like me—put on by the city Parks and Recreation Department. I'm running unattached, as I will if Luke takes me on because his team isn't affiliated with any specific school, though his athletes regularly run against the best in the state. I test the word: "unattached…" It suits me. Since when have I ever been truly attached to anything, to any one place, to even the ones I love? Leeper, Archer, the high desert, Pre's trail, even Myles Lake are but memories now. Garbage bins, a sleeping bag under a bridge or under a tent, always, always on the move – that's the reality. I'm Unattached. A drifter with no roots except a dirt track I've not seen in years. Or worse, a reluctant drifter who's always uprooted only to be replanted in a new, hostile soil.

Runners on your marks...

Toes line up. Athletes take their stances, jockeying for position. I feel the final throb of nerves just as the gun goes off and the frontrunners take off like shots. I try to stay with them, but already my legs feel like lead. I don't know if I can do this. Two hundred meters out, I'm tired. My chest heaves and my heart pounds. I have to do this. I stay with the top two girls, determined to hang on. We scramble up the rocky trail circling the water tower and my legs burn from the effort, my feet slipping on the stones and dirt. Spots swim around my head and nausea roils like a snake in my gut. It is too damned hot. Upon reaching the tower, we head mercifully downhill. My stride lengthens and I lean slightly forward, gaining momentum on the rocky trail as I push past one of the girls. I see the other still ahead, thick ponytail bouncing, muscled legs churning, arms pumping. I chase her, determined to make her work for her win. We rocket down the trail, me a stride behind. Whipping out onto the pavement behind the pool, I match her stride for stride, close enough for her to see my shadow. I am gaining strength, pushing aside my exhaustion, determined now to win. I hold pace with her as we bolt along beside one of

Portland's main streets where curious drivers must be gawking.

We are less than a mile from the school and I surge ahead, now in a full sprint. She follows suit, matching my surge and I suddenly regret I've made such a move. I can't afford now to slow down and I'm not sure I can hold this pace. My legs burn and I can taste the eggs I had for breakfast. I know that when I hit the line, I'll lose everything in my stomach, but for now I've got to hold it together. When I see the brick building of the high school, I churn my legs harder, sprinting faster and faster as we hurtle down toward the track with one lap left. Just one lap. A quarter of a mile. At the turn I hear my father's voice:

"Come on, Gina. Don't slow down. Don't look back—"

I continue to sprint, my competitor now next to me. We are neck-and-neck. It's going to come down to a strategic lean, a hundredth or a thousandth of a second. How can victory and defeat be separated by so narrow a margin? Right now it doesn't seem possible, not when I'm giving it everything I've got and how I'll feel tonight will depend on whether an inch of me is ahead of the second-place finisher. Victory is so fickle.

"Come on, Gina. You've got her. Come on—"

I close my eyes. I lean. I break the tape and, next to me, so does she. A woman at the line tears a tag off my race number and writes something on it. I wonder briefly who was first before I double over and vomit and then my embarrassment takes over. I realize when I straighten up that everybody in the world is looking at me.

My father rushes up and wraps his arms around me, smiling that stunning smile. "A damn good first race."

I swallow the remaining bile. I want to know who won but I don't dare ask.

He reads my expression, his grin broadening. "Do you think you won?"

I'm afraid to answer. Instead, I stand there, dumbly looking at him, wanting him to tell me; I can't assume anything. I don't want to be let down. I don't want to let him down.

"Well, come on; don't look at me like that. How do you think you did?"

I swallow hard, summoning the courage to speak. "I think I won."

He smiles even wider, his rugged features glowing with pride. "You done good, kiddo."

I want more. I want to win. I want to be good. I am determined now. "What was my time?"

He points over at a scoreboard with times posted. "Go take a look."

The first name under the listing for the girls' race reads: *Gina Dalton, 15 and under, 1ˢᵗ place, 18:36.* I feel myself smile. I'm first. I've never been first in my life. I won. I've never won before. Not in a race with more than one person.

I feel my dad's hand on my shoulder. "Let your pride fuel your next workout. You can do even better, I guarantee you."

*

I realize as I walk around the track, cooling down, how beautiful the afternoon is and how light I feel. Nothing can take away the glow of knowing for the first time that I'll make it, that no one can take away my drive, my will to be something better than what I am. In my pocket is a medal like my father's, only it's in the shape of a shoe with wings, gold-colored and fitted with a blue ribbon so that I can wear it around my neck when the mood strikes. I am an athlete. And I will always be at least that much.

"You've made it," Dad says, taking me out of my daydream.

I look up at him and see that he is smiling, too.

"I'm so proud of you, Gina."

I feel my face flush. "It's just one race."

"One was enough; Luke's agreed to coach you."

My breath catches. *"Really?"*

"Really."

Again, I am in my father's arms.

Archer
1989

Since becoming Linn's coach, Dad has made the mayor's life his obsession. He wants to know which times are best to drop Linn off at home, which weekends the mayor wants an afternoon alone to work and on which nights the mayor is indisposed. I don't know if he's doing it for the mayor or for Linn, if there's a part of him that wants to step in and save Linn the way he's never been saved. For all the bragging my father does about being self-sufficient and wily, there's a side of him that wants to be rescued.

Even my eleventh birthday is snubbed as the mayor's evening town hall becomes an all-day preparation, Dad making sure to have his best suit perfectly pressed and his hair combed just so. I peer at him from around a corner as he straightens his tie. He catches my gaze in the mirror along with my long face.

"What's the matter with you?"

"Can't we do something, like, *normal?*"

He smiles. "You mean you're not ready for your first civics lesson?"

"Dad, I just want to go on a picnic or something. Maybe up at Myles Lake. Can't we do that?"

He lays a placating palm on my shoulder. "You go put on your best dress and then we'll see."

*

Dad pulls up in front of Kazatimiru's and I notice his grin, wry yet expectant. I'm supposed to be excited about this, impressed. That's it—he wants me to be *impressed,* but as I gaze at the other cars in front with their glossy wax jobs and perfectly expensive brand names I realize ours doesn't fit, with its chipped okra-colored paint. We stand out in a place we don't want to stand out.

"Dad, I just want to go on a picnic. Can't we go to Myles Lake?"

I notice his disappointment, his fading smile. "You'll like it, Gina. It's Kazatimiru's."

I gaze at the pink stucco façade, the ornate wrought-iron balcony, tables outside in the afternoon sun adorned with sprays of flowers and candles, the mullioned windows and decorative strap-work, the brass-and-iron door. It's the most upscale restaurant in Archer, the place the wealthiest of the tri-county area come to socialize and do business. I feel a sudden all-encompassing sadness, the kind you never get over, never forget. I want to hang on to that place Dad said I could go anytime I felt bad; I want to feel the sweep of wild grass and breathe in the brackish scent of salt water, stark alkaline shores like a smooth line through a painting separating light from dark, land from water. But I can't; it's fading too fast and all I see is the disappointment in my father's face and the pressure to like this, to want this, to be like everybody else. He expects it from me now. I'm eleven, old enough to make value judgments, old enough to want something besides what I can dig up in the front yard.

I feel awkward as we walk in, Dad in his suit and me in my best, frilliest dress with the puffiest sleeves you can imagine. Normally I feel like a princess in it but today I feel like this is pretend and I'm in my mother's clothes playing dress-up. I feel stupid. As my eyes adjust, I see an elegant room with warm wood paneling, abstract pictures on the wall and tables draped in fine white linen, a flickering candle atop each. A slim blonde approaches, smiling, clad in a black skirt and dress top with a gold nametag that says *Constance*.

"Can I help you?"

"Two for lunch," my father says proudly.

"Right this way."

I notice the mayor sitting at a corner table against the wall near the back, by himself, familiarly clad in a suit and tie, reading glasses perched primly on the bridge of his nose as he reads. I forgot that this is one of the mayor's favorite haunts.

Arthur Busby looks up, catching my eye before I have a chance to look away. He smiles, something alight in his steely eyes, but I can't tell if it's entirely friendly or not. "Why, Robert, what brings you in here?"

I feel my father's hand tighten on my shoulder. "It's Gina's birthday."

The mayor's gaze falls on me. "Happy Birthday. This must be quite a treat for you. You're welcome to join me if you like." The mayor returns his gaze to my father.

I clutch my dad's hand, my nails digging in. I feel him flinch, pull away, the pain sharp enough for him to notice. *No, Dad, no…*

"I'd hate to disturb your work, Mayor. But thank you for the offer."

Arthur Busby nods, smiling. "Suit yourself. Enjoy your lunch…Oh, and Robert? You've really done wonders for Linn. I can't believe his self-confidence since he's trained with you. Really, you're a marvel."

"Really?"

"Really. If I could, I'd give him to you." The mayor laughs, uncertainly. "I think he's turning into a little Robert Dalton; it's awfully cute."

Dad's face reddens and I sense his tension. He tips his head politely. "Thank you, Mayor." We sit, a welcome distance away.

"Are you ok, Dad?"

There's anger in his face. "Yeah, hon, I'm fine. Let's just enjoy your birthday. My Gosh. *Eleven* already. I can hardly believe it myself." His face turns sad. "You're growing up too fast."

I wonder if he means it the way every other parent means it, as one of those platitudes, or if it's about his regret, a life wasted, dreams that never quite came true. Time going by so fast it can't be accounted for, like an assembly-line screw-up.

Then as quickly as it came, the sadness disappears, not gone, but so thoroughly suppressed you can almost believe it never was there. "So what do you think?" Dad makes a sweeping gesture. "Pretty darned deluxe, huh?"

I nod even though I want nothing more than to run out. As Constance approaches with the menus, I'm grateful to her for distracting him from my disillusionment. "I already know what I want," I blurt. "Grilled cheese."

"You haven't even looked at the menu," Dad says.

"No, I want grilled cheese."

Constance takes a sharp breath. "Unfortunately, we don't have—"

"Grilled cheese."

"Do you have a kid's menu?" Dad asks.

"Um, *no,*" Constance says. She looks at me expectantly, her drawn-on eyebrows arched.

"Let's try something really different. How about escargot," Dad says. I see a suppressed smile tugging on the corners of his mouth.

"Well, it's not exactly grilled cheese, but it's on the menu," Constance says, deadpan.

"What is escargot?" I ask as she walks away.

"You sure you want to know?"

I shake my head and I realize it's a little like old times; for a few precious moments things are light.

"Pretend it's chicken nuggets and you'll be fine," he says, still grinning from ear to ear. He tucks a starched linen napkin into my dress collar. *"Bon appetite."*

I yank the napkin out, then giggle despite myself. "How about we trade; you can have the escar-whatever."

"Who knows, you might like it."

"You won't tell me what it is; that's not a good sign."

His smile fades. "It's important to cultivate good taste early on. Eleven's a good age to try something new, don't you think?"

I feel a heat rise to my face. "What if I don't like it?"

"I think you will."

"What if I don't?"

He shrugs. "Then you don't. I just want the opportunity for you to try new things. Don't be afraid to try something new, Gina. That's what makes life interesting."

"But why escargot? Why Kazatimiru's?"

He looks away, seemingly embarrassed. "It's never too late to cultivate a sense of class. I could've had it if I'd wanted it. But by the time I came around to wanting it, it was too late for me. Do you understand?"

I shake my head.

"I could've had anything."

That's when I see it, the bone-deep hurt in my father's face.

"But you had me instead." I look down.

He takes me by the shoulders. "Listen to me. I couldn't have asked for anything more than you, but..." He hesitates, unable to look me in the eye. "I don't deserve you. I did everything backwards. I wish I'd done what I'd wanted to do first so that I could've provided well for you, so that I could've done right by you."

"You have."

"I want you to want the finer things, Gina. I want you to succeed. I want you to care about what people think. I want you to care about money. I want you to know which fork's the salad fork and which one's the dessert fork. That stuff might seem unimportant, but trust me when I tell you that from my perspective, it hurts knowing what you could've had."

"Dad?"

He stops, looks at me.

"What's it mean if I'd rather be at Myles Lake?"

He takes a breath. "Just don't think for a minute that you can't have everything you've ever wanted. Don't do what I did. Don't give up on the only thing you were ever good at." He tousles my hair, even though at eleven I want to be too old for that. "Not that you're going to have that problem. You'll be great at anything you touch."

That's when I sense another presence coming up behind me.

"Robert, I do hope you plan on coming to the town hall tonight. I'll be talking about the blueprints for the new baseball stadium."

Dad is suddenly looking over my head. "Of course, Mayor; we wouldn't miss it for the world." There is the other dad, the reverently submissive man who looks just like my father but is nonetheless a stranger.

"No curveballs now," Mr. Busby says with a wry grin. "We're talking about the stadium, not the game." He winks, an odd glint in his steely eyes. "We'll see you tonight then."

That evening, we make our way to City Hall.

"It's about civic responsibility," my father lectures as we walk. "It's about being a part of society. I want you to get involved early on. Politics can be very exciting and rewarding because you're on the cutting edge of government, of *life*. You help make the kinds of decisions that determine which direction a society goes. Did you know I was student-body president when I was in school? The decisions I made then were small compared to the responsibility you take on in government, but they nonetheless affected people. I ate this stuff up: civics, American government, politics…you know I thought about running for mayor once—years ago. Not here, of course, but in a little town called Aubin." He says it proudly, dreamily. "I could've, too. If I'd really wanted it, I could've…" His voice trails off and for a moment he's miles away.

"Dad?" I bring him back.

"I might still do it, you know? I just might. It's never too late. Your mother might have a coronary, but she'd come around eventually; I know she would." There's a wild twinkle in his eye as he slaps his leg. "Hot damn, I just might do it."

*

We arrive after Mayor Busby has already started speaking and we stand against the wall, every seat taken. I didn't realize just how tall the mayor was. He's got to be at least six feet with graying, thinning hair, an angular face, a sharp aquiline nose and eyes like steel. He's lithe and thin like his son, sleekly athletic. He shakes people's hands and nods at their questions with a saint-like grace and is soft-spoken when he answers, but beneath the genteel façade I notice something else, something quietly, privately simmering. I see it in his eyes, the only part of him that refuses to smile.

I tug on my father's sleeve, careful to whisper. "Why's he mad?"

"Mad?"

"He looks mad."

"He's not mad, Gina, he's just…focused."

"You'd be a nicer mayor."

He smiles down at me.

A middle-aged, balding man asks about the cost of the stadium and how much would come out of the pockets of taxpayers.

The mayor at his podium holds up a finger. "The revenue generated from high-profile games will more than make up for it, not to mention we'll have our own team. We're planning the third biggest stadium in the state, second only to Las Vegas and Reno. Within a summer, we'll generate enough that you'll get a sizeable tax break by spring."

"You see," my father whispers. "You always emphasize the positive. You give the customers what they want even if it means spinning your responses a little. Notice he didn't actually tell the guy how much taxpayers will lose on the front end."

"Isn't that wrong?"

"It's the game. He's not lying; he's just spinning the truth in a positive light. There's a difference."

"I don't see the difference."

"Ok. Here's an example; it's like those old cars of mine. They were worthless when I bought them. Your mother thought I was nuts. But I fixed 'em up just right and now they purr like kittens." My father winces a little, cocking his head. "Ok, maybe they roar like lions, but they run."

I giggle and Dad holds a finger to his lips, smiling, whispering: "You see, it's just a matter of perspective. Some of us are optimists, and others are pessimists. The optimists run for office, and the pessimists accuse them of lying."

"Excuse me: you in the back…"

I notice in horror that the mayor is pointing at me, at my father.

"Do you two have a question, or do you just enjoy being rude?"

I stand mute, my face flushing with embarrassment as everybody in the room turns to stare at us. I'm floored by this show of antagonism by the mayor, and I can tell my father is, too. It's got something to do with Linn becoming a "little Robert Dalton" I realize, and it dawns on me that the mayor expects this to be his opportunity to cut my father down to size, in a setting Linn is bound to hear about. But to my surprise, it doesn't take Dad long to compose himself, to lose his loyal reverence:

"This lovely lady right here would like to know what separates the optimists from the pessimists. I told her optimists run for office and pessimists accuse them of lying. What do you think, Mayor? You think ten million on the front end is worth our spot on the map as a B-rate baseball giant?"

I see Mayor Busby's face fall, the acerbic gleam in his eyes fading. I feel my snicker's insidious conception deep in the bowels of my lungs, erupting with all the embarrassing force of a loud fart in a quiet room. My father elbows me sharply in the ribs but it does no good; I can't stop laughing, my dad's defiant challenge to the mayor's antagonism suddenly so funny I can't control myself. More than that, it's relief at knowing my father is back, wiles, wisecracks and all.

"I'm sure, like everyone else, you'll be happy to partake in the spoils a baseball stadium would bring to this town, Robert," the mayor says with feigned enthusiasm. "We all know we'll have to make sacrifices on the front end; that's certainly no big secret, nor is it the illuminating piece of insight you seem to think it is."

"I'm relieved to hear that, Mayor. I'm sure you make it a priority to educate every last citizen of this town on everything that goes on in that plush office of yours after hours." Dad holds up one of Mr. Busby's fliers. "God knows these might as well be the words of the gospels."

"Please leave, Mr. Dalton."

"I'm surprised at you, Mayor; I thought these were open forums. You're not one to quell freedom of speech—especially as a man of your ambition. Since you're such a firm believer in keeping everybody informed, every person in this room must know you eventually want a shot at the state Senate. I believe that qualifies you as a bona-fide optimist, sir."

A hush falls over the room before a swarm of nervous murmuring spreads through the crowd. I realize just how much my father knows of this intimidating man and I wonder what has given my dad such courage, why he's chosen a showdown with the mayor in front of dozens. I suspect it has something to do with me, with the way the mayor called me out and Dad's rush to protect me. I feel like a queen, once again in my father's glorious stead.

"I refuse to get into a fray with you, Mr. Dalton—"

"Who said anything about a fray? I just want some open debate. I'm sure you'd agree with me, Mayor—as a man representing the people."

Mr. Busby narrows his gaze on my father, a purple vein bulging in his forehead as his face reddens. "Open debate has nothing to do with my personal life, Mr. Dalton; my future political ambitions are not up for discussion—"

"No? You don't think the fine people of Archer have a right to know where you're coming from in your decisions about what happens to them and their money? Not that bringing a baseball team to this town would have any bearing on winning a seat in the state Senate—"

"*Enough.*"

I notice the mayor shaking, his fists clenched on the podium, his angular face the color of beets. My father has gotten to him, has won. I wonder if things will ever be the same, if Linn will still stand toe-to-toe with me on the white line on Saturday mornings.

"Good evening to you, sir," Dad says, graciously tipping his hat. "My most sincere apologies if I've offended you." We turn and walk out, the room stunned silent.

*

Out in the cold, my father starts to laugh, clouds of hot hair billowing from his lungs. "Now there's no going back," he says. "I have to run."

Portland
1992

At my first practice, Luke goes over the workout, but I don't hear a word of it; Dad was supposed to be here. He was running an errand, finding food maybe, or a safer place for us to sleep, a better life in all those subtleties most people take for granted, but he promised he'd be here to cheer me on. I keep looking around, expecting to see him any minute coming around the corner of the girls' locker room or through the opening in the chain-link. *Dad, where are you? I don't belong here without you. No one else cares.*

When they line up, I line up behind them. I'm self-conscious because I stink and I know they can smell me. Since coming to Portland, we've been sleeping in the Caddie most of the time, managing a shower here and there at the YMCA. The rest of the time, if we can find a safe space with river access, we'll stretch out in the summer sun, our feet free, knees straight, toenails left to grow (we cut them short when we're cramped in the Caddie and at risk of gouging each other each time we roll over in our sleep), an icy splash from the river the extent to which I get the grime and the stink off. If anything, my stench is a testament to my fear of cold water, along with my desire to hold out for a hot shower at the Y. The other girls are clean. They're normal. And they don't think about their toenails. Their hair shines in the sun, while mine is matted and dull, no real color at all.

"Get up there, Gina," Luke says. "Toe on the line."

We're doing 400s. A simple workout. We start off at 90s and it feels slow. I pick it up, take the lead. I hear a derisive snort behind me.

"Better pace yourself, girl." I hear someone snap.

"Better save your breath," I retort.

We dash around the track, faster and faster, me and this voice, in descending splits. 89. 88. 87. 87. 86.

But I don't gain. I can't shake her.

"You think your shit don't stink? That it?"

"Not like yours." I will beat her, this voice.

"Just because you're new doesn't mean you're anything special."

"We'll see about that."

"You will, I reckon."

We are flying. I glance at my watch. 83. We're lapping all of the others, ignoring the recoveries.

"*Slow down…*" Luke shouts after us. "Crimony, you're not—" And then his voice is lost in the wind.

"Reckon we'll find out what you're made o'."

I feel her then, the heat on the back of my neck as she attempts to pass, to put me in my place. Hell no. She will not win. Will not conquer me. I speed up. 81.

"*Gina…*" Luke is angry.

But I pay no attention. She will not get me. Will not possess me the way winners possess their losers.

Because I'm not a loser.

The next lap, he yells at her. He thought I'd be an easier sell on stopping, on listening to reason, but he was wrong and he knows it now. "*Cut it out, Breeze.*"

Breeze? I want to see her face. I want to turn and look at her, stare her down, this tigress on my tail.

79. Luke grabs my arm, stops me. "You're blowing your whole season," he snaps, fury in his gaze. "You're playing her game. She wants you to blow it."

I catch sight of the damning form already on the far side of the track, a beautiful figure with perfect form, sleek and confident. She makes the final turn, speeding up as she comes to the line, stopping with a triumphant sparkle in her hazel eyes as she holds up her watch, toward me and Luke, the digital numerals reading: 1:04.58—a 64.5 final lap. Before me stands the most beautiful woman I've ever seen. Breeze is tall and freckled, with shining auburn hair, fire-tinged in the sun.

"As I say, think you better be pacing yourself out there." She winks, breathless. "You ain't seen nothin' yet."

*

As I wait for my father on the curb, my face in my palm, I hear a voice, Luke's.

His shadow falls across my feet. "You've got to be smarter than that if you want to stay in this program. You damn near blew it today."

I swallow a lump. "I'm sorry."

"Don't be sorry. Just learn from your mistakes."

I feel my face flush, embarrassment flooding through me.

"Breeze has got talent, but not much else."

I look up at him and have the sudden wish that he would sit next to me.

"She's not going to be your friend."

And that's it—the hard thumb on the bruise. I'm no one's friend. And never will be. I'm not like the other girls. I have too many secrets.

"Your dad supposed to pick you up?"

I nod.

"You tell him what time practice was over?"

The questions sound accusatory, as though Dad not showing up on time is somehow my fault.

Luke looks around. "Hmm."

"He's just running late."

"Literally, huh?" He flashes me a crooked smile, but it's not like my father's smile. Luke's seems sarcastic.

There is heat in my cheeks. I want to get mad. I want to ask Luke why it's so funny that we don't have gas in our car, but I want to be good and I want to be on his team, so I don't.

"Anyone else you can call?"

I shake my head.

"We'll give it another few minutes."

*

Luke calls him from a pay phone, Sergeant Ragland. And he does a lot of nodding even though the officer can't see him.

"Yeah, he was supposed to be here by 6. Yes, sir. Yep. I know. Well, I'll go ahead and take her home with me and—yes, she's here. Uh-huh, so when he turns up he'll know where to find her." He cups a palm over the receiver. "Did he say anything about where he was going?"

I shake my head, my mind a blank.

And Luke is back on the phone. "She doesn't know. Hmmm? Yeah. He could be just running late, but—Ok, ok. Will do. Thank you, Sergeant."

"He was supposed to watch me," I say as Luke hangs up, tears in my eyes.

He looks at me. "Watch you?"

I swallow my grief, determined not to cry. "At my first practice. He was supposed to be here."

Archer
1989

Dad makes his big announcement in the kitchen, clapping his hands the way he always does before he's about to break some bit of good news.

"I'm running for mayor."

"*What?*" My mother, at the sink, wheels around. "Please tell me you're joking."

Her voice is icy, but my father either doesn't hear the warning or ignores it. "This is it, Marie; my big break, the chance for me to—"

"My God, you're serious. *Why?*"

"I think I can win."

Mom drops the pot she's been scrubbing back into the soapy water, furiously drying her hands on a towel. "I don't believe this." She takes off her apron, red-faced, livid. "You haven't taken a good hard look at reality since 1976, you know that?"

"What's the problem here? I thought you'd be—"

"You thought I'd be what? You thought I'd be happy about this? What on God's green earth gave you that idea?"

"Why on God's green earth are you so upset?"

She lowers her head, letting her breath out in an exasperated huff. "So you're telling me you're going out to knock on people's doors and educate them on your outstanding credentials as *what,* Robert? What have you ever done?"

He takes a step back from her, hurt on his face. "I'm a hell of a coach, Marianna."

"And that's just rich, isn't it? You're coaching the *mayor's* son; did you think about that? What's going to happen to that stipend he's paying you when you go after his job? And there's absolutely no way you could ever win."

"He's running for the state Senate."

"So?"

"So if he wins, he won't be mayor anymore and there's a good chance he'll win."

"By whose account? *Yours?*"

"I've been hearing things around town." He sighs. "I'm tired of spinning my wheels, Marie. This could be good for us."

"People will tear us apart." She stops, glancing at me. "They'll make us out to be homeless deadbeats once they find out about your past."

"Nothing ventured nothing gained, right? I'm willing to take the risk. A lot of politicians come from modest beginnings."

She shakes her head. "I can't. I *won't.*"

"Why not?"

She looks at him. "Because I refuse to be humiliated. I won't go along with any more of your play-acting bullshit. You're not an ivy league hotshot, Robert."

"Just what the hell's that supposed to mean?"

"Bottom-feeders don't run for office."

Then my father does something unimaginable; he slaps my mother across the face. It's an act of violence I've never seen, something I'll never forget.

She hangs her head, her palm at her cheek, in shock, not out of hurt or submission but embarrassment. For all of my mother's modesty, she's a strong woman who does whatever it takes to survive. She looks up at him, determined fury in her gaze. "I don't need you. God knows I've never been able to rely on you. I'll go it alone if I have to, you hear me?"

Already, my father has backed away and is leaning against the wall, his thumbs in his eyes, regret setting in. "Marie, I'm—"

"Save it. Your apologies are worth about as much as that lottery ticket you bought from Moe's yesterday."

"Please forgive me, Marie. I didn't mean it. I swear I didn't mean it…" His words pour out in a hot, desperate rush as his hands shake and his eyes well up. "I just…I want you to have some faith in me. I *need* you to have faith in me; do you understand?"

But she doesn't give him an inch. "Faith is earned." Her arms are defiantly crossed over her chest. "And in twelve years you've given me nothing to believe in."

"That's not true—"

"It *is* true. Your schemes have led us to nothing but misery. You do this, you do it alone."

"Marie, just *listen—*"

"No, Robert. You want to run for mayor, you'll run as a bachelor." She turns and walks out and I know this is it. There'll be no more fresh starts, no more tentative dreams.

I run after her. "Mom?"

She turns.

"It was my idea."

A quizzical look comes into her eyes.

"I told him he'd do a better job."

She looks up at my father. "And you took the word of a child? Goodbye, Robert." She goes into the bedroom and locks the door behind her. I hear her bustle, the frenetic sounds of departure as she gathers herself, packing, pulling things off shelves, getting ready to embark on her own. My mind's a whir. Who do I choose? Do I stay with him or go with her? I know instantly I want to stay, that my father's life as an optimist is infinitely better than my mother's as a pessimist. I want to have those impossible dreams.

The door flies open and out she swoops, suitcase in hand, her curly hair falling loose around her shoulders, her face flushed, determination set in her jaw and fire in her eyes. She moves with more energy than I've seen in a long time, almost with hope. She looks at me, expectantly.

"I'm not going," I say, trying to emulate her stance, arms folded across my chest, stern gaze and all.

"Gina Amber Dalton, you get your behind in there and pack a bag."

I shake my head, a part of me terrified at what will happen. "I want to stay with Dad."

"Put the suitcase down, Marie."

My mother wheels, startled. "You stay out of this, Robert."

"Just take a minute to think—"

"I don't need a minute; I've had twelve years."

Eleven years and nine months, I think, suddenly realizing that it's still my birthday, at least by a couple of hours.

Dad holds out his hands as though trying to talk someone off a ledge. "Just listen to me…"

"No." But now Mom is in tears.

"Put the suitcase down."

"No." She shakes her head, determined to hang onto her newfound hope, clutching the handle so tightly I imagine her creating imprints on it. "I'm leaving."

"Just put down the suitcase, Marie…"

Again she shakes her head, lifting the suitcase higher. "I'm doing it, Robert, and you can't stop me."

He holds up his hands. "All I want you to do is listen to me for a minute. Just give me one minute. I don't want you to do anything rash. The important thing is to stay calm and we'll talk this through—"

"There's nothing to talk through; it's over."

"You don't mean that."

"I *do* mean that."

"Is your life with me that bad?"

"*Yes*. Christ, where have you *been?*"

"Ok, look. I'm a dense son-of-a-bitch. I'm sorry—"

"Dense?" The tears are gone now, swallowed by anger. "That's a cop-out if I ever heard it. You're smarter than that. You know better. You *knew* that those old cars would get older and you'd have to have money to fix them, or better yet, money to replace them with newer ones. I'm not stupid; I've seen the bills. Patch-up jobs won't work forever unless you find some way to get some real money for real fixes. But no, you always work *down*, not up. Because you're *afraid* that if you succeed, somebody might actually expect you to follow up on it, and that scares the hell out of you. And that's what I despise about you. You play dumb, pretend to be…*dense*. But you're not a dense son-of-a-bitch, Robert; you're just a son-of-a-bitch." She clutches the suitcase handle as tightly as she can, pushing past my father into the kitchen, that much closer to the front door.

"Please don't leave me, Marie. I love you."

"It's too little too late," she says. And that's when she turns to me. "Just remember, faith is fragile."

*

I watch her from the window, the wind riffling her curls now set free from their kerchief; she is beautiful, even as she walks out on us.

Portland
1992

I realize I'm crying as I stare out the window, my forehead pressed tight against the glass. Luke lives north on the freeway just over the Washington-Oregon border, off the first exit, eight miles east and a right turn on a climbing country road. There are wildflowers and weeds. Pine trees and the rolling green of fields not yet sold for subdivisions. It's different from the desert. Lush and tame.

The house is big, semi-Victorian, with a sweeping view of the valley from which we've come. Luke hasn't said anything the whole trip. He's nothing like my father. He is silent and sullen. I don't dare speak, terrified of the truth that will come if I do. That I'm not really good enough, that this is all a big joke and the punch line will come about the time we pull into his driveway and my father will be standing there waiting to take me back to the desert. Maybe Luke's already told Dad about what happened on the track with Breeze. Maybe this is punishment.

I remember the time Dad gave me Myles Lake, a poor man's promise. He gave the land to me that day and it felt like I held it. Today is the opposite. I hold nothing. Own nothing. Am nothing.

When Luke stops the car, he takes a breath, looks at me. "Let's try to make this as painless as possible, shall we?"

I swallow a lump, nod, not sure what he means. I look around. There is no green Caddie. No Dad in a wide-brimmed Stetson.

We get out and he sweeps me along, his palm on my shoulder. I sense his impatience; I'm not moving fast enough. As I open the gate, a golden retriever bounds up and licks my hand.

"That's Hasp. No need to be afraid of him; all he does is lick."

At the door, a pudgy woman with coiffed blonde hair appears, smiling.

Luke points at me. "Dad's a no-show. Thought she could stay for dinner."

I feel my face flush.

The woman holds out her hand for me to shake. "I'm Linda. Nice to meet you." She has a strong grip and a slight southern accent. Next to her is a girl around seven or eight years old with braces and thick glasses. "This is our daughter, Amanda Grace," Linda says.

"Hi," the girl waves.

"You want to tell them your name or should they just call you *The New Girl*?"

I feel embarrassed. Why is it that Luke always makes me feel stupid and unworthy? "Gina," I say, barely audible.

I feel Linda's arm around me. "Don't mind him; he's just a grumpy old man!"

*

Luke shows me to a room in the basement. He looks at his watch. "I suppose, at this point, you'll be spending the night."

I need someone and Luke is all I have. Merely being in his presence makes me lonely, but I have no one else. It's like dying of thirst as you stand before an ocean; of course you drink.

The bed is a single and under it is an area rug, faded and dingy, the paisley patterns tired. There are cobwebs and dead bugs on the floor. Old things litter the whole downstairs, rusty tools and forgotten toys, naked Barbies with arms and legs askew, a chewed-up tennis ball, and a racket with unraveling tine.

Above the bed is a white flag with the Olympic rings, but the white has turned a water-stained gray. To the left is a dartboard, black and red, with darts that might have come from a game that took place twenty years ago. There's also a foosball machine with dust bunnies on its fake green field. It's a game room with no games. Like those old bleachers at my little dirt track in the desert: the pretense of competition, but the real thing merely a memory in the minds of people who have long since grown up and gone home.

In the corner is a picture, half-painted, of a woman, half of her face alive, the other half languishing in pencil. It's a life forgotten. Or abandoned. Mine.

"This is your room for tonight," Luke says.

A lump comes up in my throat as I nod.

"What was that?"

"Huh?"

"In this house, we acknowledge each other. You answer when I speak to you."

I can't stop the bloom from coming into my cheeks, grief the color of violets. "Ok," I choke.

His face hardens. "Don't tell me you're crying."

At first I think he's going to comfort me as I nod, but instead he grips my shoulders. Hard. "Straighten up. Now. Do you want me to help you?"

I nod.

"Do you want to be one of the best runners on the planet?"

"Yes, sir."

"Then toughen up. There's nothing to cry about."

*

Spaghetti for dinner and the lonely clank of silverware as everyone dishes up reminds me of how far away I am from home. Wordlessly, food is passed from left to right. I think of him, of all the times we snuck moldy cheese from the dumpster in Leeper, or stale-dated hot dogs for our parties in the sand, in the weed-strewn, gravel-studded kitchen we made out of hope and hunger, when the dumpster was our deliverance. It wasn't long before I gave up being grossed out, enchanted instead with the way my father made it home. Just as he'd made a home for us beneath that bridge in Eugene and in so many other places before that, before I'd become too old and jaded and yelled at him that first day in Leeper for doing the only thing he knew to keep us from starving.

Linda's table is clean. So is her house. There is no dirt, no smudge or suggestion of imperfection, no angst, no struggle. Beneath my filthy fingers, the wood is smooth and shining. I don't belong here.

I set my napkin on the table. "May I be excused?"

"No you may not," Luke says brusquely.

I'm not hungry, my stomach in knots, but a bolt of guilt runs through me. I should want this. He would want me to want this. I dish up, eat.

And then I'm aware of everyone staring at me. Even Amanda, the skinny girl with thick glasses. She speaks with a lisp. "What are you doing?"

I set down my fork, glancing at everyone in turn. "Eating. Isn't that what I'm supposed to do?"

"We say grace in this house," Luke tells me.

"Huh?"

"Grace."

"What's that?"

At the same time Linda chokes into her napkin, Amanda starts to laugh.

"*Enough.*" Luke's booming voice startles everyone into silence. He returns his gaze to me. "This is a Christian home, Gina. Do you know what that means?"

"I think so," I squeak.

"God is top priority here."

"Who?"

Luke points an angry finger at me. "Enough with the smart remarks."

I remember this time: "Yes, sir."

Everybody's face is red. Mine most of all. I hate him. I hate this. And I hate Dad for leaving me here.

"Why don't you say grace for us tonight, Gina," Linda says cheerfully, nervously.

I swallow a lump. "I don't know how."

"Start by giving thanks to Our Lord and when you're done, say 'Amen.'" She smiles, nods, dimples burgeoning in her cheeks. She is optimistic that I can change.

I take a deep breath. "Dear God…" I look up to find everybody with their heads bowed and eyes closed. I feel as though I'm spying on them. "Thanks. Amen."

Luke looks up, abruptly. "Is that it?"

I feel my face flush hot. "Um…I guess."

Amanda pushes her glasses up higher on her nose. "Writer's block?"

"Well, I wasn't exactly writing, so…"

Again, the finger. When Luke points, I stop, nod. "Guess so."

"Do it again," he says.

Horror floods through me. I don't know what I'm supposed to say. Don't know what I'm doing wrong. "Huh?"

"You heard me. Do it right this time."

I take another deep breath, trying to calm my heart. I imagine Myles Lake, thinking that will help, but it doesn't. "Dear God…thank you for this food…and this house…and these people…" I pop open an eye, spy on them, hope this is good enough. "Amen."

No one says anything the rest of the meal. Luke is angry and everybody knows it. Linda makes apologetic sidelong glances at him, then at me, smiling weakly.

*

That night, I lie in my bed, breathe in the scent of dust and wonder where he is. Something happened, and the thought makes my throat tighten and my eyes water. Who do I call tomorrow if he's still gone?

Dad, where are you?

I feel the knot, like a pit, in my stomach. There were times I thought I hated him. I hated his wide-brimmed Stetson. I hated that stupid belt buckle. I hated his cowboy boots and the way he looked into the sun and smiled, telling me that Leeper was good enough. I hated the fact he couldn't save that doe in the ground and decided instead that it was better for her to die. I hated him for giving up on her. For giving up on me. Because he did. We wouldn't be homeless otherwise. If I was worth saving, he'd have a job. We'd have a home.

And I wouldn't be here.

Dad, what happened? Did you do what Mom did? Did you leave me?

I turn my face into my pillow and sob. *I don't hate you anymore. Please come back.* Did he leave because I wouldn't forgive him? Because he knew that I knew it was his fault Mom left? Did he leave me before I'd have the chance to leave him, too? Or was it because I couldn't tell him I loved him? And maybe I didn't? *I'm sorry, Dad. I miss you. I love you, I really do.*

*

I awaken to confusion. Where am I? How'd I get here? Whose room is this? Then I remember. Sitting up, I rub my eyes. Outside, the sky is deep blue, and in a corner of the window is a glow. It's early, 5:30 or so. I peek out the window, recall those cold mornings on the white line. Dad and his whistle. I imagine him on the front step, waiting for me. Excitement throbs through me. I dash upstairs to the front door. I don't care what time it is. Or how much noise I make. But when I open it, no one is there.

"Well, look who's up so early!" Linda says cheerfully from the kitchen. Already, she is dressed in nice clothes, her blonde hair done up and her makeup on, those dimples blossoming deep.

"Hi," I mumble, my head down as I slump into the kitchen.

"You thought he'd be here, huh?" She cups my cheek in her palm.

I look up into a face full of kindness, and burst into tears.

Her arms are around me, tight. "Luke's already called."

"Who?"

She hesitates. "The police…and the hospitals."

My heart lurches. "Have they found him?"

"Not yet. Why don't you sit down, have some breakfast?"

I look around. No Luke. No Amanda. And though she is a stranger, I feel a certain contentment to have Linda to myself.

"What would you like? I could make you scrambled eggs, a waffle…"

Simple wishes coming true amid the chaos. Even when life falls apart, there is good food and beauty. Whipped cream and alkaline lakes, those gifts Dad taught me to recognize. And reflect on alone.

"I want a waffle," I tell her. "With whipped cream."

She smiles. "You got it."

I watch as she pours the batter over the waffle iron, her slow movements made with love. I imagine her doing this for her daughter, talking to Amanda about mother-daughter things as the smell of homemade waffles fills the house. That's the gift I want. Not the mountains. Not the lakes. Not the stars. Not medals or ice-chilled mornings. I want this.

"Reddy-Whip alright?" she asks in her drawl.

I nod and feel a smile spread across my face. For now, it's enough. She sets the plate in front of me and I look down into a square face with Reddy-Whip eyes and a Reddy-Whip grin, strawberry nose and hair.

I take a bite and remember that Mom also loved waffles. It's everything suddenly. Life. Possibility. Hope. Love. A childhood reclaimed. I eat slowly.

"Does it taste ok?"

I catch her gaze, feel those tears again, salt with the sweet. She sits across from me and takes my hand. "I know this has got to be really hard. I'm so sorry, sweetie. You just let me know what I can do for you, ok?"

"This." I point at my plate. "This is perfect."

Archer
1989

Dad and I drive up to Myles Lake and sit on a boulder along the shore, facing a stark vista. We pull our coats around us for warmth as we sip coffee and hot chocolate out of thermoses, the steam making our faces damp.

"Where do you think she is?" I ask.

"Knowing your mother, she could be anywhere." He smiles. "We once jumped a freighter all the way to Portland."

"Really? Mom did that?"

"Believe it or not, she hasn't always been so serious."

"Do you think she'll come back?"

He stares out across the lake. "I don't know." For a moment, there's a catch in his voice and he turns his head, but not before I catch a glint of what might be a tear. He moves a hand across his face, then wipes it on his jeans. "Sorry," he says. "Too much dust in the air today." Only there isn't any dust, and the wind is dead calm. Briefly, I imagine his tears turning to frost in the cold then evaporating, salt left over. Like the rim of salt around the lake, except the lake is just a lake and its salt beaches have nothing to do with Mom.

Then he turns back as if it had never happened. "What were you saying?"

I pause, confused, then decide to play it his way. "What if she doesn't come back?"

"Then we'll make do the way we always have, just you and me. But that's not so bad, is it? You and I make a pretty darned-good team, don't you think?"

I nod, knowing he's trying to be strong for me—but I already see the despair in his eyes, the bone-deep hurt of betrayal. I want desperately to change the subject, to make this picnic the new start I thought it'd be. "Are you going to be mayor?"

"God, I hope so. I have to do *something* with all this spare time."

"Do you think you can do it?"

"Why not? Arthur Busby did it and we all know just how charismatic he is." My father grins mordantly. "All that old wealth and the family name—real alluring. God forbid that the smell of mothballs goes out of style."

I furrow my brow.

"I think Archer needs a fresh face and a fresh voice." His eyes dance as he flashes a toothy grin. "And I'm as fresh as they come."

"I get to be vice mayor," I blurt, Dad's excitement catching.

"I don't think there's such a thing as vice mayor, but I tell you what—I'll create the position just for you. You'll be Archer's first."

"Really?"

"Really."

"You think I'll be on the news?"

He laughs. "Maybe."

His race, like mine, is fraught. It hurts to think about it. It reminds me of my desperation to beat Linn. I pray, more than anything, for him to win.

"Can I ask you something?"

He turns to me, still grinning. "Sure."

"Why are you doing this?"

His smile fades. "I've wanted to do this my whole life. I'm living my dream, Gina."

"How'd you know it was your dream?"

"I've always known."

"Yeah, but how?"

"I know myself."

"Yes, but how?"

"I don't know." He looks at me hard. "I listen to my heart, I guess."

"I don't know how to listen," I say. "How do you listen to your *heart*? That doesn't make any sense."

"What is it you want, more than anything?"

"Mom." I feel my eyes well. Hot grief like a high tide. "I want her to come home."

He looks away. "The thing about dreams is that some work out and some don't."

"Is that why you brought me here?"

"To Myles Lake, you mean?"

I nod. "You gave it to me once. You said I should come here when I'm hurt."

"A poor man's promise…" he gazes out at the vista, "has to be rooted in the earth, in the sky, in real things. No matter what happens, you've got this. It's more than most people have."

"But doesn't it belong to everybody?"

"Yes, but not everyone knows they have it."

I think I know what he means. "Does Mom know she has it?"

"I hope so."

"I don't think she does."

"Why do you say that?"

"Because she's not here." I burst into tears, and I feel my father's arm around me. I cling to him. Want to be loved more than anything. More than this. "Don't leave me. Promise?"

His eyes are red, too, and this time he makes no effort to hide it. "Promise."

*

Back in town, we stop by the sporting goods store to pick up a ten-gallon Stetson and a pair of black cowboy boots. Image is everything, Dad says. And nobody can resist the American cowboy. At home, he struts in front of a full-length mirror, clad in long johns, boots and hat.

"I think they'll eat it up."

I make a face. The hat looks too big for my father's head and the boots…

He turns toward me. "What do you think?"

I shrug, giggling.

"What? You don't think I'm cute?"

I burst out laughing.

He speaks in a booming, formal voice: "It's what the great people of Archer have been waiting for all their lives. Rompin' Robert Dalton." He turns around, smiling at himself in the mirror. "Yessiree, you ole doggies, Rompin' Robert to the rescue."

He reminds me of a comic book character. "You need a cape," I say.

He holds up a finger. "*Aha!* I knew I forgot something." He grabs a red plaid flannel shirt and slings it around his shoulders. "Yes, that's it. The perfect look. Boots. Hat. Long johns. Cape. Now all I need is a six-shooter." He smiles at me in the mirror. "This is the American West, after all."

*

The next day, we go to City Hall and Dad asks a middle-aged woman with fluffy hair and small squinting eyes what he has to do to run for mayor. She looks at him skeptically, blinking.

"You'd need a hundred signatures just to get on the ballot," she tells him.

"Really? That many?"

"Really, that many," she says, deadpan.

"Ok. Where do I start?"

She shoves a petition in front of him, her gaze mordant. "Arthur Busby's never lost an election."

My father smiles weakly at her and I catch another glimpse of that submissive man with his hat in his hands, nothing like the superhero I saw in long johns and a Stetson the night before.

"He'll win," I blurt. "Archer needs a fresh face and fresh voice and everybody's sick of mothballs—"

"Gina," my father hisses.

The woman smiles wryly. "Really? I'll be sure and let the mayor know to change his Sunday best more often."

Dad gets up in a huff, clutching my hand tightly as we walk out. "How many times have I told you to hold your—"

"Sorry."

"This is serious business, Gina. If I run for mayor, you're going to have to keep a lid on it."

I put my head down, my feelings hurt.

He ruffles my hair. "Vice Mayor is a very important position, after all."

I feel myself smile. "Do I get to give speeches and tell people what to do?"

He chuckles. "We'll see, but first things first; we've got to get those signatures."

*

We start that afternoon, first in the Old Historic District, going door-to-door, disappointed to find that most people don't answer when we knock.

"This might be harder than I thought," my father says as he shivers, pulling his coat tightly around him.

"You think we could get them some other way?" I ask.

"We could always forge them." There's a mischievous twinkle in his eye and a wry grin on his face. "Of course, that's a treacherous route; ole Arthur Busby might have his suspicions and then where would I be?"

We try a few more doors. At one Victorian, an older man answers with a scowl on his face. My father is eager, shoving the petition at the man.

"Top of the afternoon to you, sir. My name is Ro—"

The slam of the door startles us both.

"I guess we interrupted his nap," Dad says with a smirk. "Good thing our fingers weren't in the way."

At the next house, a shrunken, chatty old woman answers in her nightgown, signing immediately and smiling a lot, telling my father just how much she'd love to see new blood in City Hall.

"I know you from somewhere, don't I?" she asks, adjusting her thick-lens glasses.

"Well, I've been known to frequent a few of the select establishments around here—Kazatimiru's, for example."

I realize he's trying to show off. I want to say, *we've been there once.* I hate the diminished superhero.

The woman looks at him skeptically. "Funny. I don't remember seeing you there." She points at him then, narrowing her gaze. "Wait a minute. I know where I've seen you. The casino..."

"What? Oh, no, no. I don't frequent casinos."

"Why not? I'd vote for anyone who supports the casino on upper Lyle River. You'd do that, wouldn't you, Mr. ...?

"Dalton."

"Mr. Dalton. You look like the type who likes to drink and gamble." She smiles brightly, her hazel eyes enormous behind her glasses. "I like a man who can admit to a bit of badness."

"Look, Ms. ..."

"Mrs. Ludlow. But you can call me Rosie."

"Rosie. I appreciate your bit of encouragement, really, but…I think you must be mistaken."

"Mistaken? No, I don't think so. Not with these babies." She pushes her glasses up higher on her face, making her eyes look even larger. "They're owl magnifiers, don't you know."

"Ok. Thanks for your vote of confidence, Rosie."

I can tell my father is dying to get out of there.

"Ok, one down, 99 to go," he says with a quiet clench-jawed sigh as we leave.

"You were at a casino?"

"She's mistaken, Gina. She's a little old lady."

"So?"

"I wasn't at any casino."

*

The next few houses yield three angry people and four no-shows. "I think we're done for the day," Dad says.

"Can't we try one more?"

"No, Gina; it's already getting dark."

"So?"

"So, we don't interrupt people during the dinner hour. If there's one surefire way to lose an election, it's standing between the good citizens of Archer and their redeye steaks."

I laugh. I want to believe he can win, that despite years of trying and failing, he'll finally succeed at a dream.

Portland
1992

Luke doesn't say anything on the ride into Portland. This is just another practice. I stare out the window and think back on when we too had lived in a house, before Mom decided she didn't want our lives anymore and changed everything. It's me this time, unwanted.

"I don't think I'm going to run today," I say, regretting my decision to go to practice.

"Your choice, but I wouldn't take too many days off. You've got to get back in the saddle."

The suburban landscape, caught in the smear of rain, drifts by. I imagine Dad out in it, like that night in Eugene, running barefoot, his face pointed toward the sky, droplets of sweat and rain clinging to his eyelashes, that grin, iridescent, in the gloom. Where does that kind of joy come from? And why doesn't it last?

"Do you like to run?" It's suddenly a burning question.

Luke glances over at me. "Of course." He answers as though my question was stupid.

"Do you run every day?"

"Every morning and every night."

"Really? Twice a day?"

"Well, that's what every morning and every night means, I suppose."

A lump swells in my throat. There are so many landmines, and I'm always stepping on them.

*

I watch her from behind the mesh of a chain-link fence as she does her repeats. Like Dad, she has perfect form. Unlike him, she shows her pain, doubling over after each interval. She's still beautiful. Still seemingly invincible despite the show of discomfort. I want to know what it is that makes her special. Why she's so fast. Why she's head and shoulders above everyone else on the track. She's prettier than me, more muscled, big for a 16-year-old, in black bun-huggers and a hot-pink sports bra. Maybe I'll be that good when I'm 16, but some insidious part of me doubts it.

She catches my gaze. "What are you looking at?"

"You, I guess."

"You guess? You blind?"

"No."

"Then there's no guessing." She walks up, nose to nose through the chain link as she grips the mesh. "I'm thinking you're confused."

"Confused?"

"You don't know anything, do you?"

My face is hot. Breeze leaves me with nothing to say. "I know a few things."

"You know what things?" It's a challenge, a dare for me to look even more stupid.

"Never mind," I mumble, turning to walk away.

"You know how to give up, I bet."

I stop.

She grins. "Can spot that kind a mile away."

"I won't give up."

"Yeah? Best you prove it, then."

I wonder if she sees in me what I see in myself—the uncertainty. The fear I want something that doesn't exist. "I'll never give up."

"We'll see."

I watch as she walks away, realizing she has something I don't. A willingness to suffer, unafraid. I wonder how she does it, how I can do it, too. Someday I'll have it. Someday I'll do it. I'll work up my nerve to run the race of my life and I'll love the labor, not just the hope, the dream, the lonely wish at dawn and dusk, hiding among those long shadows.

I wonder what it is that makes her angry. If it's something like what makes me angry. Being left behind. Squandered somehow. I watch her for the rest of the workout and think of Dad. He'd be proud of that. He'd watch her and think: *Champion. Hero. Prodigy.* And I'm nothing like her.

I feel it now, the same thing I felt with Linn, fierce and mean-spirited. I want her to trip. If I'd been anything like her, he wouldn't have left. Then I think: maybe he didn't leave...maybe something happened...It's an insidious thought because some part of me needs it to have been an accident. That would be a good reason for him to be gone, one that didn't mean I wasn't good enough, like Breeze…or Linn. Maybe he's dead. But I don't *want* him dead; I want to be good enough to have him back. Maybe he's just off getting some money for us, so that we can go back into the desert…

It's been a week, but it seems like a lifetime, as though his memory has already faded and with it, my grief. All I feel is anger. There is no excuse. Not even death. Then, unexpectedly, as Breeze does a fast 100-meter pick-up, it all comes rushing back, like a riptide I can't escape. I duck behind the trees, hide there and cry, my loneliness wound tightly in the branches of a blue fir. Luke comes looking for me after practice and I tell him about my stomachache. That's no excuse, either.

*

Every night, I wait for the phone to ring and I ask Linda what she's heard. It's always nothing. The police know nothing. Hospital personnel know nothing. There is no one by the name of Robert Dalton. The phone never rings. There's nothing on the evening news. No evidence he ever existed. Not even a medal.

At the track, I keep an eye out for him, sitting on the sidelines and watching. Maybe he's peering at me from behind that fringe of trees. Or maybe he'll be waiting around the side of the girls' locker room. Maybe he's up the street, having made his fortune, waiting to surprise me at just the right moment, as I come around that final turn on the track and then…there he'll be, arms outstretched and that Stetson pushed back on his head, his grin as large as life. I imagine it every day and every day it seems a little less likely.

*

Linda strokes my forehead before I fall asleep, and beneath that tired Olympic flag, I let her tell me things will work out. I want to believe her. I pretend I do.

"You've got your whole life ahead of you," she says. "So much to look forward to."

I want to ask: *What?* But instead I nod—because I want to believe her the way I once believed my father—that it's enough to have the wish and some chance it might come true. Is that what I have? A chance? Maybe he'll come back. Maybe he's not dead. But somehow it doesn't feel the same.

After she's gone, I stare out the window and wonder if all the stars in the universe will buy him back, as though I can bargain with God. I won't just wish on one; I'll wish on them all, trade out all of my talent and that future Linda keeps talking about to have him back one last time, to wake up to those dancing violet eyes and the tickle of his mustache on my cheek.

*

I can't bring myself to run. Not anymore. I wonder why I ride with Luke those lonely miles, often in silence, to the track in the rain. Today, I can't face even the rain, so I sit inside the girls' locker room and wait. For him, I guess. I'll hear a sound, look up, and there he'll be. There'll be another house, like that one in Archer. He'll swing an arm around me and we'll go home. This place is nothing like the desert. Even in the winter, the desert is cold and clear, the ground frozen. Here, it's mucky, the rain a bad habit the sky can't break.

I hear voices and hide behind a corner of lockers. "He's totally screwing her."

"You think?"

"Oh, yeah. She's, like, a total slut."

"Oh God, *Gross*." Squeals of laughter.

"Screwing doesn't make you any faster, though, does it? She beat your ass that first day, din't she?"

I recognize Breeze's husky voice as a hush falls over the room.

"Wha'd you say, bitch?"

"I said, she sure as hell beat your ass, din't she? You jealous or something?"

"Jealous? Are you fucking kidding? She's, like, a total quitter."

"I hear her dad left her."

"Really?"

"That sucks, Girl."

"Like, was it for another woman?"

"Girl, you are seriously *sicko.*"

"I don't mean, *like that*. Like, ok, my mom ran off with another man kind of thing—"

"You're in here talking 'hind her back. Why don't you tell her what you think to her face?"

"Um, like, no one asked you, bitch—"

I hear something. A scuffle. A shove. Another shove back.

"Don't you be shoving me around, hear? 'Cause I reckon you'll lose."

"You gonna fuck her or something?"

Laughter. More scuffling. The sound of a body thrown hard against a locker. Shoves graduate to punches. I hear gasps. Pleas to stop. And then someone runs past me, coming in through the door marked *Exit*.

It's Luke.

"Knock it off!" He grabs Breeze by the arm as the other girls dash out. "What are you doing?" he yells at her. From my hiding place, I see scrapes on her face from the fight. She spies me looking at her, glances back, expressionless.

"Look at me; I'm talking to you," Luke says.

But she won't stop staring at me.

"You know what? You're off the team. That's it. I've had it with you."

I find my voice: "Don't…"

Now Luke's attention is on me. "This was my fault," I say.

"What?"

"Breeze was standing up for me."

Luke returns his attention to Breeze. "This true?"

She shrugs.

He lets her go, his gaze hard. "Stay out of trouble or you're gone."

"Can't make any promises."

"You will if you want to stay on my team."

She glares at him as he stalks out. Then she and I are alone.

"Thanks," I stumble.

"Don't be getting any ideas."

"Huh?"

"You're thinking I'm nice to you all of a sudden, but that isn't how it is. I hate you out there." She points toward the track. "That makes us enemies, I reckon."

"Why?"

"Because you're fixing to take what keeps me here. The only reason I'm here is I can run."

"We all can, remember?"

"Why don't you go on in there and clean off that stink o' yours?"

I catch her gaze, hurt.

"It's not like it's some big secret." She pulls something out of her pocket, a lighter and a homemade cigarette. She takes a puff and holds her breath, wincing. "You've got no home, ain't that right?"

She offers me a puff, but I shove her hand away, heat rushing to my face. "No, thank you. And, yes, I have a home."

"'Cept Coach is feeling sorry for you. You're cleaning that stink off the outside, but there's no touchin' it on the inside."

"Shut up."

"Takes one to know one." She smirks.

"You don't have a home?"

"I got no folks. Same thing. I'm living at a shelter, but nobody knows. Goin' to school in the poor part of Portland, rather than that high-fallutin' suburban place Coach got you into. Kinda stupid of me, I s'pose, but you know how it goes. I live to run. Nothing else matters, not even four walls and a bed."

"Where are you from?"

"Louisiana." Though it comes out *Loooseeanna.* "You ever been to N'orlins?"

I shake my head.

"It's hot and it's real wet. You take a shower in the morning and your hair's still damp in the evening. I hid myself away down there, though, because I was a bastard."

"A what?"

"An embarrassment."

I feel my face flush. "Someone called my dad that once...a bastard I mean."

She snorts. "I came along in ugly. That makes me a bigger bastard."

"Huh?"

"My dad raped my mom and she got me. And them babies, they hurt too. They hurt being made and being born. Each of us is pain. That's what she told me."

A knot comes up in my throat, and I don't know what to say. "Oh."

"Now you know what a bastard is?"

Still my father's definition: "An asshole?"

"A child born in sin."

"A what?"

"*A what?*" Her brow wrinkles. "Girl, you seem real smart up in that head and all, but sometimes I think you don't know nothin'."

"I know enough."

"Sure. Bet you don't know how to paint the track, though."

"Paint the track?"

"In your own colors, know what I mean?"

I shake my head, already forced to concede defeat.

"All that pain…" She points to my heart. "It's got to come out. Some people are artists, and others put it all into words. I'm no good with that stuff, so I run with it instead. I push, pull, push, pull. Go fast, slow, fast, slow. It's all a rhythm, like that beating heart. You feel joy, you go. Mad, you go. Scared, you go. Sad, you slow down, take some time, recover. Know what I mean? I don' let myself feel sad that often, though. Reckon that's why I'm fast. You see those pictures, you know? All those pictures up in your head and they push you."

"I'll try that."

"You take my lead. I'll push you, pull you." She grins. "I reckon you'll get fast, alright."

"I thought we were enemies."

"I need someone pushing me. 'Sides I think you're different from the other girls."

"Different?"

"You're like me. You're lost, but you'll be findin' yo'self on that track."

*

I take Breeze's lead, pushing and pulling away from the others, away from Luke's admonishments for us to slow down, letting the faces of Archer—Dad, Mom, Linn, and everyone else I've ever known flow through my head like tides.

"Come on, you!" Breeze yells from ahead, fighting ugly. "You're tougher than that!"

I'm trying. I think of Dad and those needle-cold dawns.

"You pussin' on me?"

"No!" Dad gone. Mom gone. Anger. Hurt. Despair.

"Sure are. Run, bitch!"

Then Luke's voice: *"Slow down!"*

Breeze's effortless victories over me. Linn's, too. Dad gone. I scream it at them all. *"Fuck you!"*

"That's alright, get mad!" Breeze shouts back.

Hatred. Anger. Fear. *Each of us is pain.* I chase her until I can chase no more, collapsing on the track.

I feel his tight grip on my arm. He looks at her, his eyes red and the veins bulging in his neck. "Get the hell off the track. Now."

"You need me." Her crooked grin is aimed at him. "An' her, too. We're your team."

*

It's a return to childhood. I listen from around a corner as Luke and Linda debate my future. *What'd I tell you about eavesdropping?* Dad always said whenever he caught me doing so to him and Mom. *Not to do it, but since when have you done anything worth doing? You're a hypocrite, Dad. And you're gone; I don't have to listen to you anymore.*

"We have to let her stay here, Luke; at least until he comes for her."

"She's trouble."

"She's not trying to be. She's a good kid."

"She's a pain in the ass."

"Where's she going to go? Foster care? She could be a sister to Mandy. Especially since…" Her voice breaks, starts again. "It's time, Luke." Another pause. "We've got a lot to offer her. And you know she's got a boatload of talent— you never know where she'll take you. Why not just let her stay, for now? We can turn her around, show her what Christ has shown us. Love. Grace. If she learns those things—"

"Linda. She's trouble. We're going to have to watch her and Amanda like hawks. Family Services would take her if we asked."

"And they'd also let us keep her." She paused again. "I checked. Amanda adores her, and she's not going to be a bad influence if we show her the right path. What would Jesus do?"

Long ago, in one of my secret forays with my ear to Mom's and Dad's door, I'd heard them talk about a secret Mom called poverty, and how it destroyed their lives. But this is worse. This is borrowing someone else's home, someone else's life, and pretending it's mine.

"God has big plans for that girl."

Someone takes a breath, Luke. "You think so?"

"You've said it yourself; she might be the one."

Something swells through me. It's almost pride, but tinged with grief. It should be Dad saying such things. The words from anyone else seem hollow.

"We'll give it a try, I guess. But you've got to be prepared for the possibility it might not work. She's messed up, Lin. She's used to sleeping on the ground and eating someone else's leftovers."

My face feels hot, anger and embarrassment blazing.

"She just needs love and discipline. We can give her that."

"She's not a stray cat."

"I know that, Luke—for heaven's sake."

"They may not even let us keep her. She's a minor and more than likely has a mother who'll take her if her father decides to be AWOL forever."

Might Luke be right? Might Mom swoop in, save me, and take me home again? What would it be like, after all these years? Would she need me the way I need her? Luke's words, like an affirmation, give my hope power and an ache that brings up a desperation tinged with anticipation.

I remember how Mom told me to listen for the tooth-fairy's buzz after I'd lost my first tooth. How, from behind a curtain, I was certain I'd heard it and yanked back the fabric, only to find a fly bouncing against the glass. I'd cupped the fly in my hand to examine the blue-green iridescence of its eyes and wings, that tiny flash of color, like the refraction of a rainbow, and wondered if that was how magic might look if I held it in my hand. *Mom, I caught the tooth-fairy!'* I bellowed down the stairs. She came, took a look, and smiled. "You never know," she said, briefly turning my entire world into an enchantment. How I want that magic back, that porthole to some other, better, place, within grasp if only I could still believe in the good of the world.

"She's old enough to tell a judge where she wants to live. She hasn't seen her mother in years."

"True, but surely…well, who knows, her dad may come back."

A lump comes up in my throat. Because, deep down, I know. If he'd been able to come back, he would have.

*

Dear Dad,

You thought you were giving me everything I ever wanted, but what you did was take away everything I ever had.

Archer
1989

Mom is smiling, her arms outstretched. I run to her, but she turns and runs away. I watch as her hair, falling loose from a bun, flies out behind her, her sandals lost in a tangle of weeds, her form caught in silhouette as she chases the sun. I can't catch her. Just like I can't catch Linn. I stop, staring into the place she vanished, into that band of color now fading. I sit down, cover my face, and sob.

"Gina?" I awaken from my dream. My father has come home and I sense his presence above me. "What are you doing in bed? It's"—he glances at his watch—"not even dinner time."

"Don't feel good," I mutter.

I feel his weight next to me as he sits down and puts a hand on my leg. "Why don't you sit up? I've got something to tell you."

I turn over, but I don't have the energy to sit up.

He beams. "I've got my first public debate tonight."

I try to smile but it comes out as a smirk, half-assed and crooked.

"What's the matter with you?"

"Mom didn't want you to do this."

"Mom didn't want me to do a lot of things, but that doesn't mean I shouldn't do them. We all make our own decisions in life and this is my decision. I've wanted to do this for a very long time, and I think it'll be good for us. Don't you want this for me?"

I nod.

"Democracy's a beautiful thing. Anybody can run for office in this country. Anybody can start over and make a new life for themselves. That's what I'm trying to do, Gina. That's what I'm trying to do for you."

"What if people find out?"

"Find out what?"

"That you cheated?"

He blanches. "What?"

"I saw you write those signatures. You got tired of knocking on doors." And being told he'd been seen at the casino.

He takes a breath, gazes hard at me. "It's for our long-term good. We've always been survivors."

"Is that why Mom left?"

"What do you mean?"

"She was tired of surviving."

He looks down. "I did my best by your mother."

"I don't want to be a laughingstock, Dad. I don't want everybody at school thinking you're a joke."

His anger flashes. "Is that what you think?"

"Maybe."

The hurt spreads across his face like a stain. "That's fine if you want to believe it. But I'll prove it to you this time." He holds up a finger. "Just watch me win." He turns and leaves and I hear him rummaging through his closet. When he returns, he is clad in his mayoral attire: black knee-high cowboy boots, ten-gallon Stetson, red plaid flannel shirt, and blue jeans with a belt buckle the size of a small dinner plate. It's ridiculous. He's ridiculous. Before, I wanted to laugh at him, but now I want to cry.

"Tell me I don't look the epitome of the Old West. That's what people want—a return to the good old days, to the old ways, to an easy, simple dialogue about real issues affecting real people."

Even I know it's nothing more than a sound bite, something my father thinks sounds good but really means nothing. He's full of that stuff, full of useless, meaningless things he thinks will bring him fame, fortune, and a chance to start over. Could even his 4:07 mile be nothing but a time, three numbers on a stopwatch? I think of Linn and banish the thought. Not yet, not now.

Instead I scowl at him. "I don't like the hat."

"What? Why? That's my crowning glory."

"It's stupid."

"You can dispense with the smart-ass attitude now. I'm officially giving you permission."

"I'm just telling you before you go in front of all those people and they say the same thing."

"You thought it was a hell of a get-up the other night."

I shrug. "I don't like it anymore. I think it's stupid."

"You think everything's stupid."

I glare at him. "Not everything."

"Name one thing." He's daring me.

"Like my old life. Mom. You and me on the track. Picnics at Myles Lake. You showing us magic tricks."

"Gee. I counted five things you think aren't stupid. It seems you're on your way to being a bona-fide glass-half-full kind of gal."

I give up. I can't argue with him, can't tell him how I really feel—that all he's doing is playing a cartoon character, the caricature of a hero everyone knows doesn't exist.

"I'm a workingman, Gina. That's what people want to see. That's who they're looking high and low for, who they're starved for. Arthur Busby's all about a family name and old money. I can give this town, these citizens, so much more than that. That's all I've ever really wanted, to make a difference in the lives of average people."

Another clichéd proclamation. "Guess we better stop going to Kazatimiru's."

"I've had about enough of your attitude. Are you coming tonight or not?"

"What do you think?"

Disappointment settles in his face. "I didn't think you would."

*

I wait for him to leave before I get out of bed. I put on my coat and walk out the door. I gaze up at a crescent moon, my breath coming in hot clouds in front of me. I imagine what it must've been like for her, walking out that last time, taking one step and then another and another, her feet aching, her heart heavy, tears blurring her way. I want to feel just like that. I want to walk away forever. I head toward the trail behind the old swimming pool in Abelard Busby Park, a half mile away, in the opposite direction from my old track.

I see the pool in the dim, empty now, its pale color almost fluorescent in the muted glow of the moon. I see the shine of the ladder leading up to the tallest diving platform, the concrete all around it, the high chain-link fence keeping me from it.

I climb the fence, scraping my palms and tearing my clothes on the metal as I hoist myself over. Once inside, I climb the ladder, rung after rung until I'm on top, looking down into an empty pool. I imagine what it might be like to dive in, expecting water, feeling something else.

I hear a rustle, something in the brush. I feel its gaze and for some reason I know it's holding its breath. I sit atop the platform, too cowardly to jump and end it all. I look down, the moon's muted light throwing shadows along gray swaths of ground. I let my eyes dance along the hemline of trees as I look for whatever it is that's watching me.

"Mom?"

No answer.

"Is that you?"

Nothing.

I take a deep breath, leaning back on my arms. My despair still sits heavily on my heart, but at least out here I can dream. Nothing seems quite as impossible. Out here, I can still believe she's holding a silent vigil over me even if she doesn't show herself. Can pretend she isn't really gone. I sit and I wait for what feels like hours, then I crawl down, disappointed I haven't found the release I came out here to find. I walk home, refusing to look up at the moon any more, refusing to wish. Wishing does no good.

*

The house is still dark and quiet. He isn't home yet. I wonder how the debate is going, if he's winning or losing or if it's a tie, if he and Arthur Busby will call it a draw and share some kind of door prize for their roles as co-mayors. I just want it to be over. As I climb into bed, my mother's face traces itself in my mind. The lovely heart-shaped contour of youth, eyes the color of bluebells and hair like curled wheat. I miss her desperately as I bury my head under the covers and sob.

I hear him then, Dad through the front door. I switch off my light, not wanting to talk. It's late, too late to argue. I hear him scream. *Fuck*. A sharp, stunning word. I hear heavy footfalls coming toward my room, my door flying open, and I smell the pungent stink of liquor.

"Gina, you in here?"

It's dark. I know he can't make out my shape in the dim.

"Gina. I need to talk to you." He flips on the light, squinting into it, his face puffy and his hair messed up under the Stetson hat. "You awake?"

I sit up, furious. "I am now."

"It's over, sweetheart. I blew it."

Relief floods me, dissolving my anger.

"I just couldn't do it, you know," he slurs. "I just didn't know my shit, I guess."

"Sorry," I mutter, embarrassed of him, of his drunkenness and his stench and his ridiculous clothes.

"You were right, sweetheart; they didn't like the hat."

I feel the sudden threat of tears, heavy behind my eyes.

"You glad?"

"Glad of what?"

"Glad it's over?"

I can't lie to him, not now. I nod.

"Well, I guess I am too, then." He smiles wanly, weakly. "Just another stupid fantasy of mine. I'm sorry, sweetie. One of these days I'll learn."

I swallow a lump, don't know what to say.

He leans over, hugs me. "Go back to sleep."

Sundays
1992

"You want to pick out a dress, sweetie?" Linda's voice rises over the clank of dishes and swish of running water. "Best we do it this afternoon because you'll want to have it tomorrow morning."

"For what?"

She turns, drying her hands on her apron. "For church." She smiles brightly. "Luke thinks it's time we introduce you to the congregation."

*

"You should get a pink one," Amanda says as we drive to the dress shop in Linda's white minivan. "Mine's pink with puffy sleeves."

"I don't like puffy sleeves."

"You like pink, though, right?"

"Not really."

"What color do you like, sweetie?" Linda glances at me in the rearview mirror.

"Bruise."

"What?"

"Never mind."

"Do you like blue?" Amanda asks as she adjusts her glasses.

"Kind of."

"Sky blue or cobalt?"

"What's cobalt?"

"Like, dark blue, I think."

"Ooh, midnight blue—wouldn't that be pretty?" Linda says perkily.

I stare out the window, realizing how much I hurt. "I want to wear pants," I blurt.

Both look at me, horror-stricken, Linda from her rearview mirror and Amanda from across the backseat. "No way," she says, squinting and pushing her glasses up further on her nose.

"Gina, sweetheart, don't you like wearing dresses?" Linda asks.

"No."

"But they'd be so pretty on you."

"I want bruise-colored pants."

"Oh, pooh…" There's a scrunched-up look on Linda's face.

"Please get a dress," Amanda says. "We could look like sisters."

"But we're not."

"We could be."

Something catches in my throat. *I don't want to be.*

"Get a dress, get a dress, get a dress…" Amanda chants.

*

The Dress Shoppe is small, but chock full of everything from shiny prom dresses to cotton sack dresses and summer smocks. The sales woman, a forty-something trying to look twenty-something with coiffed blonde hair, red pumps, and too much makeup, asks if she can help us.

"We're looking for something for her," Linda says, making a gesture toward me.

"For church," Amanda interjects.

The blonde woman's gaze falls on me and there's something disparaging in it. "Oh. Well, we've got lots to choose from. Lots of different colors and prints. Paisley's always nice. What do you like?" Her voice is prim. Perky.

"Anything bruise-colored," I say.

She straightens, taken aback, voice still perky. Disconcertingly so. "Oh."

I swallow the knot in my throat, suddenly overtaken with the urge to burst into tears. I can't fight them, so I dart into a fitting room, cover my face, and sob.

There's a knock on the door. "Sweetheart?" It's Linda. "Are you ok?"

I shake my head even though she can't see me.

"Can I come in?"

I nod, unlock the door, and feel her palm on my shoulder. "I'm sorry, hon."

I look up into her eyes, the bluest I've ever seen. "I want my mom."

"I know."

"Are you going to tell?"

"Tell?"

"Him."

"You mean Luke?"

I nod. "I'm being a piss-ant."

She giggles, and startlingly, I realize we're allies: "Of course not. You're doing just fine, Gina."

I feel myself smile.

"You want to pick out a dress?"

I nod and for the next hour, I embrace all kinds of material, softness between my fingers, against my cheek, breathing in the newness of it. Some of it is fancy and shiny, cashmere and silk. Some is simple and soft, cotton and polyester. I choose a long-sleeved cotton dress with lace at the bottom, bruise-colored, but pretty.

*

It is as we're walking back to Linda's white minivan that Amanda finds it.

"Look!" she shouts, crouching. She motions to me and I feel a blitz of hope, a desperation to belong. The gesture is shocking; she doesn't know me that well, yet she beckons to me and not her mother. There is a sudden singularity between us, a sisterhood of sorts. I realize that not much separates us but for a few short years and that thin veil innocence cloaks from the reality of the world. I remember all of those times as a child when I'd call out to Mom, excitement pulsing in my determination to reveal something beautiful—and it doesn't seem like all that long ago.

I walk over and kneel down. Amanda removes her finger from a spot on the asphalt, revealing a clam shell the size of my pinky. The shell has been caught, immutably and eternally, in a patch of ground most people never see.

"How'd you notice that?" I ask, in awe, thinking of the button I once found.

Amanda smiles, and I realize that I will never tell her how that button, once found, was later lost. This is her treasure, trapped in the asphalt where she can't possibly dig it out, safe there for all time.

The square of asphalt would have been invisible to me. A knot tightens in my throat as I recall all of those little things Dad tried to show me—life in its smallest, finest detail, a mosaic of gold hidden in everyday things.

I long to live as Amanda does, for a few precious minutes each day putting away my grief for a try at something better, something without a past or a future, time and memory evaporating into the dim glow of a lamp at dusk. Mom once said that life is like a string of pearls, one after the other creating a beautiful whole. What happens when one is all you need, all you want, because the rest are gone? I want that magical minute, the one where I don't have to think, have to remember, or long for something I'll never have again. I want the shell in the sidewalk, the single pearl, the button I once held, that precious second of peace.

And as though reading my mind: "It's for you," Amanda says.

*

I do it for Linda, go to church and listen as the pastor talks about sin, redemption, and grace. Behind him are a giant cross and a choir. Everyone sings hymns, and Luke, Linda, and Amanda sing, too. I don't know how to sing even though the words are right there, plain on the page. I open my mouth, but nothing comes out. It's as though I'm mute, the words foreign. In this huge place, I've lost my voice. Instead, I look up, at all of the stained glass, at the sun making Jesus yellow with red hair. Did he really look like that? Did sunbeams really shoot out of his fingers? I feel a sharp nudge in my ribs and there is Luke's angry face. I quickly look down at my hymnal, open my mouth and lip-sync.

As the pastor speaks, I let my mind wander. How did I get here? I think of Mom and Dad. Those spikes I had when I was ten and that old dirt track. That Stetson hat and those beat-up cowboy boots Dad scuffed in the desert. Shards of brown glass he'd kick around, dusty and common, especially on Sunday mornings after wild nights when people had been there ahead of us shooting at beer bottles, the glass exploding into my next day's treasure—a fireworks of hope: a child's giddy excitement over brown diamonds.

"Are you listening?" Luke hisses in my ear.

He startles me, makes me have to pee. I squeeze my legs together hoping I don't wet my pants. "Can I go to the bathroom?"

"No."

"Please."

"Stop squirming."

"I have to go to the bathroom."

He grabs my wrist, squeezes. "What'd I say the other night about listening?"

My mind goes blank as panic takes over. "I don't know."

And that's when it happens. My bruise-colored dress can't hide the gracelessness running down my leg.

*

I lie in bed the rest of the day, beneath that tired flag.

You're going to have to learn respect, he'd said.

I wait for the slam of the front door. They're going to the park while I stay home and think about what I did. Willfully not paying attention to the pastor and his message from Our Lord. Showing blatant disrespect for God's word by letting my eyes wander over the church and everyone in it. Lying about having to pee when called on to listen, then peeing just to spite what I was told to do—in my new dress, no less, and having to greet my fellow parishioners, "May Christ be with you," with a giant urine stain showcasing my lack of character.

I stare up at that flag, now gray. The Olympic rings look like they're all the same color, dirt-smeared, shit-smeared. I wonder what would happen if I tore it down, shat on it, and showed it to Luke. It's what I want to do, what Dad would want to do.

My cowardice makes me lethargic, so I lie there and I look at all of the pictures, Luke as a young man running down the lanes of an Olympic track in some foreign country, a grimace on his face, pain caught eternally in a single second, still palpable twenty years later. Maybe that's what has always drawn my father to greatness—not the medal, the fame, or the fortune, but that single, tangible moment, captured forever, eternally observable, impossible to forget or discard—the ultimate possession. Yourself at your best. Proof of your worth even when you're no longer on the podium.

Then there is Luke. It occurs to me that he doesn't seem happy. I wish I could tell Dad just how much I loved him (and took him for granted). *I don't need you to win. It doesn't matter, anyway. Look at Luke. He's not happy, either. Besides, I'm better than that stupid 4:07 mile, better than that medal. I'm your greatest accomplishment.*

Anger overrides my fear. I tear down the flag, yank it with my teeth until I'm breathless, all of my fury concentrated on that brittle, musty cotton. But it's stronger than it looks; it doesn't rip. So I stomp on it, making sure to leave recognizable treads, then I get a more dangerous itch. Luke's pictures. I grab them, slam them onto the floor, shattering the glass and cutting myself as I pull the photographs out of the mess, a thrill pulsing through me as I tear them to shreds. All of those moments, those pinnacles, those eternal bests, gone.

I don't stop there. I shatter the mirror, shove over the dresser, tear out all of the clothes, stomp them, kick them, find my new (urine-soaked) dress and ruin that, too (unlike the flag, it tears), pull everything out of the closet and break, stomp, and throw whatever isn't too heavy. I find Luke's golf clubs and crack one across the foosball machine, destroying its perfect green field and bending the club. I take the club to what remains of the mirror and the dresser, knock the dartboard off the wall and crack it. I break the window, knock plaster off the ceiling, and put a dent in the wall. I think for a dangerous moment about taking the club to the rest of the house, but my anger is spent, my biceps burning as I try to catch my breath.

I lie back on the bed, high and exhausted, the room a mess. What will he do to me now? I want to stare into those furious brown eyes and tell him he'll never break me, will never possess me and to hell with the best in the world.

Maybe he'll kill me. Maybe that's all that's left for him to do.

*

For hours, I await the inevitable. I'm not running from this. Not apologizing. Not hiding. This is me. My fury goes beyond my father's righteous entitlement or my mother's pious despair. My hatred is clean. There is no dilution or impurity in it. It's not tainted by any other insipid emotion, love or pity or empathy. It is pure. And it is purely me. It's who I am above and beyond my mother and my father. It's not strong, it's overpowering. And it's original; I doubt anyone hates quite the way I do, as a habit of thought and as a lifestyle, as surely as breath is regularly taken into my lungs, a world growing within me that can't be quelled or conquered. It's unlike the transient hatred that's all too typical, cloaked in anger and jealousy and fear; mine is unequivocal. And it is infinite.

*

Funny how it evaporates the minute I see her horrified face. "Oh my God," Linda gasps as she walks in. "What have you done?" She is suddenly crying. "Why, Gina? Why did you do this?"

Her sobs make my stomach lurch and I'm suddenly terrified, suddenly sorry. "Someone broke in."

"*What?*"

"I didn't do this. Someone broke in."

She stands there with her mouth open, horror-stricken. "We can't let him see this." She shuts the door, locks it, and goes to work, rushing around, grabbing each ruined scrap, plastic, paper, cloth, shoving it all into the laundry bin. I wonder why she is doing this for me.

"Help me, Gina. We've got to get this cleaned up."

Something in the back of my throat closes up. "Why are you helping me?"

"Never mind that now. We've got to get this cleaned up before he gets back."

We shove everything under the bed, into the ruined drawers of the oak dresser, into the closet. "I'll tell him you're asleep when he gets back, ok?" she says. "We'll figure something out."

*

I hear their muffled voices upstairs. She's trying to save me, though I don't understand it. I wouldn't even save myself.

I lie on the bed for hours, watching as the radiance outside turns from light to dark. Above, the creaks of footsteps and life as usual keep me tethered to the reality I'm hiding. My angst has gotten tougher to bury; it's strewn and broken, powder on the rug.

*

Linda comes down with a plate of food, covered with a cloth. "I hope it stayed warm."

I pull off the cloth and breathe in the smell of roast beef. I think of Dad. Moments in the desert, moments not captured. Nothing like the now ruined photo of Luke's pained sprint down the track. Six months from now, I won't remember this. I take a bite and burst into tears. I feel Linda's palm on my shoulder and for what seems like forever, we don't speak. I eat and cry. She sits with me and that's all.

Finally, I work up my nerve: "Why are you doing this for me?"

"You're a good girl."

"No, I'm not."

"You did something bad. That's not the same."

I think of Luke and his sprint down the track. He should be happy. I would be. But maybe that's not him, either. "I'm scared of him," I say.

She purses her lips. "You shouldn't be. He sees great potential in you. He cares about you, believe it or not—it's just that he doesn't always know how to show it."

"That's not true. He hates me."

She cups my face in her palms, gently, as though holding a butterfly. "He wants to see you succeed, Gina—and sometimes he thinks that takes some tough love." She hesitates. "Tougher sometimes than it needs to be, but he has his reasons."

I shove her hand away. "Why are you defending him?"

"I know him."

I think of my father. I knew him, more than anyone else. I knew the man behind the Stetson and cowboy boots and was constantly defending him, too.

*

For the next month, Linda tells Luke and Amanda that my room is off limits while she redecorates it and surprises everyone with the makeover. She waits until Luke is gone to take all of the ruined things out, buys a new dresser to cover the hole in the wall until she can figure out how to patch it and browses home stores to replace the drapes I destroyed. There will be new paint. New trim. New closet doors. It has become her hobby to fix my room. Little by little, she does it. And little by little, I surrender. I wonder what Mom would think. Would she forgive me? Would she protect me? Would she be jealous of Linda, knowing that I'm beginning to need her, love her, more?

Devastation
1993

"May I speak to Gina Dalton?"

I swallow a lump as I stand at the door, the police officer facing me obviously nervous, preparing to tell me something I don't want to hear. "I'm Gina Dalton."

He fidgets with his hat, like Dad used to. He reminds me of Dad, just a little—with a mustache and kind eyes, boyish, paradoxically paternal and youthful. I feel someone come up behind me and put a hand on my shoulder.

"Can I help you?" I hear Linda say.

But the boy-officer can't speak right away. He stutters, doesn't know how to tell us as he moves his hat round and round in his hands.

"For heaven's sakes, come in," Linda says.

Then finally, after an eternity between the front door and the couch: "We found him."

Amanda appears from around a corner. "Mom?"

I want to slap her. I want to jump up and scream *Go Away!*

"Could you go up to your room, sweetheart? I'll be there in a minute."

"You found him?" My voice is not my own. "Where?"

He catches my gaze and I can tell he's sorry, so sorry. "About fifty miles west of Portland, in the state forest a few miles off of Highway 26, next to a quarry."

My face is hot and my mind goes blank, his words barely making sense. *What's a quarry?* I close my eyes, will back tears. Fury. Grief. "What happened to him?"

"We're not completely—"

I stand. "What happened to him?"

"We're still waiting for the coroner to—"

I realize suddenly that I'm screaming: *"What happened to him?"*

*

I recall the night in Hayward Field, his blood in the rain, hidden in the gloom, shocking in the light as trails of it went down the drain. He'd been proud of it then.

The fingerprints come back as belonging to Victor Moun, recently caught when he was arrested for a convenience store robbery. I imagine him every night as I drift off to sleep, an evil-looking man with yellow eyes, a handlebar mustache and bushy eyebrows. But the picture in the paper shows a pudgy, round-faced man in his twenties with a sad little-kid expression. He's not what I imagined. Not the monster I thought I'd see. He looks like the kind of kid Dad could've beaten up—or worse, the kind he would've helped.

I imagine Dad with his Stetson pushed back on his head, driving his green Caddie all over the countryside looking for an old treasure at a yard sale, some glittering opportunity, with an arm hanging out, freckled in the sun. He spots a young man with his thumb out and pulls off onto the shoulder, offering him a ride the way he once offered Linn a hand…

You're so stupid, Dad. How could you be so stupid?

There is tragedy in the irony. It was a robbery-gone-bad on a man who had nothing. I can't stop crying. I think of Dad and his alkaline water. Victor couldn't steal that. Couldn't steal Hayward Field. Couldn't take those desert stars and that long-shot wish. I didn't want his life, but I don't know how to live without him. And all so that I can have a dream he walked away from.

"Sweetheart?" It's Linda. "I've got something for you."

I'm in bed and I make no attempt to move.

"They found the letter in your dad's car, in the glove box. And the baby picture…"

I sit up, breathless.

"They found it when they took the car apart. It must have been on the dash and slipped into some crack years ago. It'd been in there a long time."

I grab them from Linda's hand. My letter:

Dear Mom—

We're in Eugene, Oregon. Do you know where that is? Dad says it's a place where everything starts. Have you ever heard of Steve Prefontaine? I wish you were here. I miss you. Maybe you could ride a train to Eugene. I wish you would. I'd wait for you at the station. And things would be ok again.

Love,

Gina

And the baby picture, which I'd never seen before: a Polaroid of me in a frilly white dress and black patent leather shoes, Mom holding me up, joy on her face, her curly hair long. Linda has a plastic bag, too. With my stuff in it. Tiger tube socks from Mom and long johns Dad bought me before our first extended stay at Myles Lake. I feel my face dissolve into tears, Linda's hand on my shoulder, but I shrug it off.

"I'm so sorry, sweetie."

"He said he'd mail it." I tear the note to shreds, pencil-lead-laced snow on the carpet. "He said he would. He said he'd find her. He promised."

"Come here, let's just—"

"*No.* They didn't care, so why should you?"

"I care about you, Gina."

I turn over, away from her. "No you don't. You're pretending, like they did. The only reason you're letting me stay here is because the state's paying for it."

"That's not true."

I won't give her anything—certainly not the chance to decide I'm no good. "Go away."

*

Linda brings me beautiful meals on a TV tray. The smells fill my room. Chicken noodle soup. Apple pie. Beef stroganoff. Pepperoni pizza. Nachos. Fresh fruit. Hot chocolate. Blueberry cobbler. All enticements not to give up. But the smells always fade as the food gets cold and I hear her come and clear the dishes, each meal, like the evening's color settling into gloom as the day grows dark, gets cold, old, and soggy.

"Gina…" I feel her hand on me. "Please eat."

But no delicious dish can make up for it. Nothing Linda pulls off the griddle, or out of the oven can save me now. Not even waffles or lasagna or grilled cheese will change my mind. I don't move. Can't. I'm caught in the grip of rigor mortis, already gone. Like my dad, who'd been dead for six months when they found him.

"Gina, I need you to look at me."

But I can't.

"I want you to call upon the Lord for strength."

I turn over, glaring at her, my strength momentarily miraculously restored. "That's such bullshit."

There is hurt on her face. "I think you need to pray, ask Christ for help in getting through this."

"I'm not going to get through this," I shout. "I don't want to get through this."

"Of course you do—and you will."

"I won't. I can't. And Christ can't do anything. I don't believe in that shit."

She closes her eyes and puts a palm to her mouth, the other on her heart. "Please don't say that."

"Why not? Because it scares you? Because it puts doubt in your mind? If there was a God, this wouldn't have happened."

"Oh, Gina…"

I shrug off her hand. "Stop telling me how to think." I turn away from her, refusing to believe any God could have let this happen. I think of the doe, the one Dad couldn't save. He wasn't the magician I thought he was. He couldn't save the house or those old cars, either. He couldn't save Mom. Couldn't save Linn. Can't save me.

But the next time she brings food down to me, I rouse myself enough to flush it down the toilet. Her desperation to save me should make me feel guilty, but it doesn't. The toilet can eat it. It's a hell of a lot better than arguing with her about it.

Archer
1990

I see Linn in front of his locker, alone, his back to me and I think of the medal. I was wrong when I thought I didn't need it. I do need it. It is my father at his best. My father in his dreams. An identity he's been trying his whole life to recover.

I skip class, following Linn instead. I want something I can hold when everything else is gone, something of Dad's that will remind me of what he once was, of what he once had, the one tangible thing that proves dreams can come true.

I'm careful to hide around corners whenever he lollygags, as he drags a stick along a picket fence, making it *ratatatat*, as he kicks a rock through an alley, as he skips and spits and takes his time.

I wonder why he's leaving school early. Is he sneaking in a workout? Is he sick? Or just tired of being picked on?

I realize as he crosses Main Street that he's going home.

I wait in the alley next to his house, listening for the squeak of the screen door as he goes in. Once I hear it, I peer around the fence and dash through the yard, in hot pursuit. I imagine socking him in the nose and grabbing my father's medal. Or kicking him in the knee, and diving for that shining piece of gold as he doubles over. But where would he keep it? Where would I begin to look? Despair floods through me, but I still have to try.

His house seems bigger standing in front of it than it did waiting in the backseat of my father's Cadillac and it seems older, too. From the road, it looks impeccable, but as I tiptoe up the steps, I notice tiny faults, cracks in one of the windows and chipping paint, a torn screen, rusty hinges that creak when you open the door. It doesn't look like a rich man's house to me.

I take a deep breath as I push open the door and walk into the front parlor. Above, there is an elaborate chandelier draped in cobwebs and I notice the pictures on the wall, not family photos, but renditions of paintings by famous artists, the colors washed-out despite the fact there is little light. Even shadow can fade color over decades, I realize. The whole place feels tired, subdued by age, dust caught in cobwebs so old they look like silk. There's no sentimentality of any kind here, no reminders that this is a home.

"Linn?" I'm suddenly scared. Maybe he isn't here, after all. Maybe it was another little boy I followed. Then I see his shoes at the bottom of the stairs, the stained Keds he always wears. "Linn?" I start up the steps.

At the top of the stairs is the mayor's study, an extravagant parlor, high-ceilinged with bay windows and warm wood paneling. His enormous oak desk sports tassel-draped Victorian lamps, another wisp of spider web shivering with the displacement of air I create. The desk is flanked by a large leather chair, the same chair I've seen him sitting in on frigid Saturday mornings when Linn was already out front waiting for me and my dad.

And then—under a pile of paper, just a corner sticking out, a flash of gold! My heart lurches as I spot it. What is it doing there? Did Linn put it there? Did the mayor? Why? I notice other things too, on this small corner of oak, a squad of tiny green soldiers and a tiger's-eye marble, Linn's things, claiming this outer island on his father's desk. Did Linn put them here as a means to be close to his father, just as I chose the track to be near mine? Dad and me. Me and Dad. Only this seems sad. The corner is so small. And I can't really see Linn trying to stake out a corner that way. Maybe this stuff is here because his father took it from him, the marble and toy soldiers confiscated because they were things Linn was supposed to outgrow. And if the medal's here too, it must've meant something to him. Enough that his father took it away from him. In a blitz of grief, I know he and Dad really had shared a bond I'd thought was mine alone.

I tug at the flash of gold, pull it out and pick it up, my heart hammering as I turn it over:

Robert Caleb Dalton, May 13, 1976
Mile, 1st place, Petaluma, CA, 4:07

The words are so familiar, fixtures of my life—as much a memory as my mother's face. I trace their furrowed shapes. They seem fragile here, as though the gold has turned to glass. The medal feels small in my palm, insignificant.

From downstairs, an angry voice splits the air. "You better have a damn good reason to be home at this hour."

I panic and hide in the closet, peering through a slit in the door as Linn dashes in and dives under his father's desk. But the minute Mayor Busby walks into his parlor, he sees his son's guilty foot sticking conspicuously into view. Despite the man's regal façade, the newly pressed suit and wingtips, his crimson face gives away the primal fury riding shallowly beneath the surface of refinement. He is not the man of quiet resolve people see in his town halls.

He grabs his son's foot violently. *"You come out of there."*

"No, wait—" Linn is breathless, terrified, and pitifully small next to his father. "They were after me again…"

The mayor pulls him up by an arm. "Who was after you? Your classmates? Stop being a sissy and they'll leave you alone. How about that?" Arthur has his son by the collar of his shirt, shaking him roughly. "And what have I told you about staying out of this room? You stay out of this goddamned room, you hear me?"

"Yes, sir." Linn is sobbing.

My heart is in my throat, racing as I cover my mouth. I close my eyes, panicked. I can't believe this is happening, can't watch any more. A picture of Linn in the closet soaked in urine flashes through my mind. I think of the way my father saved him, wishing he'd save me, too. Then I remember something he said: *Be that person I have all the faith in the world in. That's who I want to show to Linn.*

I take a deep breath and push open the door, my heart hammering. They both startle, look over. The mayor has his son by the arm.

"Let him go," I try to say, but the words come out like squeaks. I don't sound tough. Instead, I sound scared.

"What the hell…" Arthur Busby's face is crimson.

Seeing his father's distraction, Linn pulls out of the mayor's grasp and runs from the room. I've saved him, but have doomed myself. I'm awash in a cold sweat as he approaches me.

His face is tight. "What's this?" He whisks the medal out of my hand, holds it up as though looking at something small and squirming, a rodent. "Oh; this is your father's?" He grins, but it isn't kind. "Linn said he found it in the dirt."

I swallow hard, somehow manage to speak. "It's mine. He took it."

Arthur Busby snorts. "A sissy like him wouldn't have the balls." He glances at the inscription. "And there's no way your dad actually won this. Not a half-ass screw-up like him. He's the stupid bastard who thinks nobody can check signatures against voter registrations." He looks at the medal again. "He's lucky he lost so quickly. I bet he walked into a second-hand store, bought this thing for a couple of bucks, and carved his name on it to impress his friends."

I can't hold it in any longer; the sobs escape against my will.

"Disappointing to find out the truth, I know." I feel his breath in my ear. "Listen carefully. Leave now or I'll make sure the world knows what kind of people you and your father really are. And don't say a word about me or my son to anyone, ever, or I'll have you charged with breaking and entering and sue him for what little he has. Do you understand?"

Then, he holds up my father's medal, the 4:07 mile that once made him a hero, and throws it in the trash.

Portland
1993

"Tachycardia with BP well below normal... Damn near starved herself to death... Potassium levels are in the basement." Voices float in and out of a vast white space. *Dad? Are you there?* He smiles, those half-moons dancing. "I'm right here, sweetheart."

"Where'd you go?"

"To hell and back." He laughs. "Let me tell you, it's crazier than you think."

"Really?"

"Really. No fire and brimstone, just a hell of a lot of sun."

"What?" I squint up at him, my voice a croak.

He grins. "Sun. It's just too damn bright in here."

"Dad—is that really you?"

"No." Something in his face starts to change and I close my eyes before I see it. I don't want to see it, whatever it is. Someone is screaming. There's something on my wrist. A claw. Is that Dad's hand or the devil's? Or God's? "Stop, please stop…" The voice is shrill, panicked. There are faces in the white and all I see are eyes. Blue ones, brown ones, and some with lines. Older and younger.

"Calm down, sweetie; we'll get you stabilized."

"Dad, stop. That *hurts.*"

"I did this for you and all you can do is tell me I'm stupid."

"I didn't mean it."

"Sure you did."

"No, I didn't. I was angry. You left me."

I open my eyes and there is Luke. He's wearing a mask as the doctors work on me, his brown eyes locked on mine. I don't know what I see, but it's something beyond anger, beyond pity, beyond desperation. It is something wild, something I've never seen.

"We've got to stabilize her heart rhythm. Potassium chloride, please."

"It's not working."

"Goddamn it, get that crash cart up here!"

*

"You don't want to die. Just trust me on that."

"Because there's no God?"

"Because there's just too much damn sun."

"Go away; you're scaring me."

"Then take a breath."

"I'm trying."

"Try harder."

*

"She's returning to a normal sinus rhythm."

A what?

Someone's holding my hand too tightly. Crushing it. *Dad, you're hurting me.*

"Ok—we need everybody to clear out."

I try to open my eyes, but I can't.

"She's stabilizing. We've got her."

"Clear out, please."

I open my eyes and everyone is gone.

*

The next two days are a blur. There are flowers, well-wishes, and cards. Linda drops by with Amanda, who gives me a Cabbage Patch doll with braids, freckles, and a blue dress. I drink a bunch of 7-Up and eat a lot of Jell-O, among other light, bland things like Saltines and dinner rolls.

"Is Luke coming by?" I don't know why I'm compelled to ask, but it's a burning question.

Linda looks quickly at Amanda, tries to smile. "I don't think so, sweetheart."

"After what happened to Olivia—"

"*Amanda.*"

It's the first time I've ever heard Linda's voice turn hard. And Amanda flinches, looks away.

"He's mighty busy right now with practices," Linda continues quietly.

Who's Olivia? And what's she got to do with me? I feel my face flush. I want him to care. "I almost died."

"I know. He just…" Again, she glances at her daughter. "He doesn't do so well with this stuff."

"What stuff? Death?"

She takes out a Kleenex and wipes her eyes. "That's right. He just doesn't like to talk about such things."

"Doesn't he believe in God?"

"Of course he does."

"Then why's he afraid?"

"Goodness gracious; everyone's afraid of death."

"I'm not."

She stares at me. "Sure you are."

"No I'm not. I could die right now and I'd be just fine." I stick my chin out for added effect.

"Well…" She stands. "Most people wouldn't be."

"Where are you going?"

"It's time for us to be heading home."

"Don't go." I'm shocked at my desperation. She's not my mother.

Linda takes my hand and sits back down. "Of course, honey. I'll stay as long as they'll let me."

*

I name the Cabbage Patch doll Olivia. I thought I'd outgrown dolls, but I like this one, with her freckles and braids. She reminds me of Mom, or of what I'd guess Mom might've looked like as a little girl. I hold onto her through the night and it surprises me just how far a little nylon and cotton will go to soothe the loneliness that settles in with the dark.

Archer
1990

It's long after dark, and the mayor's words course through my mind like a pulse: *Leave now or I'll make sure the world knows what kind of people you and your father really are.* But for Dad, the pull for something else, something new, something better, is already moving in like a tide as he bangs into the kitchen with a smile, whistling a nameless tune. He throws his Stetson on a hook as he sets down some large take-out containers.

"Who thought we'd be dining on sashimi and caviar?" he says, lighting a candle and setting it on the table, pretending that it's for atmosphere, rather than something we've done off and on for a year. Even my studies have to be done early or by flashlight.

"At least for tonight, you and I are royalty," he says. "Do you prefer to be a Queen or a Princess?"

My throat tightens. He's trying so hard, but I know where this must have come from. "I don't want it."

Disappointment settles in his face. "It's sashimi."

"It's garbage."

"I had a little extra money saved up. I got it to celebrate our new start."

But I know better. I imagine the dumpster behind Kazatimiru's, the one that smells like Myles Lake when the water is low. I shake my head. "I don't like sashimi."

"Have you ever had it?"

"I've smelled it."

My father stands defeated in the middle of the kitchen. "Gina, I got this for you. Will you please at least try it?"

I gaze down at the fillet, nudging it with a fork, noticing that part of it has been eaten. "How do you know it won't make us sick?"

He looks away. "I saw them throw it out. It's fresh."

I return my gaze to the fillet, wondering who has taken a bite out of it, knowing it's someone with money, someone with influence, someone with respect. Somebody my father would tip his wide-brimmed Stetson to as they walked by him on the street. I take a bite and then another and another; I was hungrier than I thought.

"What do you think?" He looks at me expectantly.

I shrug. "It's ok."

"Just ok?"

"It's pretty good."

"Royalty good?"

I smile a little, nod. I want to make this special, want him to know it's ok.

"Queen or Princess good?"

I think for a moment. "Queen good."

"Queen good? Really? Now that's taking it up a notch."

I smile, loving his sense of magic, even now. "How about you? You think it's King good?"

He takes a bite, narrowing his gaze at the fillet. "Pretty darned close."

"Duke good?" I laugh.

He shakes his head. "Better than that." He ponders a moment. "I think it might even be Divine." He smiles, holds up his water glass. "To new starts."

I hold up mine. "To new starts."

"We foreclose tomorrow."

So this is it, our last night in this house. And this is his way of breaking the news to me. I set down my glass, despair flooding through me. "Will I still be able to go to school?"

"Of course. Your education is top priority. We'll do everything we did before. You'll go to school and I'll find odd jobs to pay for gas to get you there. We'll live our lives the way we've been living them—minus the roof and the fridge." He smiles. "We'll find a place."

I glance around. "Where are we going to put everything?"

"We're not."

I look at him.

"It all goes with the house." He takes a deep, weary breath. "We'll start off with nothing, but nothing is good. We'll have a completely clean slate, nothing to remind us of our old lives. It'll be like a bright white canvas. You ever painted in art class?"

I nod.

"Just think of it that way, like that big white canvas; you'll have the palette in your hand and you can paint it any color you want."

I nod, think muted, blue and green and white. Water and land and sky. Our new home.

He holds up his glass. "To the empty canvas and the blank page."

I nod, holding up my glass, wordless.

"Home" Again
1993

Linda's put up pink and purple streamers and a big, loopy-lettered sign that reads: *Welcome Home, Gina!*

"I made the sign," Amanda says proudly, her smile so big I see her braces in their entirety.

"I like it. Thanks."

"I've never met anyone who *almost* died before." She looks away as though to say something else, but instead sits next to me on the couch and pushes her glasses up higher on her nose, continuing to smile.

I smile back. Awkwardly.

"Who wants hot chocolate?" Linda says, jumping up. "I've even got Reddy-Whip and those mini-marshmallows to put on top."

"Me, me," Amanda says, thrusting her arm up. It looks like a toothpick in contrast to the fat, pink puffy sleeve from which it comes. I almost laugh.

"You seem like you're in a good mood," Linda says, grinning at me.

"I feel pretty good today."

"Nothing like a tap on the shoulder from our Lord to wake you up. Life really is beautiful."

She leaves to get the hot chocolate and I'm alone with Amanda. I wish she'd stop smiling.

"Who's Olivia?"

That takes the smile off her face, as her glance darts toward the door. "Don't tell anyone, but she was my half-sister. Dad was her dad, too. She didn't live here but we saw her all the time."

I think of Luke, remember that he's someone's father. Apparently not just Amanda's. "What happened?"

"She died. For real."

I feel my chest tighten. "How?"

"Dad said it was leukemia. She was really sick and kept going to a special hospital all the time."

"I'm sorry."

"Thanks." The smile returns. "She's walking with Jesus now."

In too much damn sun.

"Ok, Girls. It's time for a treat." Linda returns, holding both cups up, frosted high with whip.

"Did you get me the dog one?" Amanda asks excitedly.

"Yes, hon—I know you like the dog cup."

"And Gina gets Prairie Polly," Amanda says. "I love Prairie Polly. I used to be so into that when I was little."

I look at the cup. There's a little girl on it wearing a pink dress and bonnet who I guess must be Prairie Polly and she's letting a deer eat out of her hand. *Just don't chase it over a cliff.*

Amanda takes a sip of her hot chocolate. "Mmmmm!" And furiously kicks her feet. "SO GOOD!" She looks at me. "Drink yours, drink yours, drink yours."

Irritation flashes through me, but I take a sip. "Mmm. It's good."

"It's not good; it's GRRREAT. Who am I?"

I shrug.

"Tony the Tiger. Don't you know? He's on TV."

"I don't watch TV."

"Why?"

"We almost never had one."

"Because you were poor?"

"Amanda Grace." Linda glares at her daughter. "You know better than to ask such questions."

*

We eat lunch in silence after church. It's been three weeks since my discharge from the hospital, and Luke still won't look at me. Until he says to Linda: "I want you and Amanda to get out of the house this afternoon; Gina and I need to talk."

My stomach lurches. Is he going to yell at me? Is he kicking me out?

Linda wipes her mouth. "You sure? Why don't we all get out and do something as a fam—"

"I want to talk to Gina alone."

*

I wait for him in my room and when he comes, he brings something in a pillowcase. He pulls over a chair so that I'm facing him as I wait on my bed. He sits down, takes a breath, and looks me in the eye.

"Do you want to die?"

I think for a moment about being a smartass before deciding against it. "No."

He sits back. "Good."

"What's that?" I nod toward the pillowcase.

"This?" He holds it up. "Prove yourself and I'll show you."

"What do you mean?"

"Prove to me you're worthy."

My heart speeds up. "Worthy of what?"

"Of doing this. Of going for it." He looks at me as he dangles the pillowcase. "You may die trying."

I wait, nervous, for an explanation.

"We're going to the track."

"Now?"

"You want it or not?"

*

I stand, toe on the line, as the sky opens up. I feel the rain on my face, rolling down my cheeks like tears.

"Go," Luke says. "Hard."

"How hard?"

"81s."

"Are these 400s?"

"Go."

"How far—"

"NOW."

I push off, gliding at first. I hit the first 200 meters in 39 seconds. But Luke isn't telling me to slow down. These have to be 400s. I go hard through the line, stop.

"Why the hell are you stopping?" he shouts. "I said 81s."

"But…"

"Go. You do an 84 on this one, you'd better do 78 on the next one."

I start again, hold the pace. It's still ok. Maybe they're 800s. I come around again in 83.

"Next one better be in 79," Luke shouts.

"I can't–"

"Bullshit."

I pick it up, but now it's starting to hurt. I hit the line in 80.

"I said 79."

The pit of my stomach has become the surface of a storm-stirred sea. I come across the line in 85.

"You're digging yourself a hole, Gina. Do the next one in 77 and you can stop."

"I can't," I puff.

"Then you're not stopping."

I push as hard as I can, my breath now coming in spasms, but I still hit the line in 82.

"Do the next one in 80 and you can stop."

But I can't. My legs won't go any faster. "Please…please…can I…."

"No."

83.

"I need a 79."

86.

"Next one in 76. The slower you run, the more you'll need to make up."

"Luke…I *can't*—"

"Stop whining."

"Please, I—"

"Go or you're out."

87.

"The next one had better be a 74."

I fall to my knees.

"Get up." Luke is standing over me.

"I can't."

"You can. And you will."

I stand, wobbly.

"Go. Now."

87.

89.

92.

I don't hear him anymore. I've failed, but I keep running anyway.

91.

93.

96.

97.

All there is in the world are my legs. My heart. My breath. My eyes shut against the sky and then that cramp. I run some more, rain mixed with tears running down my cheeks.

98.

99.

99.

101.

104.

110.

143.

I'm staggering, my calves cramping.

"You're done," I hear him say.

I collapse. Luke picks me up and walks me to the car, his arm around my shoulder. He's gentle. Gentler than I've ever known him to be. I lie in the backseat under a wool blanket, shaking. He hands me the pillowcase. Something in it is hard and cold.

I don't look. Don't care. I close my eyes and concentrate on not feeling the cramping in my legs. "Oh, when's this gonna stop?" I groan, anticipating the next charley horse.

"Never," he says from the front seat.

*

I carry the pillowcase to my room and fall down on my bed, curling into a ball under a pink comforter, the shy glow from a bedside lamp making everything soft. I close my eyes, exhausted and still shaking, my legs and back stiff. I reach into the pillowcase and pull out a medal. It's gold and on it is the carving of a man, arms stretched to embrace the sky, chest thrust forward as though he's looking to hug a giant. Who? God? Or destiny? He's won and he's reaching to claim a star. Any star. But there are so many. How can any one star be special?

I'm deflated. Tired. Discouraged. I don't want the medal. It is lost to me as veritably as my father's. I throw it onto the floor and turn over.

And there in the doorway is Luke. "It was hers, you know."

I sit up, startled. "Whose?"

"Olivia's."

My stomach lurches.

He sits on the bed and I suddenly can't look at him.

"She was anorexic."

I swallow a lump.

"You don't want to die like that."

Back to School
1994

The numbness settles in like a fog. I try just going to school and realize I've turned into a pariah. Everyone's heard the rumors. I'm a crazy-case. People either ignore me or snicker as I walk by. When I sit down at a table in the lunchroom, everybody gets up and moves. I sit alone. I eat alone. I walk alone.

But it's not as bad as you'd think. For the most part, people don't care. Most of them simply pretend I don't exist. I keep to myself, pretending to be the black hole I know deep down I am. I am finally, purely, myself. After everything that's happened, being liked by other people is a small affair. I don't want to be liked. I don't need to be liked. And I'm smart enough to know that if people knew me, I mean *really* knew me, they wouldn't like me anyway.

Everybody seems to be moving on with their lives, happily progressing both here in school and across the river in Portland, where Luke's team is gearing up for spring track. I have the bizarre impression that I've been asleep and am now just waking up to a reality beyond the lightless tunnel my own life has become. I like this other world despite the ostracism and the ridicule, despite the pervasive feeling I don't belong and never will, despite the fact I'm only a spectator. I look forward to school every day, vastly removed from the hope-turned-despair that brought me to this point. I realize I've missed simple, innocuous things like math and global studies. I missed the gentle reprimands of frustrated teachers, their bland threats of sending transgressors to the principal's office a welcome respite from death runs and police officers delivering bad news as it's getting dark.

This is so easy. If I could, I'd stay in school forever, spending my time working complicated math formulas and pouring liquids into beakers. I'd read all the greats and pontificate on them for hours. I'd study every area of the world and learn all the capitols, the demographics, the languages, the religious affiliations, the climates, the mountain ranges, the plateaus and plains, deserts and steppes. I'd know the state birds and state flowers. I'd name every American president. I'd know the difference between a homophone and a synonym and an antonym and an adverb. I'd know everything—except for all the bad stuff, the nightmares, the humiliations, and all of those damning secrets poverty inspires.

My mother was right; education really is freedom. Dad had quit because that was ultimately the easy way out. Dream so big that when you fail you can tell yourself it was always impossible anyway. Mom had quit for love, then had gotten trapped when love wasn't enough. But education is also escape. You can steel yourself against anything when you're educated. When things get rough, you can focus on the narrowest angle of an isosceles triangle and figure out just how much space you have to squeeze through to escape or study Einstein's theory of relativity and ride a beam of light right out of the darkness. You can play the odds, using statistics to determine what the likelihood is you'll survive or pick up a ruler and measure the number of feet it'll take to walk right out of town. I sit by myself in the back, as far away from the other students as I can get, relishing the smell of chalk, old linoleum, and adolescent sweat. I take lots and lots of notes, pages of them, more than anyone else. I stay long after the bell has rung and the others have left and the teacher looks up at me from behind a giant desk, a quizzical expression on her face.

"Do you have any questions, Gina?"

I always shake my head.

"You're going to be late for your next class."

I don't care. I'll be late and the teacher in the next class will glare at me as I slouch in and the other kids will snicker a little and I'll take my seat in the back and I'll sit there and take notes and relish the old smells I used to take for granted and thank God I'm here and not there. Not collapsing from exhaustion on the track or headfirst in the dumpster behind Lamb's. Not at home in a lamp-lit basement listening to lectures about how Jesus walks with me; I just don't see him. Life is fine. I'm not worried about any pissed-off teacher talking to any pissed-off principal. And if they ask me, I'll tell them I don't care. Because all I care about is being here and not there.

*

It's nice to get home after school and find everyone gone. I ride the bus since I'm no longer going to practice with Luke. I love the silence crawling along the walls. I love sneaking something out of the freezer to have all to myself. I love those unexpected goodies Linda will sometimes buy. The occasional six-pack of Coca-Cola or package of Totino's Pizza Rolls. I don't hesitate to help myself, aware that all the nights spent hungry more than make up for my gluttony now.

I get to know this family, little by little, as I find their preferences in the fridge. It's like looking them in the eye without that uncomfortable flinch I feel as they look into mine. This is anonymous, yet intimate. I get to know them yet keep them at arm's length. It's easy, then, to snoop elsewhere. What is hanging in their closets? How about the desk and dresser drawers? What about that space under the bed? I'm so glad I ride the bus. Like exploring an undiscovered country, I'm excited about what I find. Those intimacies no one else knows or notices. The worn lace on Linda's bra. The baby blanket of Amanda's she keeps folded neatly in the top of the closet. The old naked Barbies with ratty hair and chewed-up feet that vaguely smell like bathtub in the toy chest Amanda never digs through anymore. I should feel guilty, snooping, but the things I find remind me too much of Archer, forgotten gems, the stuff of life, but quickly dismissed and left behind. My memories and theirs both have smells. Sagebrush and bathwater. Cut grass and mothballs. Unlike the ethereal dreams of greatness, these are coarse and raw, imperfect.

*

It's the imperfection that starts to reawaken me as the weeks and months go by, details reminding me that I am, in fact, alive. Hunger. Cold. Bright sunlight through curtains and the response to turn over and crawl into a dream. The sight of Amanda's ratty nightgown on the floor, and a bunny's cotton-ball nose from an arts-and-crafts class she had in school. The smell of wet pavement and loam on a spring day. I don't tell anyone about Olivia's medal, in the same way I don't talk about Myles Lake or Kazatimuru's King-great sashimi. Because words don't work. They are experiences captured only in images and feelings that words can't touch.

*

One day, when Linda and Amanda return, giddy from a spring stroll through the zoo, I feel something I haven't felt in a long time—a desire to be a part of the world. I never thought I'd fit in here, but maybe that's changing. Maybe I can live again. Even happily.

They rush in, a flurry of unwrapping scarves and thrown-off jackets, their cheeks rosy from the chill. They bring with them the smell of crisp air. Easter air.

"Oh, it was gorgeous—flowers everywhere, yellow, pink, and red. Cool sunshine," Linda tells me.

"I picked some for you," Amanda says, handing me a bouquet. "Aren't they pretty?"

I nod, grateful for the gesture as I put my face in them and breathe. Loam and rain. *Don't forget to smell the air.*

"We saw the elephants *up close*," Amanda says. "They were feeding right next to the glass. They're so big. Even the babies are big, huh Mom?"

"They sure are."

"I'd love to see them," I say.

Linda's cheeks flush and I can see her hope in her clasped hands. "We'd love to take you."

*

It's a cold and cloudy Saturday at the zoo. I pull my coat around me for warmth, something that Amanda gave me as a present—quilted pink silk with fake-fur white sleeves and neckline. I look stupid, feel stupid. But what does it matter?

We walk down a ramp, past the gift shop and I wonder suddenly what I'm doing here. It'd sounded like a good idea the night before, but like the dream that seems brilliant in sleep, it has lost its shine in the light of day.

"Mom, can we get some cotton candy?"

"Maybe later."

"I want mine to be pink." She looks at me. "You can get pink, blue, or purple."

"I guess blue."

"Ooh…ooh…" Amanda jumps up and down, pointing. She looks like a marshmallow bouncing on toothpicks in her huge quilted coat. "It's the Better Burger. Can we go there?"

"Maybe for lunch."

"But I'm hungry."

"*Now?*"

"Yes!"

Linda looks at her watch. "Well, I guess. Are you hungry, Gina?"

I shrug, indifferent. I wish I was like Amanda. I wish I could get excited about the little things and think those things were neat. I remember when Dad bought the house and I got excited about that bald spot in the yard, when I wasn't much older than Amanda is now. That button I'd dug up had been treasure back then. What would it look like now?

I feel Linda's arm around me. "You ok?"

I nod. "I'm kind of tired today."

"It can take a long time to get your strength back."

I want to say *that's not it*. She didn't know about the workout Luke had subjected me to, would probably be furious if she did know. Physically, I was fine, had been for months. On my own, I sometimes walked for hours in the hills above the house. Steep hills. Green hills. Hills where it rained all winter and I had to fight mud and brambles to get to windy viewpoints high above the river, places nobody else went. What I needed was a strength I'd never get back: joy, innocence, life as it should be, not as it is.

The crowds seem happy; they smile at the animals—at the leopards and the elephants as they pace, as they swing their heavy heads, back and forth, behind the glass. I wonder why they sway, why they pace, and I realize it's because it is all they are able to do. They have forgotten who they are. The people don't notice and are never bored by the animals' repeated movements. They don't seem to realize that the leopards and the elephants aren't really like that, not out there. In those wild, private, hidden spaces, they are different—something else, something better, more thrilling, more fantastic. I think of Dad, of who he was in the sun, on a mountain range or a desert plain, on the track in the rain, and how different he could be.

"How do you know who you are?" I ask Linda as we walk toward the restaurant.

She looks at me, knits her brow, and I realize it's a baffling question, like asking where you were before you were born. "What do you mean, sweetheart?"

The words come out of nowhere. "I don't know who I am." Because I don't. I don't feel like myself anywhere. I'm pacing and swaying behind my barrier, and I don't know how to break it down, don't know how to be myself in the wilderness.

"Sometimes it's hard to figure out," Linda says. "You're young; you have lots of time."

But it doesn't feel that way. It feels urgent.

"They were supposed to show me," I say, mostly to myself.

"I want a cheeseburger, Mom."

"Ok." She looks at me. "Gina?"

"Grilled cheese."

"With fries!" Amanda pipes up.

"Ok. One cheeseburger with fries and a grilled cheese."

"I think they come with fries," Amanda says, bumping my hand. "You'll get fries with yours, too. If you don't want them, though, I'll eat them. But only if you don't want them. If you want them, that's ok, too."

"Thanks."

"So is grilled cheese your favorite?" Amanda pushes her glasses up higher on her nose, but they keep sliding down.

"Yeah."

"I like cheese with meat. That's why I like cheeseburgers—and pepperoni pizza. I could eat them every day, like forever. If you could choose just one thing to eat for the rest of your life, what would it be?"

"Worms."

"Huh?"

"I think I'll go eat worms."

Amanda makes a face. "*Gross-O.*"

"I'm just kidding."

"Grilled cheese, then?"

"Yeah, I guess." I remember my birthday at Kazatimuru's when all I wanted was grilled cheese. "Actually, escargot's my favorite."

"Escar-what?"

I'd asked the same thing. "Snails."

*

We eat our lunch, and my mind keeps drifting back to Dad, his death a secret I'll never know. Never understand. I'd felt this way before, on the times I'd heard Mom and Dad arguing in their room, before she left and Dad decided that we didn't really need a roof. Secrets are like bullets. They poke holes in you. Take vital pieces away and depending on where they hit, make you mortal.

"Aren't you hungry, sweetie?"

I stare down at my grilled cheese. It seems limp and small, the bread thin, with what looks like Velveeta oozing out. Ironic that, once, cold like this was exactly how I wanted it. "I don't feel good."

"You want snails instead?" Amanda giggles.

Linda makes a face at her.

"Or worms. With ketchup."

"Amanda, that's enough."

"I'm just trying to cheer her up."

"She just said she's not feeling well; you think references to snails and worms are going to help?"

"Maybe. If she laughs hard enough." She picks up a fry and dramatically dips it in the ketchup, making a ghoulish face. "Deep-fried *worms*…eeewwwaaaahhh…"

Linda hits the table and both of us startle. "That's *enough*."

There's a moment of shock on Amanda's face before it turns red and her eyes well up. "Sorry."

I'm shocked at Linda's sudden anger. It's not like her and it strikes me that I cause trouble wherever I go, without even trying. "I think it's funny," I say. "Really. Deep-fried worms—eeeaaaahhh!"

Through her tears, Amanda smiles, those big braces flashing.

Do you want to die?

This time there isn't any hesitation. *No.*

Don't forget to smell the air.

I decide to try what Dad's shown me all along. How to breathe and forget the rest.

*

I invite Amanda to sit on my bed, and Linda brings us tea. Maybe we could be sisters.

"That's a really cool braid." She points at my hair. "Did you do that?"

I nod and hold up Olivia, the Cabbage Patch doll. "We're matching."

She giggles. "That's neat. I have a Cabbage Patch doll, too. Want me to show you?"

"Yeah."

She jumps up and dashes up the stairs. Maybe it's all a matter of relearning how to live. Maybe I really could be like her. Maybe innocence isn't lost, but buried. Reclaimable, like that button I dug up so long ago.

"Here she is." Amanda skips into my room and plops onto the bed. "She's a corn silk doll."

"She has pretty hair." I stroke the blonde curls. "Where'd you get her?"

"Dad bought her for my birthday." Amanda glances around before cupping a hand to her mouth and whispering: "I think she looks like my sister."

"Really?"

"Yeah. Olivia had blonde hair, too. And she was really pretty."

"I'm sorry that happened to her."

"Me, too. Jesus is taking good care of her now, but it's still hard."

"Do you really believe that?"

"What?"

"That Jesus is taking care of her?"

She makes a face and pushes her glasses up higher on her nose. "Of course; he takes care of us all."

*

When the pastor asks if anyone has any requests, Linda stands. "I want everybody to pray for Gina."

My stomach lurches, and I feel my face flush as everyone's eyes are suddenly on me.

"As you all know, she's lost her father. Pray that the Lord give her strength and that she finds peace in her new normal. Pray for her father's spirit as we send it unto Jesus."

I look down, heat in my face. I imagine Dad walking beside a man with shoulder-length hair and a long, white robe. I think of the way Dad would tip his Stetson and shake the man's hand. What would Jesus think? Would he be angry at Dad like Mom was? Would he tell him to grow up, to stop living in 1976?

That night, I ask Linda: "Do you think Jesus likes my dad?"

She strokes my hair as I lie on my bed. "Jesus doesn't just like your dad; he loves him."

"Loves him? Are you sure? Mom didn't even really love him." At least not any time I could remember.

"That's what makes Jesus different; he loves everybody, even when we make mistakes."

"Even bad people?"

"People aren't born bad; they're taught. And even then, they're not 'bad' people; they're simply misguided." She takes a breath. "You think your father was bad?"

I consider that for a moment and feel a knot in my throat. "Sometimes."

She pats my shoulder. "We all make mistakes. That's part of being human. Jesus knows that. We must learn from our mistakes and ask the Lord to forgive us our sins."

"How do you know that's how it works?"

"It says so in the Bible."

"But how do you know?"

"Faith."

"Faith?" I think of Dad and his cars, and his certainty with every new project that there was a pot of gold just around the corner.

"The belief in something we can't touch, hear, see, or feel."

"I know." After a year of church Sundays, that part I understand. *But how do you know it's there if you can't touch, hear, see, or feel it? What makes you think anyone's taking a tour of the Universe with Dad—especially when, down here, no one but me could stand him? Why would Jesus be any different?*

"It's ok to have doubts."

I catch her gaze. "What do you mean?"

"A lot of people don't believe. Faith takes time." She smiles and gives me a kiss on the forehead. "See you in the morning."

*

I turn the light on after she leaves. It's the first time I've had the courage to really look at the picture the police found in the bowels of my father's car. Me as that six-month-old in my mother's arms. My hair appears as burnished wisps and my grin reveals a bottom tooth. My eyes are my dad's and my smile, my mom's. I am shared. Loved. Forgiven. I may have been a hardship at first, but I can see in my mother's eyes that I am wanted.

So what happened? I go to the bathroom, look in the mirror, and there's that baby with a few more freckles and darker hair, smile gone, attitude to replace it. Would she love who I am now? Could she have imagined back then the me I see today? I stare at the picture and something swells through me. Grief and love mixed. Absolution. I don't know about God, but I believe in moments captured, spared, and kept somewhere sacred. In some other dimension I'm a child in my mother's arms. I feel myself smile as I put the Polaroid under my pillow and turn off the light.

*

I get up early, brush out my hair, and tie it up. Outside, it's barely light, the clouds gathered, gray and rumpled, like a dirty blanket in the corner. I wear my tights, fleece hat, gloves, and a jacket. I recall the way Dad once told me to take off my jacket and warm-ups before track. I hated that. Hated those first few minutes of bitter cold and the jangle of nerves, the promise of speed hanging like the Sword of Damocles over my head, the combination of cold and nerves sending bolts of anxiety through the pit of my stomach.

I relish having my jacket on as I sneak out the front door, as I breathe in that first sweet scent of spring. There'll be no relinquishment this morning. If I want to run in a down coat, I can. I can run slow, 9-minute miles or not at all. I can run a mile and stop and walk. Or I can head toward the edge of town, taking in the lonely city streets caught in the shine of an early morning rain. The street lamps cast orange globes on the sidewalk and I remember a time when I thought I could scoop them up and hold them in my hands, shining Easter eggs caught in the combination of rain and darkness. Of course, when I got to them they'd vanish, but that didn't stop me from trying. I do that this morning. I run hard toward each globe and stop, then walk a bit, turning my face skyward to catch raindrops on my tongue.

I think of the story Mom told me about Dad's freedom. No one telling him to go to school or brush his teeth. There's beauty in solitude even if it's heartbreaking, but this morning it feels good to be alone, running solely for myself, on my own terms. Like the way I used to on that dirt track in the desert.

I pass a diner called "Lumpy's" and smile, thinking of Dad in his wide-brimmed Stetson. That's where we'd belong.

I pick up the pace a little, skipping and jumping, running willy-nilly. This is running at its best, without expectation or a clock to chart my worthiness. Here, worthiness is measured in joy, the smile forced skyward, hair wet, lashes brimming with beads of rain, the soaked cotton that was once a shirt clinging to my skin, cold and hot at the same time, the smells of wood smoke and loam bringing back memories of better times, the briny taste of my own sweat, mud-splatter on the backs of my legs as I take a detour through the park, my own biochemistry mixing with the rain; joy, sorrow, anger, and hope all caught in the sweep of an April morning. I take a breath.

I get it, Dad.

It's what they chase.

It's also what they lose.

I think of the night Dad ran at Hayward Field in the rain, no one cheering. No one there but me. And even when I clapped, he didn't seem to notice. I didn't get it then. Now I do.

*

Every morning I chase the globes of shining light. I chase the bush on the corner of Hall and 6th. Then the gray brick building on 27th and the red van always parked in front of the A-frame on Miller's Lane. There are prizes caught in the branches of the bush and in the wheel wells of the van. Minutes and seconds like diamonds. How many of them can I collect?

*

I break the silence at the dinner table: "I'm ready to get back on the track."

Everyone stops, looks at me.

"You sure you're rea—"

"She's ready." Luke nods. "Good deal. We're on for tomorrow."

"Well, wait a minute—she hasn't even been run—"

"She'll do just fine, Linda." He looks at me. "Way to get back in the saddle."

Something swells through me. Maybe it's pride or maybe it's gratitude, but it's something I haven't felt in a long time and want more often. I feel myself smile. Maybe things will get better. Maybe my grief hasn't cut too deep. I remember Mom telling me once that grief is like a glacier; it cuts deep and even when it's gone, there's still the scar.

*

"Where the hell've you been?" Breeze's husky voice carries over the hill as she walks toward me from the track.

The sight of the track with its neat white lines takes my breath away and leaves my legs full of lead. "I can't keep up with you now anyway."

She is nose to nose with me through the chain-link. "Didn't you know those muscles never forget?"

A lump comes up in my throat. "I'm not sure I can do it anymore."

"I reckon you're the biggest bullshitter I ever saw."

*

In the locker room, I stare at myself in the mirror, a freckled girl with knobby knees and bee-sting breasts. My eyes are the only striking piece of me, my father staring out, the color of violets. At least I have that. Like those places Dad gave me as gifts. Myles Lake and the mountains. Things that can't be unwrapped or quantified. Like this, speed, gold in the soles of my feet. I put on my singlet, club colors. Red and white. Flesh and bone.

*

As we walk down the hill toward the track, Breeze says: "You ready to kick all those other bitches' behinds or what?"

But I keep thinking about that girl in the mirror.

"You're gonna paint the track today. It's your canvas and you're the brush." She is beautiful in a one-strap hot pink sports bra and bun-huggers. She is not modest, never shy. But she has no reason to be.

I envy her, shrink away. "I'm not feeling good."

"You pussin' on me?"

"No; I just—"

"You afraid of him?" She nods toward Luke. "Lemme tell you something—he doesn't know shit."

Dad thought he did. "He knows more than you think."

"Trust me. You don't need him. You've got everything you need right there." She points to my heart. "That's you."

I believe her suddenly. More than I've ever believed anyone. I need to believe her. Need to believe someone.

"You stay right behind me. I'll be breaking the wind for you."

"Are we taking turns?"

"Taking turns?"

"Leading?"

Her grin falls crooked along her square jaw. "Shit. You're not ready for that."

I'm defensive as I think of what I once was to Linn, always second-best. "You don't think I can lead? Or you just want to be the one to win."

She snorts. "Win?"

"It's obvious; you want to be the fastest one out there. You want to be the one to win." Dad's dancing violet eyes flash through my mind and with them, all of the angst and anger. "He gave up his life for me to be the one out front."

"Wait…who? What?"

I stop, realizing what I've said. "Never mind. It's…nothing."

"You don't win workouts, anyhow."

"Sure you do."

"You want to win the workout or you want to win the race?"

"Duh."

"Then let me lead."

*

I let her all right. Immediately off the line, I fall back, way back.

"You're staying right on my heels, Girl," I hear her yell. "You're doing what I'm doing."

But soon her voice is lost in the wind as I drop to the back of the pack. Then I hear Luke's voice. *"Gina! What are you doing? I didn't ask for 2-minute laps."*

I see her glancing over her shoulder now and then, looking for me. But I don't want to give her what she wants. I don't want it myself anymore.

"Pick it up, Gina!" Luke shouts. *"We don't have till next Christmas."*

Luke doesn't like dilly-dallerers. Is that a word? Dallerer? He uses it, so it must be. I think about that for a minute. Next Christmas, almost a year away. I could go a long way in a year.

"Come on, Gina; let's go!"

But I don't. Won't. I'm tired of being told what to do by people who know nothing about me. I'm sick of taking orders from those who think they know what I need, who I am, and where I'm going. *You're not my mother,* I tell them. *You're not my father. I don't have a mother or a father, so I'm sure as hell not taking orders from you.*

I slow until the other runners lap me. Until I'm walking. Those pictures Breeze keeps telling me about have evaporated, as though the darkroom door has opened and all of the images that were supposed to motivate me have turned into something overexposed and meaningless.

"I quit," I yell toward the track and all of the athletes upon it, to Luke and to Breeze, to Dad and to Mom, to everyone I've ever loved, ever hated, ever believed or questioned. I'm done. Done trying. Dad was wrong; it's not enough to have the dream or the talent to achieve it. It's not even enough to believe you can do it. You have to believe it will be enough once you get there. If you don't have that, you don't have anything.

"Where you going, bitch?" And then I see her angry face, sprinting off the track after me.

"Go to hell."

"You're telling *me* to go to hell? What the fuck?" She rushes up, breathless. "You a quitter, that it?"

I catch her gaze. "Yep."

"That's all you've got to say?"

"Yep. I'm done."

"No you're not. You're never done. You're not done until you're dead."

I feel my face flush, emotion behind my eyes. "I am dead." I burst into tears, bury my head in her arms.

She pushes my face up. "Ain't stinkin' yet."

"It's not funny."

"Don't even smell like BO. Girl, if you're out there working, at least you can smell like BO."

"What is this?" Luke says, walking up. "A powwow? Let's get back out there."

"She needs the day off, Coach."

He looks at me, and there's something in his gaze I've not seen before. His voice borders on gentle: "Why don't you shower up."

The thought makes my throat swell. Maybe he does care, if only a little.

She looks at me. "You're stupid if you give up now."

She comes from the same place I do. From loneliness and doubt. From tragedy. "I don't want to give up."

I feel her arms around me, sweeping and soft, palms on my back, warmth on my cheek. I hold her, filled with a desperation I can't describe, can't quantify. It is bottomless, limitless, infinite. I need. Simply and ceaselessly.

Then I hear her in my ear: "You won't."

Racing Again
1994

It's cold. Low-slung clouds hang over us and piss. It reminds me of those dreary dawns in Archer. I wonder why I'm doing this. Is it to win? Or is it to prove to myself I'm ok? Am I doing it for him? Or am I doing it so that I'll be occupied by the pain and the nerves of a race and not by life? Those butterflies, ever restless? I don't know why. I never know why before the gun goes off.

I shake out my legs. It's the moment of truth. I hold my arms around me for warmth. It's close enough now that I've taken off my sweats. This is the part I hate, the waiting. The cold and the nerves making my stomach churn. I hop on one foot, then on the other, trying to stay loose. Count to 10 and down again. Soon, there will be a real countdown. *Runners on your marks*, then the gun and all those nerves will evaporate in a blitz of adrenaline.

"You ready to paint the track?" Breeze says.

I nod.

"Don't seem too convinced."

"I'm ready."

She catches my gaze. "Get mad."

But fear and anger are mutually exclusive, at least they seem to be. Right now I'm just scared.

She positions herself ahead of me, looks back and winks. "Just keep your eye on the booty."

It is a little funny. I feel myself smile. The starter walks across the infield, a blue jacket flapping in the wind, unzipped, an orange band on his gun arm. "Ready, ladies?"

There are a few scattered affirmations. Mostly silence. We're all in the same solemn, anxious world. I feel raindrops on my arms. Soon they will mingle with my sweat and maybe my tears. There's a reason gray is a sad color.

We line up. I hear a collective intake of breath as though we're all preparing to swim to the bottom of the pool. It's how it feels when you're not ready. Like you may just take that fateful breath before you get back to the surface.

"Ladies take your mark!" Then a step to the line and the *BANG* of the gun.

"Chase me," Breeze shouts back.

And I do. I hang onto her, that booty and those dreams. But she pulls away and I want to tell her to wait. Wait for me! Then I remember that this is a race. She's supposed to leave me behind.

There's a distinct loneliness that comes with being dropped. It's a cross between jealousy and despair. The feeling that you're not measuring up and here is the gut-cramping proof as the other person glides past you and on to the ethereal part of the track that seems unreachable, the next bend or the straight on the other side. To be there and not here would make me elite, something other than what I am, something infinitely better. It's not that far away. Two hundred meters. So why is it so hard? Why is half the length of track as seemingly unattainable as the summit of Everest? That's how it feels as she leaves me, on the other side now, nearly a minute ahead.

I slow down. Take my eyes off her, no longer chasing. I can't chase what I can't see. I coast in, 18:53 on the clock.

She holds a hand out to me. "You gave up, didn't you?"

"Not quite."

She holds my gaze. "Almost."

"Almost doesn't count."

"It does if it's *almost* every time."

*

I can't eat. At dinner, I pick at my food and Luke notices. "Not hungry?"

I shake my head.

"We're not worrying about our weight, are we?"

Linda snorts. "For heaven's sake, Luke; if she's not hungry, she's not hungry."

He catches her gaze. "Stay out of this, Lin." He looks at me. "A weight problem is not what happened out there today."

Linda jumps on it immediately. "What happened?"

"My stomach hurts," I say.

"Are you going to puke?" Amanda blurts, expectation in her eyes.

"Oh, for heaven's sakes." Linda throws down her napkin. "Not at the table, Amanda."

"What? Puke's not a bad word, Mom."

"It's not something we say at the table."

"Yeah, but it's *still* not a bad word."

"I didn't say it was."

"You told me not to say it."

"At the table."

"Yeah, but you said that was only bad words we're not supposed to—"

Luke's voice cuts through the fray. "Knock it off, Amanda."

She sets her fork down, her large eyes registering shock behind her thick glasses.

"Is it nausea or gas?" Linda whispers, cupping a hand over her mouth, though I wonder why she bothers because everyone can hear her.

"Nausea, I guess."

Amanda starts to titter. "Gas means you need to fart."

"Amanda Grace."

"Well, it's true."

"Enough of this." Luke stands, points a finger at Amanda. "Go to your room."

Amanda drops her head and slides out of her chair, slinking away as Luke follows her. I stare after her, envious. She still seems like a little girl. Still laughs at farting and gets excited about zoo animals and pink dresses.

I feel Linda's hand on mine. "What happened today?"

I shrug, my face flushing, tears threatening. "I just didn't have it."

She puts her arm around me. "Didn't have what?"

Courage. Drive. Hope.

I shake my head. "Nothing, never mind." And it really is nothing. Until suddenly, it's everything. I want Love the way I once wanted her waffles. I want to eat until I'm sick. And I want to push it all away.

*

I'm still sore from the race, so I trot in the rain. There are sun breaks through a weather-smeared sky. Dad would've thought it resembled a painting, something uncaught, even in the millions of attempts on easels around the world. He'd be right. There is nothing like this. Breath in my lungs. Rain on my face and Dad in my mind. That smile, charmed and indescribable. If only I could have this at the line, just before the gun goes off, the smile and the sky, uncaptured except in a place halfway between joy and grief. Victory.

*

The Tuesday after the race, I watch her at practice, loose-limbed and beautiful. Alive. *I came along in ugly.* How is that possible? It's beauty she seeks—and finds—on the track. Same as me.

In contrast, I don't feel a part of anything. Warming up, I observe from the back, not wanting to be out front anymore. I don't belong there anyway.

Her voice cuts through the distance. "Gina!" She's looking for me, pushing others aside. "We're doing 400s today!"

Twelve of them, in fact. Three miles' worth. Almost a 5k. I'll string together a few 88s and pretend that, maybe the next race, I'll catch her. Because catching her will be like catching her beauty and I need it, too.

"What's going on?"

I turn and there's Luke. I shrug, unaware that my doubt was so obvious.

"Relax, Gina; you're doing fine." I feel his palm on my shoulder. Dad used to do the same thing. "It'll be your turn very soon."

*

"I got something to show you," Breeze says after practice. "Something that might change your mind."

"Change my mind about what?" I follow her off the track.

And she glances after me, over her shoulder, as though to flirt. "You'll get it once I show you."

I follow her to an old gray building with a broken sidewalk and a leaning railing out front. Inside are rows of cots, sleeping bags on top, some with people buried up to their noses in a worn reprieve.

She turns to me. "Wanna see where I live?"

I swallow a lump, nod, butterflies alight in my gut. She points. "That one right there."

I see an old Army-surplus blanket like one Dad used to have, a scratched-up medal, and a dog-eared teddy bear missing an eye. Something compels me to hug the bear to me, feeling the soft, mashed stuffing, old, worn, eternally familiar somehow. I breathe in the scent of something well known, a whiff of old childhood.

"It's all I got left of her," Breeze says.

"Who?"

"Mama." She takes a breath. "My face just got too painful, like I burned her every time she saw me."

My throat aches. "I'm sorry."

"It's why I got this." She holds up the medal, small and diamond-shaped, gold paint chipping off. I think of Dad's medal, that thing that also kept him willing to dream. "I won this when I was 11, right after I moved here," she says. "Nobody ever wanted to take me in the way Luke did you, so I got so damned mad, I sprinted the whole thing, and fell down after I crossed the line almost like it wasn't really me who ran it, but this other real mean gal who didn't want anybody telling her what to do 'cept run. It's what kept me goin'."

There's more buried in that than I know how to respond to. *I'm sorry,* I want to say, but I know it would be exactly the wrong thing because I realize she's smart in the way only outcasts can be smart. The way Dad was with his alkaline lake and I was with the tarnished button I once carried in my pocket.

"Why do you stay?" I ask instead.

"This is my life."

"It doesn't have to be."

"I've been doing this for five years. The first year I wanted to die, but I got to know it. I don't know where I'd go if I left. S'ppose I'd just crawl under a bridge or something, but I got outta the habit of the rain and cold a long while back. I like having a roof and potato soup. We get potato soup every Tuesday and Saturday night. You ever eat potato soup?"

I nod.

"It's your favorite, then?"

I shrug. "I think grilled cheese is my favorite…Or maybe escargot."

"*Grilled cheese? Escar-go?* You're kidding me! Girl, there ain't nothing like potato soup when it's made right."

I nod, laugh a little, realize it's the first time I've laughed in a long time.

"Tell you what? You go an' ask that coach of ours if you can stay for dinner."

"You mean potato soup?"

"Girl, you said it. Prepare to be knocked onto that skinny behind."

*

As we eat in the mess hall, one giant room with long tables, cooks behind an assembly line of people, some of whom live here, some of whom come in off the street, I gaze at Breeze. I remember the way Dad used to dig food out of the dumpster and smile, convinced he'd found a flash of gold in a pan of gravel.

But this isn't day-old dumpster food. I take a tentative taste and there's an explosion of flavor on my tongue, enough so that the next bite and the next occur in quick succession. "This is really good," I say.

"Told you." She nods toward the bustling line of cooks. "There's a genius in there somewhere."

I sit back and wonder suddenly: "What was it you thought would change my mind?"

She looks at me, grinning playfully. "This." She points with her spoon at her soup. "This is everything."

Back in the Saddle
1994

I tuck my baby picture in my shorts before my next race, an affirmation. Joy and hope are tenuous, and I need more than a thought to cling to. I want those words to mean something: *You are a good girl...* I stare at the picture and I realize that I was.

*

She slaps her butt as she positions herself. "Ready to hang onto it this time?"

I think of her potato soup, of the *everything* she seems to think is out there somewhere. A different kind of *everything* from what my father uselessly chased. The kind I want to find.

I smile, but inside is the familiar flutter of nerves. I gaze into the sky, into the wind-whipped tails of cirrus clouds. Brush strokes. An already-blue canvas with the start of something wilder. Today, the possibilities are limitless.

I pull the rubber band from my hair and let it fall around my shoulders. I want to feel the wind, to watch it dance with every turn of the track. The gun goes off and I feel the tips of my hair licking my back and shoulders, brush strokes of strife as I chase her. I won't catch her today. I already feel the fatigue setting in as I watch her pull away, the magic vanishing with her. That belief in myself is so tenuous. It occurs to me that I may never catch her, that I might be as fast as I'll ever get, and as good as I'll ever be. It has to be enough, because if it isn't what will I do then?

I cross the line, my head down and I feel a palm on my chin. I meet her gaze. "Throw out the sadness," she says. "Those colors are poison."

*

Heading home from the race, I gaze out at the folds of land leading east and I imagine him, somewhere in those trees, green canvas draped on a limb and a crackling fire. I want him back so bad. I want to show him how far I've come and how much I've grown. Because I'm not his little girl anymore.

"You've got to fight for it, Gina."

I look over at Luke.

"You're not working hard enough."

My heart sinks. Because he's got to know the heartbreaking truth, the same truth my father knew and walked away from. "Yes I am."

"Maybe in body, but not in mind. Not in spirit. You defeat yourself before you start. I see it."

A lump swells in my throat. "What do you see?"

"You in the front with your head down."

I turn from him, stare out the window.

"It's not about Breeze."

I feel his gaze on me.

"It's about believing you can do it. Not believing you can win or that you can beat her, but that you can do your best and be happy with it. Don't worry about her. Don't worry about the clock."

I turn to him. "You did." *Hypocrite.* "You made the Olympic Team."

"And I hated every minute of it."

Something catches in my throat. Shock. Grief. "Then why bother?"

"If you hate it, don't." I see a flicker in his brown eyes. Anger? Sorrow? "Don't waste your life on a dream. Love it first. Love the process. Love the race, win or lose. If you don't love those things, you're wasting your time."

"I want to win."

"I know you do. Problem is, everybody does. That makes first place very popular and only one can be first. You're going to run a lot of races and the faster you get, the faster your competition will get. You won't always win, not if you go to the kinds of places you want to go. You think I had a snowball's chance in hell of winning Olympic gold? You're always going to lose, Gina. It's just a part of racing. Even the best get beaten."

I think of Prefontaine and Dad's wish to be great. "I want to be great."

"Why?"

A million pictures flash through my mind. Windswept prairies and alkaline lakes. Desert valleys and the far-off peaks of mountains. Dad's vision, freedom. His dream, to be the best in the world. To be Robert Dalton, the hero. I think of the contrast. Myles Lake and the packed stadium on the other side of the world. An anonymous drifter with the potential and the belief that he could've been a household name if only he hadn't given up. What must it be like to go from one to the other? I think of all of those nights spent staring up at the stars wondering how it would feel not to have to worry anymore. My dream, to know how it feels.

"You haven't answered my question. Why do you want to be great?"

"Because I will have made it."

"Made it where?"

"To the top."

"There is no top."

"From here, there is."

"Even at the top are good days and bad days."

I cross my arms, refusing to believe it won't be any different. "More good days than bad, I bet."

"That depends on who you ask; there are plenty of world-class athletes who are miserable." He pauses. "I was one of them."

*

That night, I notice a small addition to my room, a little wooden cross above my bed.

"You like it?"

I turn toward the voice. It's Amanda's and she's smiling, her blue eyes large behind her thick glasses.

I nod.

"That way you'll know, morning and night, that Our Father is watching over you."

I have a father. Had a father who did just fine. "Thanks," I choke, toeing the line.

Dad never toed the line, but he never made it, either.

It comes in waves, this grief. I want to forget my father's face and those dancing eyes of his, but every time I look in the mirror, it is both a gift and a curse, for there he is staring back. As I've gotten older, I look more like him. My mother's likeness has seemingly shrunken back within me, that pale skin disappearing under my father's tan and that curly hair turning burnished and straight. I don't want to look too closely at the reflection for fear that my sorrow will make me never want to see myself again.

Go away, Dad; just let me move on with my life.

As I lie in bed and think about the little wooden cross above my head, I conduct a test of my own: *Lord, take away this pain.* I'll give it a week. I imagine God's to-do list, my name at the bottom. A week is a long time.

Districts
1994

I remember my father's words: *Toe behind the white line*...Luke is watching, his eyes narrowed on my form, a stopwatch clutched in his hand. I can't let him down this time, can't let myself down. If I blur my vision just a little, I can almost make out a different image, those dancing violet eyes flashing whimsically.

I wait for the sound of the gun, Breeze beside me. "Get mad," she says.

The gun goes off and she is ahead. Too far ahead. She must be pissed. I chase her. She is my shining globe, the one I can't catch, will never scoop up, as unattainable as my father's wish.

Something thick catches in my throat and my emotion erupts. In a blitz of heartbreaking clarity, I know what Dad always hid from me—a certain desperation that he'd spent his life banking on a bet he'd lost. He left me because he realized I wasn't good enough, would never be good enough.

Without another thought, I start sprinting. I can't let him down. 200 meters in 35 seconds, blowing past Breeze as her voice cuts the air: "Girl, you a bat outta hell?"

The first lap in 72. The next in 76. I hear Luke's shouts: *Gina…* 79. I'm on a national-class pace. All on pure emotion. 79. Hatred. 80. Fury. 80. Jealousy at what she can do. 83. And at what I cannot. 85. At what I will never be. 87. And at what dispirited destiny I've been left to accept. 88. He wasted his life and his death on me. Because I will never be the winner he imagined. Breeze passes me, fluid and calm, as I begin to stagger, unable to go any farther.

*Gina, stop. Gina stop Gina stop…*I hear his desperation. But it is my father's voice I hear, not Luke's. He is witnessing a suicide. I will never be good enough, no matter how hard I try. I stumble off the track, as I feel my tears. Smell them. Ammonia. My whole body stinks of it.

I hear her then, somewhere through the fog of exhaustion: "Girl, I tol' you to get mad, but this is some kind o' pissed-off I reckon is new."

*

"Gina?"

I open my eyes trying to remember where I am. I'm in bed. I look up to find a steaming mug of mint tea sitting on my bedside table.

I turn my head to see Luke sitting beside me.

"What the hell were you thinking?"

For a brief moment I consider the possibility that I might've run a national-class time. Then I remember it doesn't matter; I didn't finish. My essence is traced in the hieroglyphics of minutes, seconds, and quarter-seconds.

Things that, to me, embody everything from alkaline water, tall dead grass and clear blue sky, to starlit evenings spent dreaming, hoping, grieving, and regretting, a blitz of bittersweet, and the flash of a badge delivering a tragedy. Desperation to win and a longing to die. Things that, to anyone else, wouldn't mean a thing.

"Why?"

I'm drawn back.

"Did you hear me?"

I catch Luke's troubled gaze and I realize that he's angry. "Why the hell do you care?"

"Pouting never got anyone anywhere. You want this or not?"

I feel the sting of emotion in my eyes as I realize that I'm as trapped as I've ever been. I shrug.

"I wanted you to prove yourself."

"To who?" I snap. "To you?"

He shakes his head. "To you."

Something in my throat tightens.

"You were going to die for grief." Luke says. "Might as well die for glory."

I catch his gaze and there's something on his face I rarely see. Sorrow. There's a pulse in his jaw, something contained. Leukemia had been the story he'd told Amanda. Luke's panacea. Or his salvation. Had he pushed her too hard? Wanted too much for her to win? Reliving his old glory, a shot at a dream that never quite came true? He made the Olympic Team, but never stood on the podium. Did she die for his dreams or for her own? Did she die on the track? In his arms? Or quietly in her sleep after she'd told him for the thousandth time that she just wasn't hungry?

He looks at me. "You've got something to show the world, so show it. You need to run under 16:30 to qualify for the World Junior Championships, but that's going to take a hell of a lot of control. You need to rein in your emotion, Gina. Use it. It's a tool."

I think about what Dad once said about needing to earn a parent's love on the track; he'd tried and failed with his own father. Running fast can win you a lot. It can win you money and medals, but it pays its biggest dividends in all of those rare things we want more—hope, love, and happiness—the belief that we will finally, one day, get there.

I think about painting the track and what Breeze said about how pictures color your whole workout, making you run faster or slower, joy and hope trading places with fear and anger, taking their turns at breaking the wind. I wonder if I'll ever let joy out front again.

There used to be joy, way back when I ran on my dirt track and Mom and Dad watched from the bleachers, clapping each time I ran by. The little podium, where Dad gave me his medal, his 4:07 mile, his greatest achievement, that was joy. Hope, even. Where did it go?

There is no room for joy at the front of a race. "What if I can't do it?"

"Do what?"

"Run 16:29?"

I remember what Dad would've said. He would've shrugged. He would've patted my shoulder and told me: "You'll do your best and if you do it, great. If you don't, the world won't change. It'll be you and me and it has always been you and me." He'd smile. "And you and me are pretty great."

My world blurs.

Because Luke doesn't say what Dad would've: "You've got it if you want it, but you've got to believe it."

*

"You're starting here." Luke has taken me to the far side of the track from everyone else and positioned me at the 200-meter start line, half a lap behind the others. "Today, you're running by yourself."

I feel a pit in my stomach as I stare at the line. The workout is a two-mile time trial and this feels like punishment. "No one starts here."

He catches my gaze. "You do."

"Why?"

"You'll never catch them from here."

Anger flashes through me. "How do you know?"

"It isn't possible."

I don't want to believe it can't happen. I want to remember what Dad once said: A part of sport is having impossible dreams. "It's possible."

"No. It isn't. Not unless you suddenly become the under-16 national 5k record holder."

"I'll do it."

"Do it, then. Just don't let them catch you."

"What?" I gaze across the infield at the clutch of athletes on the other side.

"You aren't just chasing them; they're chasing you."

A cold sweat traces its way down my body. I don't want to do this.

"In fact, I've told them that, if even one of the boys catches you, I'll take everyone out to pizza."

I feel out-of-breath already. "I can't beat the guys."

"You don't have to beat them. You're just trying to stay ahead of them. You're getting a 200-meter head start. You should feel really good about that."

"I can't do it, Luke."

"You just said two minutes ago that you were going to catch them, even if it meant breaking the national record. You either believe in yourself or you don't."

I take a deep breath. "I do."

"Believing in yourself has to be more than a defense against fear. Believe it because it's possible and you're willing to do the hard work to get there. If you want to run 16:29, you can't let them catch you."

"Ok."

"You're a wolf, not a rabbit."

"Huh?"

"Stop running scared."

I watch as he walks back across the infield toward the crowd. I listen for the whistle. Am I a wolf or a rabbit? I want to be a wolf. Luke's whistle sounds and I take off, hard, mouth dry, legs dead, heart in my ears. I'm still a rabbit. I make the first turn and there is Penstamon Tucker, the fastest boy on the team, on the straight on the far side of the track, up 10 meters already. I'm losing, but I dig in. Harder. I try desperately to imagine myself as the wolf. The girls are only 200 meters ahead; I can close that gap. I don't care what Luke says.

But like a dream vanishing in dawn, I can't hang onto that fragile faith, my belief in myself as precarious as my father's hope. I can't do it. Can't run any faster despite my anger. Despite my determination to prove Luke wrong. I can't do it.

My legs and lungs burn. My stomach churns. I will hang on for as long as I can. I'm gaining on most of the girls, but not on Breeze, and not quickly enough on most of the others. Penstamon is 50 meters behind. Then 30. Then 10. Before I know it, I hear his cleats and his breath, even. He is in control. His form is perfect. He is barely working. I think of Dad at Hayward Field. Know, finally, that to wish on my father's star is futile because I will never be that good.

As he passes me, he gives me a thumbs-up. "Good fight, Dalton."

"Thanks," I puff. I tried.

When I come to the line, I drop my head, exhausted. I've failed, but it doesn't feel as bad as I thought it would. Some part of me is relieved. Proud even. I did my best. I feel a hand on my shoulder. It's Breeze's. "Way to go, Girl." Others follow, a million palms on my back, affirmations, glimpses of glory in a not-so-glorious finish. I look up at Luke.

"How do you feel?" he asks.

"Good."

"Better than you thought?"

I nod.

"You did it, Gina."

"What?"

"Lost."

*

"Hey." She hangs around the corner of the locker room. She's waited for me, I realize. I'm always the last in the shower, wanting the other girls gone before I shut my eyes against the stream of hot water as it washes away my sweat and my tears. After the shower, I'm relieved the workout is over and am ready to go home, clean.

She smiles when she sees me, her auburn hair loose around her shoulders as I clutch a towel, my cotton shield. "You're getting faster, know that?"

"Yeah?"

Her smile fades. "You still have doubts, huh?"

Do I tip my hand to her? Dare tell her the truth? *Doubts? You think these are doubts? They are truths. I'll never be what you are.*

"You know what I think of when I have doubts?"

I won't tip my hand, won't admit it even if I don't disagree. "What?"

She grins. "To compete means to seek together, did you know that?"

I shake my head.

"When it starts to hurt, I want to remember why. She wants to win and so do I. Only one of us can, but we're both willing to suffer. Remember your courage. Remember hers."

*

The pizza parlor is buzzing, Friday-night festive, patrons celebrating a two-day liberty. Luke orders a large pepperoni, a sausage, and a veggie. I eat ravenously, remember Breeze's potato soup as I watch my teammates laugh, and realize it's a perfect moment.

Moment of Truth
Hayward Field
1994

My heart hammers as I shake out my legs and trot around the outside lane of the track. *This is it, Dad. That track you thought was magic. What do you think of it now?* I remember him that night in the rain when there was nothing and no one, just us and the wind, and I pray for that kind of joy—the kind that will carry me, that will give me the courage to do what he always believed I could do.

This is a twilight meet, so the sun has set. I stare at the glow in the west and hope this will be one of the biggest nights of my life. Around me, other athletes warm up, doing strides and bounds. Coaches pace the infield. There are hundreds of spectators in the stands. A photographer positions himself on the northeast corner of the track, hoping to snap some dramatic pictures as we whiz by, vying for a lifetime shot to be the best in the country.

Don't forget to smell the air...

I haven't forgotten. But I'm too nervous to pay much attention.

"Relax, Gina." I hear Luke's voice behind me. "It's only 12 ½ laps." I feel his palm on my shoulder. "You'll do just fine. This is practice. That's all it is."

Only it isn't.

He takes me by the shoulders then, like Dad used to. "Listen. You know this. You've done this. You've got this."

*

I take a deep breath. Jog. Catch the westward glow and try to remember what my father once said. I close my eyes. Focus on the scent of rain.

"You're gonna whip the other broads' butts." I open my eyes and Breeze is there, smiling. "'Cept mine." She winks. "You and I gonna go one-two."

"Gina! Breeze!" Luke is motioning us toward the track. It's time to line up. But my legs are heavy and my motivation is in the basement.

"C'mon girl—time to roll." Breeze is excited, confident. I wonder how she does it.

Above me, people sit forward in their seats. The photographer on the far side of the track is poised with his telephoto lens. I think of Linda and Amanda in the stands, hands clasped, thrilling for the sound of the gun. I remember the way I once ran for Mom and Dad that long-ago day I tested my mettle on the little dirt track in Archer, no gun, but my Dad's shout to *GO!* and the way I went hard from the start, fearlessly. And I want to do it the way I did it the first time. Boldly.

I stare at this big red track and think back to my old dirt one in the desert. That small place where a big dream was born. I wonder what might have happened had I never seen it, had we moved to a different house in a different neighborhood…

*

We line up, all of us girls in our singlets, showing off our school and club colors—peacocks in a pen. In the west, the sun has set, leaving in its wake a twilight I'll never forget. Thunderheads gather in the south, capturing both the pink of the setting sun and the black of impending lightning. It's how I feel. I look down at the line at my feet and realize that I'm staring at a destiny.

"Good luck," Breeze says.

I take her hand. "Good luck."

The gun goes off. But instead of bringing on the lightning, it magnifies the fear. I can't do this. Not for 12½ laps. But amazingly, I don't back off. I didn't in that impossible race against Penstamon Tucker, and I won't here. I keep digging. Struggling even though I no longer have the help that once made me great. My father's faith. Now it's only me.

"Hang in there, Gin," Luke yells. *"Come on, pick it up."*

I shake my head, puffing. *I can't …*

77. 76. 76. The colors flow. Dad and that Stetson. Scuffed cowboy boots.

"Come on, Gina. Gut it out. This is the biggest race of your life."

77. 77. 80. Mom and her paisley kerchief and Dad's dancing eyes. Blues, greens, yellows, and reds. Violets, too. I see his face pointing skyward that night in the rain, a smile on it, joy thrown in every direction with every turn of the track, color, a rainbow in the dark. *That happened here,* I remind myself.

"You're fading. Come on, Gina—this race is tough, but you're tougher."

79. 80. 82. My little dirt track and Dad on the sidelines cheering me on.

And then there was loss.

And the stars above.

And Breeze. She's still ahead of me, but not by much.

I think of that Caddie, too. Green in a desert of brown. An oasis. And all too often a home. I want more than that now. I'm in third and I want more. I push harder. I'm gaining on her. She's 20 meters ahead, then 15. I can do it. I know I can. And I will.

"Good job, Breeze," I puff as I pass her. *Two faces. Two wills. One victor. Remember your courage.*

But she doesn't look at me. It's as though I don't exist. She stares straight ahead, her eyes glazed as she chuffs, her breath coming in ragged gasps as she hangs on and doesn't let go. I surge, but she is right there with me, my shadow as I once was hers. *Remember your courage.* This hurts. Bad. *Remember hers.* We come around another bend, Breeze off of my right shoulder. *Each of us is pain.* I throw in another surge, but this time, I falter. I don't have enough left. I know it now. And there is still nearly 1200 meters left in the race.

You've got it if you want it, but you've got to believe it.

How is that possible?

I feel my legs burn, my stride shortens as I slow down. And that's when I hear her: "Get mad."

Because it isn't enough to be fearless.

I recall those cold mornings, that stubborn wish, realizing I don't want it anymore. Being beaten again and again by Linn because no matter what I did, I was never really good enough, whatever excuses my father tried to make for me. Because that was all his life had been: excuses. And yet, I continue to fight. Why? Because it's all I know how to do. The only thing he taught me.

I hate you.

I'll break her yet. Again, I surge and she cannot catch me.

*

There is just one more girl. I have to pass her. I'm a wolf, after all. And she's the only one standing between me and my dream, a blue-eyed blonde with a ponytail like a golden comet—the only one standing between my father's hope and the reality he always talked about in that desert oasis below a rash of stars. My dreams, now, are left on the banks of a lifeless lake, and in a restaurant where we didn't belong. I need more than the dream.

"You can do this, Gina. Go get her."

I know I can. So why can't I?

82.

"You have to want it, Gin. You have to want it bad."

79. *I do.*

"Want it, Gina. Want it more than anything."

There are 200 meters to go. *I want it more than anything.*

I hear the crowd. They are on their feet. They will carry me.

I surge and I pass her, the golden comet, 100 meters from the line, the last lap in 72 seconds. I think of my father's medal, the object that for me epitomized success, something I know now represents just one illusory part of a wasted life. I need more than that. And I need it desperately. I catch sight of the clock: 16:14.

I fall to my knees. This is it. The biggest moment of my life. Because I have just qualified for the World Junior Championships.

Press Time
1994

People rush up to me. Spectators. Coaches. Journalists with cameras and microphones shoving recorders in my face and asking how it felt to qualify for the World Junior Championships.

But I still don't know. I keep thinking of Breeze. She should've made it, too. I should've let her.

I look for Luke, but his face is not among the ones I see.

"I need to find my coach," I say to no one in particular.

"Did you know you were on world-class pace?" one journalist asks.

"I didn't think about it."

"You didn't think about it?"

"I just ran."

He snorts. "Wow."

"Was it a difficult race for you, Gina?" someone else asks.

"No." I walk away, wanting desperately to find the one man I think will care.

"Gina!" I turn, and he is waving. Something in my heart catches. Pride? Joy? A moment of clarity? This is me. What I've worked my whole life for. For now, it's enough. He's proud of me and he is smiling.

I feel his hand on my shoulder, his voice loud in my ear over the din. "Way to go, Gina. Way to go." I can almost hear my father's voice.

"What's next?" another journalist asks.

"The World Championships," I blurt, grinning.

"I mean, after that." Microphones are bigger than you think and the lights are brighter. Everyone is looking at me, waiting for an answer.

But my mind's a blank. I've never been here before. It's always just been a dream. Dare I say *The Olympics?* But dreams come true; this one has. "The Olympics."

A chuckle goes up in the crowd. I'm cute. An ambitious kid with a long-shot dream.

I feel Luke's hand tighten on my shoulder. "Watch this one," he says. "She may just do it."

I believe him now. Walking doesn't feel like walking. It feels more like floating. Luke's hand is still on my shoulder as we walk to a tent on the far side of the track so that I can pick out my Team USA gear. Penstamon Tucker strides up beside us, lithe and beautiful; he has qualified, too. "Good work, Dalton," he says, grinning. "Way to blow 'em out of the water."

My heart lurches as I catch his gaze and I feel a familiar heat. "Thanks. You, too."

"You know how many athletes dream of wearing Team USA on their jerseys?" Luke grins down at me and he looks a little like Dad. Sounds like him, too. "A lot. A lot of them dream and most never get here."

I've gotten here. I've crossed the line from good to great. I try to remember what I thought that'd feel like. I thought it'd feel like nothing would ever matter again. But I was wrong. Things still matter. Like Dad being gone. But it still feels good. At this moment, it feels like it did my first time on that dirt track when Dad put his hope around my neck and told me I'd won. And that it was only the beginning.

"Extra small," Luke tells the officials in blue coats. One of them brings out a singlet and shorts, warm-ups and a jacket. All blue. All with letters: USA.

"Your name?" The woman with curly hair looks up, a pen in hand. She's also wearing a USA jacket.

"Gina Dalton."

She puts out a hand. "Brenda Voegel. I'm the assistant coach. Welcome to the Team."

"Thanks." I feel Luke's hand on my back, joy and pride swelling through me.

"Luke Havelock," he says, shaking her hand. "You've got a winner here."

Her gaze falls on me. "I can see that."

"She's the toughest fighter I've ever seen." And I hear in Luke's voice something as subtle as the brush of a feather. A tremor. A hint at emotion. A lump comes up in my throat. *I'm a winner and it's not just my father who thinks so.*

Brenda is looking at me. "Do you have a passport, hon?"

"A what?"

She smiles. "Doesn't sound like it." She looks up at Luke. "She can go by the post office for an application and get her picture taken there. You should request that it be expedited."

"Will do," Luke says.

"We'll be meeting as a team in Newark on August 18th. We'll assist in getting the flights arranged. From there, we'll travel as a team to Bonn." Her eyebrows go up when she says *Bonn.* A fancy name. A place where dreams come true.

Celebration
Portland
1994

"To the World Championships." Luke holds up his water glass at the restaurant. It's loud. Michael Jackson is playing and people are laughing. I smell the air—BBQ ribs and shrimp scampi. Somewhere near the back, I hear waiters sing Happy Birthday.

"To the World Championships." Linda and Amanda both hold up their glasses.

I feel my face flush. "Thanks." I think of my father's King-great sashimi celebration and Breeze's potato soup as my eyes water.

I try to take it in. I've made it, haven't I? I could walk into Kazatimuru's and belong. This is the dream Dad talked about on those nights in northeastern California under a canopy of stars. This is what he'd dreamed of as a kid when he'd run to school and home again, hoping his own father would be awake when he got back. What he talked about on storm-smeared days at Myles Lake when all we had was a tarp and a package of hot dogs. This is what kept us going. This. I look around and it doesn't seem like much.

There's a lump in my throat that makes it hard to speak. I feel Linda's hand on my arm. "I wish he was here," I manage.

"I know."

I made it, Dad—did I tell you? I did what you always wanted to do. I'm a world-class athlete now. Maybe I'll turn pro. Maybe I'll go to the Olympics. Do you love me, Dad? Are you proud of me yet?

I order a cheeseburger, a Coke, a slice of cheesecake with raspberry drizzle, and I eat.

*

As we leave the restaurant, I look up into a rash of stars. After all of those nights spent dreaming, I've finally cashed in.

Then I hear a voice in the dark. "Hey." And there she is. Breeze. I realize that her shelter isn't far from here, that Luke must've invited her tonight and she decided not to come. My mind races. Is she angry? Hurt? Or just disappointed? Was it that she thought it was a celebration for me just to share with my new family, knowing what it's like not to have one, and to want one desperately?

"Congratulations." Her eyes are glued to mine. "You made it."

"Yeah. Thanks."

"You happy?"

I feel my throat swell. "Yeah."

There are tears in her eyes.

Remember your courage. I step toward her. "I painted the track, just like you said. I thought of my dad."

She nods, tears spilling down her cheeks.

Dad flashes through my mind. He needed it, too. "You'll do it, Breeze."

"We'll see." She holds my gaze. "I'm really happy for you, Gin; I knew all along you'd do it."

A gift, I realize. Her sacrifice. "Why'd you let me win?"

"I didn't."

A part of me is prouder than I've ever been. The other part doesn't believe her. "I got mad."

She smiles. "Good."

Journey's End
1994

Luke stands in the doorway and it occurs to me it looks nothing like him. I'm not used to seeing Luke Havelock sad.

"You did it."

I think about that for a minute. I did it. I made the Junior National Team and in three weeks, I'm leaving for the World Championships in Germany.

"I wish Dad could've seen me."

"I know. Listen." He sits down on my bed, the light from the lamp softening his face. "I know it's been a bumpy road, but…" He looks at me. "I'm proud to be your coach."

I glance down, at my hands, my face hot.

He takes a breath. "I won't be going with you to World's."

I catch his gaze. "What? I thought—"

"You've got team coaches, Gina. Remember Brenda? She knows what she's doing. Besides, individual coaches aren't always all that welcome."

I'm suddenly teary.

He puts a hand on mine. "I promised Amanda two months ago that I'd be at her recital on the 21st. She's been practicing for months. I've got to be there."

The lump in my throat swells and pops. Because I'm not his, will never be his. Then I wonder if this has something to do with Olivia. Maybe he just can't watch anymore. I feel his hand on my shoulder, shocked that he's not angry at me for crying.

"You've made it, Gina. You don't need me. You don't need anyone. Not anymore."

Only I do.

*

It's the first thing I pack, in the bottom of one of Luke's duffel bags. Olivia's gold medal.

*

Standing in line with Linda at the Post Office, I muse on what it'll be like to have a passport. Dad never had a passport. All he did was drive that green Caddie around the desert. Back then, the desert was the whole world. How far I've come from that dusty windshield and those mud-caked wheel wells to this, a flight over the ocean and an upscale hotel. Kazatimuru's is nothing.

Linda squeezes my hand. "Are you excited?"

I nod.

"I told Luke when you first came to us that the Lord had big plans for you."

I feel myself smile.

"You've done us proud, Gina."

I look up at her and realize that she has forgiven me, unequivocally. There is no doubt in her mind that I'm worth saving, worth believing in, even for all the hardship I've caused. I notice that her eyes are full of tears. "Are you ok?"

"I'm just in awe; there are still miracles in this world. Praise Jesus."

The big woman behind the counter looks down at me over her spectacles. "Can I help you?"

"I need a passport."

She points to a rack full of forms. "Bring it up when you're finished."

"Yes, but I also need to have my pict—"

"Fill out the application and bring it up to me when you're finished."

Even dreams come with hassles.

*

There are hard questions. Like where I live. It pops into my mind before I have a chance to think: 14 Emlyn Street. Archer, Nevada. My real home. The place where Dad gave me my first pair of spikes. The place I dug up that button and called it treasure, only there'd been no audience, no expectation, only me, that blade of broken glass, and the dirt.

My pen hovers over the paper. "What's our address again?"

Finally Famous
1994

"Gina, come quick!"

I rush into the living room, toward Linda's frantic voice and there I am, on TV. I recognize the reporters—and the questions. I feel my face flush.

"Was it a difficult race for you, Gina?"

"No." I'm looking for someone. *Dad?* No, he isn't there. I'm looking for Luke.

"What's next?"

"The World Championships."

"I mean, after that."

My face is blank as the camera focuses on my confusion. "The Olympics," I say finally, lamely.

I turn away. I don't like myself. I can't possibly be that dorky. It doesn't help that Amanda has already dissolved into peals of shrieky laughter.

"Amanda Grace," Linda snaps.

"Your voice sounds really funny," Amanda gasps. "Oh my gosh, that is so *funny.*"

My cheeks burn and I'm not sure if I'm about to cry or hit her.

"Amanda Grace, now you apologize this instant," Linda says, her hands on her hips and her head tilted in that I'm-not-kidding way.

For a moment, Amanda straightens out her face, but it's like one of those don't blink-don't laugh games where the longer you try not to do it, the harder it gets. She holds it for a second, and then there are the snot-shooting snickers, the kind that come when you can't not laugh, so every muscle in your face, throat, and tongue contorts to make noises far worse than laughter.

Then her mother in her drawl: *"Amanda Grace! What did I just say?"*

"I can't help it."

"Yes, you can."

"No I can't."

"It's ok," I say. "It was dorky."

Immediately, protectively, Linda puts up her hands. "No, no, hon. You were great. You did great. That's not an easy position to be in. You've got all these cameras and folks asking you all these questions. I wouldn't know what to say. I would've just stood there."

"Yeah, you did great," Amanda parrots, gamely trying not to giggle. The fact she's trying so hard makes me feel loved. She reminds me of me as I might have been if I'd not been babysitting my mother's sadness and protecting my father's untenable dreams.

"Thanks."

Linda puts a hand on my shoulder. "Most people can't do what you do, will never do what you've done. You've got nothing to prove, Gin—to anyone."

I believe it for a moment and I let myself be hers. Her hug is genuine, motherly. Here's where I want to stay. In a place where it doesn't matter. It didn't matter to Dad, either, not really. He wanted me to make it, but he loved me even when I didn't. Even when he was a desert whirlwind, blowing one way, then another. Though Linda and Amanda have always blown in the same direction. Luke too. The consistency caught me off-guard, made me slow to accept it.

We separate and she looks at me. "Your dad would be so proud of you."

"You think so?" I am hungry. Needy. I want her words as much as I've ever wanted anything.

"He'd be the proudest father on the planet, I'm sure."

"Really?"

"Really."

"You think he's looking down on me, huh?"

She smiles and her dimples blossom. "I sure do."

*

It comes in the mail, my passport. In it is a picture of me, plain-faced. There is no smile. The photographer said that to capture my true likeness, I had to be straight-faced. Me, my joy, stripped.

In the picture, I see my father most of all. Those violet eyes and the slightly crooked mouth, asymmetric. I miss the grin. I don't think I ever really saw him straight-faced, because even in those moments he wasn't smiling, there was that tug on the corner of his mouth, the suggestion of a joke or a surprise in the works. When Dad wasn't in the middle of making some big announcement, he was planning one.

Though he imagined it, I wonder if he ever could've really believed it. Me, on TV, telling reporters I hope to make the U.S. Olympic Team.

*

I shut my eyes against the sun, my last workout finished, Luke now on the far side of the track and silenced. I'm done. There will be no more calling out splits or pleas to go harder, faster. There is nothing more to do except taper.

A voice cuts through the quiet, Breeze's: "You like grilled cheese, that right?" She's walking across the infield, a grin on her glorious face.

I nod, feeling the joy spread through me.

"Well, you see this here?" She hands me a grease-stained white sack with the gold-printed words *Sadie's Snack Shack.* "This is your everything, I reckon. Thought you'd be hungry after your last workout."

I gaze at the bag. "How'd you...where'd you get this?"

"I call it a rainy day fund." She smiles.

I smell it, cheesy and rich, hot. I feel like wolfing the whole thing, the way I ate Linda's waffles, ravishingly, cramming every last steaming, ambrosial morsel down my throat. It's hope. It's love. It's sustenance, both physical and emotional. It's a rescue rope thrown over a cliff. I open the bag to find a face-sized sandwich on Russian rye and draped in extra cheese.

"You best be tryin' a bite if you're up for it," Breeze says, grinning. "I've been tellin' myself for the last half an hour not to touch it and if you don't eat it, I surely will, 'cause, me, I'm an eating machine." She pats her belly. "And God knows I don't need it the way you need it."

I laugh. "Why don't we share it?"

"I like that idea, alright."

*

The night before I leave, we celebrate with a pajama party in front of a Hallmark Hall of Fame family movie. Only Luke opts out, choosing to stay in slacks and a polo shirt while he reads the paper. Linda wears a fluffy blue robe, while Amanda cuddles up with a teddy bear and wears her special Strawberry Shortcake jammies. Me, I wear my green long johns, the ones Dad bought before our first extended stay at Myles Lake. They've got holes in them now and are too small, but they're still as soft as ever.

"Get the blankets, Mama," Amanda calls out. She smiles at me. "I like your socks."

I put up a foot and examine it. "Thanks." They're tiger tube socks Mom bought, orange-and-lavender-striped.

The living room is warm, lamplight making everything soft, the hot smell of popcorn and the cheery sound of it popping in the kitchen turning this place into the closest thing to home I've ever had. It occurs to me suddenly that I've earned this.

"Here we go." Linda sings as she brings with her a heap of brightly colored comforters. "Popcorn's almost done. Are we ready?"

"Hot chocolate!" Amanda says.

"Oh, that's right. What's a movie night without hot chocolate?"

"And M&Ms!"

"Of course. What's popcorn without M&Ms?"

I look at Amanda. "Popcorn and M&Ms?"

Her face drops so much that her glasses slide down her nose. *"You've never had popcorn and M&Ms?"*

I shake my head.

"Oh my gosh! Mom, Gina's never had popcorn and M&Ms!"

Linda smiles. "Well, it's time she tried it."

"The sweet and the salty are so GOOOOOOD!" Beneath the blanket, Amanda is furiously kicking her feet.

"Amanda Grace…"

She looks in the direction of her father's voice, her eyes big behind her lenses. Luke is sitting, invisible until now, in the rocking chair. He's staring at her over the top of his reading glasses. "Can we tone it down a little?"

"But Dad, Gina's never had popcorn and M&Ms!"

He glances at me. "She's in for a treat, then."

"Here we are," Linda says as she brings in the popcorn and cups of hot chocolate topped with whipped cream. "Everything we need for a pajama party and movie night."

I take my cup, Snoopy wonderfully warm in my hands. I sip at the whipped cream, sweetness on my tongue. I think of Breeze. She'd love this, too. Joy the size of someone's palm.

The movie starts and there's a man coming through the front door at the end of a hectic day, kissing his wife on the cheek. I wonder if it's ever really like that. It never was with Mom and Dad. It isn't with Luke and Linda. Love isn't quite that gift-wrapped. Love is torn.

My mind drifts. Tomorrow my life will change and it will change forever. How can I be on my own? Someone's always taken care of me. There's always been that kiss on the cheek, though not as neat and as straightforward. Still. There's always been *someone*. And once I cross that threshold, one foot on a plane destined for the next day and a whole world, how will I feel?

I'll look up at the moon and they won't see it. For them, it'll have set. Or not have risen at all. My eyes burn. Faraway has never felt so far away. I didn't expect to bond to anyone else, ever. I never thought there'd come a day I wouldn't want to leave.

"You ok, hon?"

Linda's eyes are on me and so are Amanda's. "I'm just being stupid," I say finally.

Linda turns down the volume on the movie. "Nothing you do could ever be stupid." She gets up, sits by me. "What's the matter, hon?"

The words come out, unexpected. "I don't want to go."

She smiles, her arm around me. "You're going to see so many things. Amazing, wonderful things."

But this is better. Love. Home. Routine. This is what I've always wanted.

She squeezes my shoulder. "This is a gift, Gin." And I let her hold onto me. Because this is what I want. Someone's arms. Someone's heart.

*

I tuck it in as an addendum to my passport, my true likeness, me in my mother's arms.

*

As I pack, a knock on the door startles me. "Hi." It's Amanda, lingering around the doorjamb. "I want to give you something, for luck." Her hands are behind her back. "Close your eyes."

I do.

"Put out your hand."

I feel something smooth and cool in my palm.

"Open your eyes."

I look at a silver tube, tiny flowers etched around the top and bottom.

"It's rose petal," Amanda says. "It was Olivia's."

I swallow a lump. "And you're giving it to *me*?"

"She used to wear it all the time even though Dad wouldn't let us wear makeup." Amanda grins. "It was her secret, too." She takes the tube from me and pulls off the silver lid, uncorking a petal-pink thumb. "It's light enough no one noticed she was wearing it, but there's this sparkle..." She holds it next to the lamp. "See?"

I nod as I spot the flecks of gold and silver in the light, tiny stars.

Amanda smiles. "I could always tell."

On the Wings of a Dream
Flight 605/Destination: Newark, New Jersey
1994

As we walk through the revolving doors of the Portland airport, Linda and Amanda are on one side of me and Luke's on the other. I have an entourage. In my mind, Mom and Dad each take a hand.

Remember that day on the track when you were the only two watching, the only two clapping?

I breathe in the scent of cinnamon rolls and coffee, and something else, perfume or incense, something floral. The airport's like a mall with gift shops and snack shacks.

"Did you want to buy a magazine?" Linda asks me. "It's going to be a long flight."

We go into a gift shop and I gaze at all of the magazines. On each is a beautiful woman. And in each are articles about how to love. I reach for the blonde woman whose hair is blown behind her as though it's windy where she is. I've always liked wind. It reminds me of the desert.

So does love.

*

"Mom, can I get a cinnamon roll?" Amanda asks.

"Sure."

Suddenly, she's jumping up and down. "I *love* cinnamon rolls; they are THE BEST!"

"They look pretty big; how about you and Gina share one?" Linda gazes up at the illuminated menu.

"Want to share one?" Amanda asks me excitedly. "I've had them before and they are SO GOOD!"

I nod, smile.

Linda orders one of the pinwheel-sized rolls and the cashier cuts it in half, wrapping each piece in pink wax paper.

"Oh my gosh and they're *pink!*" Amanda says.

*

We eat on a little wrought-iron table outside the café and I watch as passengers walk by. I wonder where they're going and what their story is. Is it anything like mine? Do they want to start over? To find the self they know they can live with forever?

"Are you ok, sweetheart?" Linda asks.

I nod, choose simple. "Just nervous."

"Nothing to be nervous about, hon. You'll do great like you always do."

"I've never been on a plane."

She smiles. "Oh, that's right. You know, I'd say it's like riding a bike, but it's easier; all you do is sit there." She cackles like I've never heard her cackle.

"I think maybe *you're* a little nervous?" Luke says to her, an eyebrow arched.

"Oh, for heaven's sake, of course I am. This little girl's going to the *World Championships.*"

*

I feel Linda's hand on my shoulder as we approach the gate. "Good luck to you, Gina." She glances at Luke, then back at me. "We love you."

The words make my stomach lurch. And I can't stop them, the tears. Her arms are around me and her hands are rubbing my back as I bury my face in her shoulder. I want her to sit beside me on the plane. I want to look up into the stands and imagine her there. I want her clapping for me. Cheering me on in that final stretch of the track. I don't want to be on the other side of the world alone.

She cups my face in her palms and wipes my tears with her thumbs. "We're so *proud* of you."

I know.

Luke squeezes my arm. "Go get 'em."

You think I can? You think I should? I have so many questions. So many doubts. Instead, I nod. "I will."

Over the crackle of a loudspeaker I hear: *Flight 605 now boarding.* I muster a smile as I look at them, my new family, proud of me. Loving me. I blow them a kiss and I turn. I don't look back.

I walk down the ramp, think of Dad's old Caddie and again realize just how far I've come. The flight attendants smile, say *welcome aboard.* I see the pilot, too—a graying man with a mustache and brown puppy eyes. He nods and says hi to each passenger. If he wanted to, he could end all of this and I'd never make it to the World Junior Championships. Instead, I'd be an almost, like Dad.

I get a window seat and look out onto the tarmac. It's a gloomy day, not uncommon for early morning in Portland, even in summer. It was never like this in the desert. It occurs to me that maybe I'll go back someday. Even though they're gone. I miss the crisp feel of the air, the smell of sagebrush, and those familiar silhouettes, Archer's hills. The landscape of childhood. A good one, I realize. *Don't forget to smell the air.* Did he ever figure out that the best air is Archer's?

One of the flight attendants closes the door and we wait for the signal to take off. Butterflies explode in my gut. What will it be like to fly? Outside, the tarmac moves. We turn and are aimed down the runway now, and then I hear the engine, feel a surge of power, and we are moving, faster, faster, until there's a little jolt, and I see the ground drop from beneath me. Something in my gut falls. Never before have I been lifted from the earth.

Then I think of the star I wished on years ago and realize that the only way to touch it is to fly.

I gaze down onto the gloomy ceiling I've grown used to. Soft and gray, like a blanket. Up here, it's bright and the sun flashes off the wings. Excitement throbs through me; I've finally escaped. I'm not a part of the gray anymore. Not that girl sitting, awkward, in Kazatimuru's. Not the one always daydreaming under the night sky. This is it. My moment. My dream. Everything I've ever worked toward. Here. Now. Mine.

"Mind if I sit here?"

I look up, startled—and smiling above me is Penstamon Tucker.

I'm flustered as I feel my face redden. "Sure."

"You looked great at Nationals," he says, grinning, confident. I wish I had what he has.

"Thanks. You did, too."

"Did you think you'd make Worlds?"

I shrug. "I hoped I would. But I'm not sure I really believed I could do it. Did you?"

He sits back. "Yep."

I swallow, trying to think of something to say. He reminds me a little of Dad.

"I always knew I could do it," he says. "You have to believe it yourself, you know?"

"Yeah. I know."

"You're faster than you think."

I feel myself smile. "I guess I am."

"I meant that generically."

"Oh."

"Is this your first World Championships?"

I nod.

"Excited?"

"Yeah. You?"

"Well, this isn't my first time, but sure, yeah, I guess I am."

I gaze out the window, wishing he'd leave. I don't want to talk right now; I just want to feel. Talking, for some reason, is taking the magic away. I think of Dad. Know that magic exists.

"Well, good luck," he says, finally standing to leave.

"You, too," I say without looking up.

*

Newark, New Jersey: Outside is a myriad of lights, the city beyond the airstrip, skyscrapers all but silhouettes in the settling dusk. I'm still alone, but not for long. There will be four team coaches, the coaching staff, and a lot of other kids full of dreams. I wait, gaze out the window, realize that, out there, are a hundred Kazatimuru's.

"Gina?"

I turn and there's Brenda Voegel, the Team's assistant coach. I met her after the National Championships race. She looks different in slacks and a Team USA blazer. Heavier. And the humidity has given her blonde hair tighter curls.

"Come this way," she says, smiling, and I follow her toward the next gate. "You excited?"

I nod. "Everybody's been asking me that."

She chuckles. "I'll bet. It's a big deal."

The deal of a lifetime, Dad would've said.

"You're going to be sitting next to Jessie Weston. She's a senior at Allderdice High School in Pittsburg."

"Has she gone to Worlds?"

Brenda nods. "Twice."

Something in me withers. It seems like everybody but me has been here before. "Is there anyone who hasn't been to Worlds?"

"Robyn Foresythe from Smith Rock."

"Is she nervous?"

Brenda smiles down at me. "Why don't you ask her?"

I shrug, embarrassed suddenly.

"I'd be willing to bet she is. And that's perfectly normal. It means you care about your race."

We walk down a narrow corridor and there they are, the whole team, as everybody turns to look at Brenda and me as we approach. I feel my face flush and tuck behind her, but she turns and puts a hand on my back.

"Team, this is Gina. And this is her first World Championships."

There are some scattered hi's and mostly stares. Penstamon is there, too, and I marvel at how he managed to get off the plane so fast.

I glance over all of the faces and wonder which one is Robyn.

As we enter the crowd, Jon McCarroll, one of the head coaches, shakes my hand, hard. "Welcome to Team USA." He's a bear of a man with dark hair and a husky voice. Like Brenda, he's dressed up in slacks and a Team USA blazer. So are the other two coaches, a man with flyaway black hair and a woman with too much rouge and a red ponytail. Each shakes my hand, says *welcome to the Team. The Team.* I've finally made it.

Penstamon is the only one I know, so I sit next to him as we wait for our flight. "Have you ever been to Bonn?"

He shakes his head. "The last Worlds was in Italy."

"Oh."

He looks at me. "You?"

I shake my head and look around at all of the other athletes, most of them lost in themselves as they listen to music, headphones on, cut off. It strikes me suddenly how lonely this is. In this sea of strangers I want, desperately, to find a friend. "I've never been overseas."

"Never?"

I ignore Penstamon's exaggerated show of disbelief. "Never. Ever been to Nevada?"

"Never."

Words run out as I try to describe it. Hills bare but for knots of sagebrush. Lonely streets and dawns that stretch the sky to infinity, no clouds to interrupt. Wind with a desert scent, dry and fragrant, even in the winter. The smear of steel above alternating with the bluest sky you've ever seen. Dad's crackling radio and those scuffed cowboy boots. Dreams found on tracks forgotten.

"So what's it like?"

I realize I haven't said anything. "Amazing. Sad."

"Sad?"

I catch his gaze. "I grew up there."

He gets it. "Oh."

*

We hear the first boarding call and line up. A woman at the front is checking everyone's ticket and passport. A thrill pulses through me. Bonn. Once my turn comes and I step across that threshold, I'll have one foot over the border.

She smiles, marks my ticket, and I walk down the corridor toward the plane. There's a crack in the floor and through it I see gloom, twilight seeping in. It's the last I'll see of America for a while. A patch of gray-tinged blue.

I sit next to Jessie Weston from Pittsburg, try to smile. "Hi."

"Hi," she says.

My mind a blank, I stare out the window.

*

As I gaze south over the Atlantic Ocean, the sea a dark curve yawning into a night full of possibilities, I think of him. This is his dream. This is what he wanted when he ordered escargot for my birthday. This is what he held out for me to take when he put his inspiration around my neck that day on the track. This is him. His mistakes and his misguided attempts to recapture the day he threw away at the State Cross Country Championships. His habitual imprisonment in 1976. His one shot at greatness.

This is me.

Maybe he's still out there. That's the thought that keeps coming back. Maybe it was someone else's body they found. Maybe he wanted to free me. Maybe he wanted to wait until I'd lived my dream so that he wouldn't drown me with his. Maybe I'll see him on that track in Bonn.

But even as I indulge the fantasy, I know it won't come true. Some dreams are simply impossible. Funny now how my father's presence is less attainable than an Olympic gold medal.

"Anything to drink?"

I look up to see a stewardess pushing a drink cart. She is young and pretty with too much makeup and coiffed blonde hair stiff with hairspray.

"Root beer."

She smiles generously and I can tell she is sweet. I wonder if she is someone's mother. "You got it."

I watch her pour the pop as the ding of the seatbelt light goes on and I hear the voice of the pilot over the intercom: "We're going to be hitting some mild turbulence, folks…"

"Enjoy your drink." She grins and I watch her move on. I wonder where she grew up and if her father loves her. Is he proud of her beauty? Of her kindness? Of her having made it as a flight attendant? I hope so.

Jessie reads a magazine. She's pretty, with shining nut-brown hair tied up in an elaborate chignon. Her features are delicate, smaller than mine, and despite being thin, she's got more than beestings and her knee joints are proportional to the rest of her body. I feel a sudden, riling jealousy. I'll bet she's got a mom and dad, real ones. And I'll bet she's never had to eat sashimi out of a dumpster.

I make quick glances to see what she's reading. *His O Secrets Unlocked.* What are O secrets? I mean to ask, but a different question comes out: "Are you nervous?"

She looks up at me as though startled and I notice how blue her eyes are. "Nervous about what?"

"World's."

"Um, *no.*"

"Really?"

She makes a face. "Really. It's not like I haven't done this before."

This is old hat for her, nothing worthy of excitement at all. So much for asking about O secrets.

I want desperately to talk to someone, to share this with someone, the night wrapping itself around us as we hurtle east, the anticipation of the biggest event of our lives, a destiny that for me will last all of sixteen minutes.

Then what? A lifetime committed to a quarter of an hour.

Then maybe the Olympics and another quarter of an hour. When it will be just like this, a flight across an ocean, a movie playing on the too-small screen five rows ahead of me, as actors, like mimes, make silent pronouncements and live silent lives. I watch the faces, happy then sad; he's telling her something she doesn't want to hear.

I close my eyes. *Dad, do you see me? Do you know where I am? Where I'm headed? I did it, Dad.*

And it's funny how suddenly small Kazatimuru's seems.

*

I give up on Jessie as the darkness lulls me into dreams and I see her face, vividly painted in browns and grays, shadows of grief, Breeze's sad memories. In the dream, I find her in a garbage-strewn, weedy spot, a half-mom-half-Breeze girl in an alley. It has become a haven for us. We level with ourselves out here, confide here, escape from Luke and his expectations, eat, drink, cry, and laugh, feel sorry for ourselves and our lot in life and, conversely, feel grateful for what little things we can get, evidence of our indulgence often blowing out across the parking lot when the wind picks up, Styrofoam beverage cups, hamburger, French fry, and candy-bar wrappers, empty potato-chip bags, and smashed Hostess cupcake boxes carried end-over-end like tumbleweed on a blustery day. Something about all the trash gives me comfort, as though it has formed the structure of some insidious nest, a cocoon layered with both need and want, loneliness cloaked in the hunger for something salty or sweet, greasy, tangy, or bold, strong or burnt or grade-A. We understand the nuances of want and need, the ways in which we feed our addictions for extra-salty French fries, ooey-gooey strawberry cupcakes, or especially greasy hamburgers. It's all a part of a newfound language—something a naïve person might call desperation.

But it no longer feels like desperation. Instead, as I sit with Mom-Breeze eating a donut, it feels more like a kind of amnesty; I am done running, done with hardship. I have found what will save me.

I ask a heart-pounding question: "Why do you hate me?"

"Hate you?"

"For winning."

"Same reason you hated me, I reckon."

I think about that for a minute. "I did at first, didn't I?"

"Sure did, 'fore you got to know me." She looks at me. "You had to know that part didn't matter, right?"

"What part?"

"The part about bein' faster. Bein' faster doesn't mean your life is better."

The shelter flashes through my mind. "I thought winning would save me."

She snorts. "Only you can save you."

*

I wait, wanting the white seatbelt light to go off so that we can make our way to Germany. It finally does and we file out. I breathe in and something smells different. Spicy. Potpourri? Or pumpkin pie. My first glimpse of Germany. Outside, it's bright. Sunshine with wind-whipped clouds. In the desert, you always look up. Then I remember this isn't the desert.

In the airport, we're greeted by illuminated pictures of women in black petticoats, *Seien Sie schön!* A girl points to the sign, says: "Be beautiful!"

"You know German, Allie?" someone asks.

The girl, a sprinter from the look of her, or maybe a pole vaulter—tall and muscled—nods proudly.

Be beautiful. I stare at the women, thin with short black hair, dark eyes, and white skin. I think of Kazatimuru's and how it seemed in a desert full of routine. Glamorous. Exotic. Unattainable. It's the same kind of beauty. Worthy of daydreams. Like this one. I feel a blitz of hope.

Not unattainable, because I'm here.

*

I hear a voice and to the right is a young man in a gray-green uniform. "*Das ist der Weg, bitte.*" He is motioning to us. "This way, please." We lay all of our belongings on a belt being eaten by an X-ray machine. I watch my small bag disappear into it and see its skeleton on a monitor above the man's head. The contents of my life, the ribs of a comb, the femur of Amanda's secret tube of lipstick, and those silver nail-clippers Dad bought before my first meeting with Luke, that day we caught air in the back of an old Chevy truck headed for Portland. "*In Ordnung,*" I hear the man say to another as my bag reappears on the belt behind the machine.

Other men in uniforms check our passports and direct us through a narrow hall to the baggage claim. "Welcome to Germany," one says, as he stamps my passport. "What brings you to Bonn?"

And I don't know what to say. I'm here to do what I've always wanted to do, but I don't know how to tell him that. "I'm competing," I say finally. Then the best part: "I'm a runner."

A knot gathers in my throat as I wonder what Dad would think of all this, an experience he missed, the details of a reality unknown to him. Dreams are limited. So is imagination, I realize. I recall the days in the Caddie as we kicked up dust in the desert and dreamed. It'd all been shiny then. Ethereal. But there are real smells and real sights. Real things that have nothing to do with crowds, lights, and medals. I take it all in. The reality, not a dream anymore.

*

I find it in the bathroom. *Ich liebe dich.* Black loopy letters enclosed in a Sharpie heart. He could never have imagined this. A 5,000-mile certainty he could never have seen, never have known. The heart gives it away. So do the three words.

Ich liebe dich. I should have said it more often.

*

We board a bus for *Der Heidel Haus,* the hostel we'll be staying in, bouncing along on a country road out of the city. I listen to the locals as they speak, their words unknown, realizing that, here, everything is different.

*

There's something love-worn about the peeling wallpaper, blue with white daisies and the smell of dust and old linoleum. The hotels in my mind were grand, with crystal chandeliers and walls made of marble. The armoires in the rooms were made of bird's eye pine and the sheets of silk. That's what Dad had imagined, too. I knew it the day he took me to Kazatimuru's for escargot.

I think of our house, of the way it was when Dad found it, with its broken windows and water-stained floors. It had been ugly, but Dad came along and made it beautiful. This place is like him. Dad had big dreams, but when things came up short, he made do with a whistle and a smile.

There are all sorts of things like that here, tarnished buttons I could grow to love. Things that remind me of him even though I'd never meet him here. I sit down on a bed with an ornate wrought-iron frame, a child's, and I go back to those nights before things went wrong, when he'd tuck me in, brush a finger against my cheek and tell me I could do anything. Those were the times the stars seemed brightest, when what I had was my father's faith. Before Mom left. Before frigid evenings spent huddled around a spark on a wasteland. When I thought a medal was really a summit from which to look down on the world. And here is where it all led, to a place like the one where I began, hope wrapped in broken glass and the brittle curls of a paper garden.

Dust motes dance in a beam of sun and I remember the window in the attic of our old house, the sill with the carved pronouncement: *JL was here*. I wonder suddenly if JL is still out there, the way Mom is, in that vague anywhere. I'll go back someday. I'll go back and trace those letters and remember what it was like to be a child and how it came that I made even bigger pronouncements on the dusty track across the street. I am here. I scratch it with a fingernail on a sill bright with sun, the letters barely visible, unknowable to anyone but me. I look out over the farm, a henhouse right below me and a pigpen across the path. I feel myself smile. There will be no distinguishing dessert or salad forks tonight. Because it doesn't matter here.

*

Two nights later, there's a knock on the door and Coach Voegel peers in. "Gina, Luke's on the phone."

I follow her out into the hall with the red velvet carpeting to an antique table with an old-fashioned telephone. The white receiver is laying there, ready for me.

I pick it up. "Hello?"

"Gina?"

"Hi."

"How are you doing?"

"Good."

"Feeling ok? Still jetlagged at all?"

I shrug even though he can't see me. "A little, I guess - but it's ok."

"You feeling strong?"

"Yeah."

"How are practices going?"

"Good."

"You like Coach Voegel?"

"Uh-huh."

"You don't sound too convincing."

"I'm just nervous."

"It's pretty overwhelming; I understand."

Then I remember; Luke once made an Olympic Team.

"You're gonna do great, kiddo."

From 5,000 miles, he could almost be Dad. "Thanks."

"We'll be proud of you no matter what."

"I know."

*

I think of Luke and his sprint down the track, an Olympic berth. I wonder if the memory ever carried him, knowing that bright spot has long since faded. I pull out the Polaroid of me in my mother's arms. Everything fades. Even perfect finishes. Even love. And it is what I'll carry onto the track, what will paint it in those darning colors. Not grief over hardship, but grief over what becomes common. The used-to of wonderful. The has-been of grace. Pastels have a place, too.

*

Coach Voegel comes in when the other girls have gone. "How are you feeling?" she asks, sitting beside me on the bed.

I look into her face. "Nervous."

"That's normal."

"I know."

She seems to search me. "You know a race won't fix everything, right?"

My stomach flops; this isn't what I expected. "Is this some kind of pep talk?"

She purses her lips. "I've coached a lot of kids. And they all have something to prove. The problem is, you can't prove it in a race."

I'm defensive as I remember my dream. "What are you talking about?"

"What you feel you need to prove has nothing to do with running. Do it for yourself, Gina."

*

My heart hammers as we walk into a holding area to check in. I look around at the athletes and notice that each has a different flag over her breast. They are all lanky and beautiful. They stretch, graceful, fingers to toes, legs up as they bend, seemingly in half, laying their pretty faces against their shins as they breathe, calm themselves. Insecurity flashes through me. I don't belong here.

There is no one I know. I'm the only American in this race—the other American qualifier, the golden comet from nationals, opted for the 1500. A knot comes up in my throat. These people don't even speak my language. I'm a one and only at long last, but not the kind I thought I'd be. They're all faster than me. Prettier than me. Taller than me. Real runners versus…what am I? A child still at play. Is that all? I remember the day on the track. It had all been pretend. Me running like an Olympian, Dad's medal, not my own, around my neck and me on the podium, closing my eyes against the sun as I imagined their claps carrying across the desert, turning somehow into a crowd's. I wanted then for it to be like it was on TV and now all I want is for it to be like it was then. But they're not out there. No one is.

A girl with a black face and bright eyes nods and smiles. I nod and smile back, wishing I could talk to her. *What's your name? Are you scared? I am. What if I can't do this?* As though reading my mind, she comes up to me, grins, and extends her thin hand, firm on mine. "Goot…Lauck." I look at the flag on her jersey. ETH, it says.

I smile, stumble. "Good luck." Something in her face reminds me of Breeze's, but her eyes dance like Dad's and I wonder what memories will carry her through this, as the crowd cheers and those digital numbers fly upward, as the pain sets in and the last mile becomes the longest of her life. Will she remember where she came from? Will she think of her parents? Will she remember who she was at the beginning?

I hear a baritone voice over a loud speaker: *Willkommen, Athleten. Viel Glück!* Hosts in black suits and white gloves open the doors for us as we walk onto the track. All the color in the world has been washed to the west as another night mutes it. Everything is soft despite the bright lights of distinction.

I take a deep breath as I walk out and gaze into a thin crowd. I have imagined this moment so many times and in my mind, it has always been packed. I'd look up and stands so tall they touched the sky were full of cheering people, the roar of their anticipation deafening. There was music, too. Always an up-tempo beat. There were flashbulbs and people on their feet as two or three of us abreast sprinted down the final straight toward the line, me suddenly out front by a hair, triumphing by the length of my big toe, the feat effortless. I've found myself living it in dreams and in brown studies out the window on slow Saturday afternoons. I've thought of it as I've closed my eyes before practice, breathed in deep, expecting to smell something foreign and floral, only to discover that it was the dry desert air I smelled and there was no crowd.

I didn't forget, Dad. The air smells like apples. Can you believe that? Apples.

But there are no huge grandstands. The crowd is modest. There are coaches out on the field and a few photographers. I imagine families in the bleachers. Parents. Grandparents. Brothers and sisters. I gaze up and catch sight of my team. They are all here to watch me. Coach Voegel gives me a thumbs-up and a spasm of adrenaline throbs through me. I hope I don't let them down. But what do they want, really? What do I want? The thought is reflexive: To win. But what if I can't win? What's next? To make top three? To bow my head as an official puts a medal around my neck—a real one, my own this time? How will that feel? Will I finally be whole? Like a part of me has been put back?

I think of Dad's medal and I doubt it. Funny that it calms me. I know I won't feel any different.

A giant black rectangle with 00:00 in red digital numerals sits next to the start. Butterflies take flight. What will it say when I'm done? Will I be proud? Will he?

*

We line up. The crowd is silent. Cameras flash. I take a breath, wait, my heart hammering. The Rule: Three steps forward and one step back. Toe behind the line, not on it. Foul and you're done.

This is it, Dad. You believed in me once.

When the gun goes off, I let joy lead. Let memories paint the track in those colors from the good days. Faded summer denim and freckled skin, Dad in that dusty Caddie driving down the road with a blade of grass in his teeth and his arm hanging out, a finger on the wheel. God, I miss him. There are wings on my feet, invisible now, but for the smile on my lips as I remember a happy childhood after all. For now, I'll let my grief go. I'll tease myself into thinking it was perfect and when the race ends, I'll use a bit of Dad's magic. That acceptance he used to talk about. Because it wasn't perfect, will never be perfect, and I want to be happy anyway. Colors run wild. Reds, oranges, and yellows lick those sore spots, extinguish the pain of blue.

You were going to die for grief. Might as well die for glory.

Never.

I sense her then, off my right shoulder. Hear her breath. Feel her heat, her strife, my own. She is suffering. Struggling. *Remember her courage.* I hear her uneven gait, her form falling apart as she fatigues. *Remember yours.* This is the race of her life.

"Get mad," I say, though I can't see her face. Those memories tumble out. Mom. Dad. The desert's clear sky. I looked up at it then and dreamed of something bigger. This. I surge and, amazingly, she stays with me, unshakeable. Breeze flashes through my mind. I broke her and understood that everything is breakable. Even people.

I imagine her shatter, this shadow of mine. Myself as I once was to Breeze. And to Linn. *But you don't exist anymore.* I throw in another surge, look over my shoulder, and she is gone.

The crowd is on its feet and I imagine Mom and Dad among them, clapping the way they did that day in the desert. I push harder. Joy is tough. Tougher than it looks. Tougher than it seems. It can break the wind better than anger or fear. I think of Hayward Field. Blood in the rain. A smile in the dark, pointing skyward, known only to God or to Fate. Dad's dream realized, with no one watching but me.

The words flash through my mind on the final stretch, reflexive: *Ich liebe dich. I love you.* And there it is, a destiny, mine: 15:44, :45, :46… I will break 16:00 and to do so will mean I'll become the new National High School 5k Record Holder. I sprint, dive, feel the grit in my palms as I fall, and that's when I see him, the man by the clock. He's wearing a hat, a Stetson with a silver rosette, and he takes it off for me.

"Dad? *Dad!*" I rush to my feet, and fight through the crowd, through the reporters, blood on my hands. *"Dad wait! Wait for me!"*

But he's not there. I stand, dumbfounded, still staring at the clock as it clicks upward, 16:04, :05, :06…," my destiny long gone.

There's a tap on my shoulder. *"Entschuldigen Sie Frau Dalton. Zeit für den Drogen-Test…"*

I turn and there is a raven-haired woman in a black suit. "Huh?"

She looks at my jersey and holds up a finger. "Ah…time for…*drug test.*" But first, she takes my palm, gazes at it. Her eyes are green with flecks of gray. She looks at me. *"Du bist verletzt, komm ich helfe dir."*

She leads me into the bathroom, turns on a faucet, and holds my palm under the tepid water. I watch as my blood goes down the drain and I think of my father's that night in the rain. It's the same blood. He's here if only in alleles. In the hieroglyphics of DNA.

I close my eyes and see clearly the man tipping his hat, my father the way he was that night at Hayward Field, joy on his face and not a medal in sight. There's a purity to running without regard to who else is on the track or how far they are ahead. It's like eating waffles when all you are is hungry. There is nothing else.

I smile at the green-eyed woman, realizing that she is as close to him as I'll ever get. This moment, mine to claim as sure as a prize on a podium. Relief spreads quickly as endorphins pump. I'm happy and there is that star, tangible in her kind face and in the throb, now dull, as she wraps my palm with clean, white gauze. I've done it. I've done what I've always wanted to do. I'm what I always imagined on the dirt track across the street, what, deep down, I wasn't sure I could ever be. I am my impossible dream.

*

"Goot Jop," she says, grinning, as we stand together on the podium. She is beautiful, her smile vibrant, her gold medal swinging like a pendulum around her neck. I feel the weight of mine too, remember that this isn't a dream. I reach up to touch it, my bronze, as I take ETH's hand. There are flashbulbs and clapping. Below, my team cheers for me. I will go home not just the bronze medalist, but the new high school 5k record-holder.

Athletes' Party
Bonn, Germany
1994

I take a deep breath as I stare at myself in the mirror, clad in a diamante evening gown the color of periwinkles, bought at the same shop where I once picked out my bruise-colored dress. I'm wearing gold hoop earrings I borrowed from Linda and my hair is done up in a French twist. I pull out the lipstick tube Amanda gave me, Olivia's beautiful secret. I unscrew the cap and stare at the sparkled pink thumb, look at myself in the mirror and wonder if I'm pretty enough for this. I smile. Because I am. I put it on and see a sister's secret sparkles. I imagine inspired giggles, whispers in the hall, and shy hands over snickering faces. This, a treasure and a celebration. I think of Mom and the way she dressed up for that Polaroid. To me, to my father, a gift.

This is what Dad meant, I realize. What it's like to know the salad fork from the dessert fork. It's a world apart from that pastel landscape where it all began. A lifetime removed from those brush strokes of air and water I thought were mine.

I have a pretend conversation with Breeze before I step out. She would've been honest. "You think I'm pretty?"

"Sure are gorgeous, yessiree."

"You don't think I look like Daddy Long Legs?"

"Daddy Long who?"

"Someone who looks like a spider."

"Don't look like a spider with only two legs."

"Thanks."

*

As I take a deep breath and step out, I hear the words to an upbeat song. Breeze would have loved this. The disco ball, light falling along the walls, a cascade of stars, and that huge table in the middle with a giant crystal bowl of punch and baby frankfurters, desserts and cheese, all set up on an ornate silver platter. I walk up to the table and sample one of the little franks.

"Good job today," I hear someone say.

I turn and there, in a suit and tie, is Penstamon Tucker. My smile is reflexive. "Hi. You, too."

His face reddens and I notice that he's not smiling. "Actually, I didn't do so well."

I swallow a pit. "Oh. I didn't see. I was off in drug testing. I'm sorry."

He takes a breath. "Yeah. Me, too."

"You ok?"

He shrugs and I see Dad, the vulnerable kid who got himself to school. "Want to dance?" he asks.

I let him wrap an arm around my waist as we sway to Lionel Richie. "You remind me of someone," I say.

"Who?"

"A guy I used to know."

"I hope he was good-looking."

I smile as I think of him that night in the rain, doing his private dance on Hayward Field.

We stop and he looks at me. "I lied to you; this was my first World Championships."

"Oh."

"And I blew it."

And that's when it happens, the unfathomable. He bursts into tears. And it all comes back. Dad and his walk-away day at the State Cross Country Championships. Mom and her regret over a life far from Juilliard. Failure and hurt. Disappointment. This was what Dad had been terrified of. The moment of glory that comes and goes without you.

I walk with him up to my room, next to the window with my scrawl, an anonymous declaration, and the moon.

"I'm sorry," I say. I see the boy my dad once was, scared and disappointed, on the edge between realizing his dream and walking away. "Don't give up."

He snorts. "I'm a senior; I won't get this chance again." He gazes at me so that my face burns and it takes everything not to look away. "I've wanted to do this for so long and I've trained so hard."

I know. Me, too.

"I don't know what happened. I went out too fast, I guess. I couldn't even finish."

I touch his cheek the way Breeze touched mine, hoping it helps. It helped me. That tactile hope. What I want to say I can't put into words. What I want to show is the sky, my dad's happy face, the desert's hoar frost on the shingles of our old house, and that rash of stars we used to wish on.

Believe in yourself, Dad always said.

"You still ran the race of your life," I tell him.

"Yeah? How?"

I think of Breeze. "You got this far."

*

I follow the familiar red carpet, my yellow brick road, a far cry from the sand and the gravel that brought me here, to that white telephone. On the other end of the line, 5,000 miles away, it's lunchtime.

I dial her number, someone summons her, and she answers.

"What are you eating?"

"Gina? *Gina! Is that you?*" Her voice is faraway, crackling and kind, astonished. There's the hiss of something, of distance.

"I wish you were here." I want to laugh, not cry.

"Girl, I wish I was, too. How'd you do?"

"I broke the national high school record."

"No shit!"

I laugh as my eyes well. "No shit."

"Well, hell, we'll have to celebrate!"

I feel a blitz of joy. I can't wait to go home to the tactical genius who taught me to see it all in color. "Potato soup sounds pretty good."

Despite the hiss and the distance, the brightness of her voice comes clear: "Throw in some A1 Sauce and it'll be perfect!"

*

I gaze out the plane window as we leave Bonn, my dream realized. I could make an Olympic Team and it will be just like this. A high point of joy and fading color, dusk settling after an extraordinary day. I realize it will always be like this. A pinnacle before picking my way back down so that I can start over, look up again. I think of Breeze's potato soup. What comes after victory? Life does.

*

As I get off the plane, there are reporters waiting. They've heard about me. The World Junior bronze medalist. The new national record holder.

And those same questions: "Was it a tough race for you, Gina? What's next for you? Who will you be running for next year?"

No one, I think, then remember that I count. I'll be running for myself. To say it out loud would sound stupid. But it won't be for him. Not anymore. He's gone and I'm all that's left. *Do it for yourself, Gina.* I'll have to.

*

I hear them clapping before I see them. Linda, Luke, and Amanda, their voices carrying across the terminal.

"Way to go, Gina!"

They hug me and it's real. I think of Dad's acceptance, that magical thing that makes life great even when you aren't, and I feel myself smile.

*

I take one last look at it, the medal I once thought would define me, define my life, and make me whole. I shine it with a sock, hoping it will work the kind of magic Dad's medal did. I draft a letter:

Dear Breeze—
I want you to have this because you taught me how to see it all
in color. Thank you.
*   Gina*

The medal I keep isn't mine.

*

Luke takes me to the track, even though I'll have no more practices for several weeks. But it's not the track I want to see. I walk down to that old, gray building—the one with the broken sidewalk and crooked railing out front. I find her sitting on her cot, reading, a haven in a blanket and a book.

She glances up, startled, then smiling. *"Gina!"*

"I wanted to give you something." I've put it in an envelope as though it's a letter and, in a way, it is. "Thanks for the potato soup."

She takes it. "What's this?"

"My dream."

She catches my gaze.

It's not the *everything* I thought it was, but it's enough to nurture a dream. I think of my father's medal. For a while, it carried him. And then there were those snow-capped peaks and that alkaline lake, Kazatimuru's King-great sashimi and all those aluminum cans we collected for a can opener and packages of hot dogs. Potato soup and grilled cheese. That ethereal hope turned into so much more than what sparkling two-dimensional dreams can yield, the simplicity of glitz.

"Is this…?" Breeze pulls out the medal, agape. "Gina, I can't…"

"I want you to have it."

"Why?"

I feel myself smile, recalling the day she first opened her home to me. "You changed my mind."

"About what?"

"About what *everything* means."

*

That night before bed, I tell Linda I want to go home. "I need to see Archer again."

"I figured you would." She tucks a strand of hair behind my ear, like Mom used to. "I think that's probably a really good thing."

"You think so?"

"You haven't forgotten where you came from. That's good. Most people have to be reminded."

I smile. "I have to do this alone, but you know I'm coming back."

She hugs me. "I know."

Archer
1994

I get off the train, and breathe in. *Don't forget to smell the air.* It's home alright, the same air I've always known, dry and sweet, sagebrush-scented.

I walk toward the road alone. It's early morning, but the stars have faded. As a little girl, I thought morning meant I'd lost my chance to make a wish. In the dark, there'd been so many stars, so many opportunities, but as they dissolved into a daytime sea, the wishes and my belief in them vanished. Now I know the wish never dies.

I head toward what for me is Archer's heart, that dirt track, the place I once thought would be the only one that would ever make me truly happy.

I think of my father's pinnacle, that 4:07 mile embodied in a medal, now lost. I think of my dirt track, know, finally, that wishes are simple. I want something else, to find my own way in the world and to not make the same mistakes. I break into a run, come around the corner of the middle school, and there it is. My track. There are dandelions and daisies and tufts of tall grass. Unremarkable and yet an inspiration still. And there is that little podium I stood on after winning my first race, a race with one entrant and an audience of two. I close my eyes, remember. Wish he was standing here now with that medal of his poised above my head. I would give anything.

I go to the bleachers and sit. What must they have seen back then? A ten-year-old trying desperately to hang onto something… A childhood? A belief in herself? Hope? Redemption?

You knew me, Dad. What was it?

*

I know, finally, what my father meant. I look at these hills and they are mine, each bump and curve a memory. My life is written here, fanning out like the desert's dry tributaries, the forgotten landscape of time and desolation rediscovered by my stumble through a hope and a dream that were not my own.

Each time he comes to mind, I think of that green Caddie in the morning sun, imagine the dust in the wheel wells and the dirt on the windshield. Remember the smell, a hint of WD40 and Armor All, my father's loving touch. Imagine his wear on the steering wheel, at ten and two, where he always gripped it, evidence of him everywhere, on everything I see, in everything I am. I stand on the track now felted by grass and moss, the gravel beneath like that button I once dug up. Forgotten. There are hundreds of toadstools, arbitrary markers charting a damp spring and summer rains. I take a breath. Stand, poised, one foot forward and the other back as I push off down the straight.

This track has no lines and there is no way to draw any, not anymore. I don't imagine heated competitions here, don't see the fiery lights of distinction, or imagine any sprint to the finish despite the empty bleachers where Mom and Dad once sat. Instead, I see hair, unbound and left to the wind. I see arms pumping, yet outstretched, Olivia's faceless runner. I see freedom. I don't count laps. Don't keep splits. Don't even care about those angry colors anymore. Instead, I claim this too. A forgotten hue rediscovered and a long-ago wish granted. Joy.

Acknowledgments

Like Gina, my first encounter with running was on a dirt-and-gravel track, though mine was in Charlo, Montana. My first race, at age 5, was only 100 meters. And like Gina, I was fascinated by treasures. Mine were pretty rocks, and I kept stopping to pick them up. By the end, I'd spent so much time treasure hunting that I finished dead last, in tears. But my mother came to my rescue, telling me there's more to life than winning and that treasures come in many forms. Since then, I've run in track and cross-country meets, marathons, trail races, road races, and even a master's national championship. Running and sports have come to mean adventure, and I have been fortunate to have discovered that, win or lose, there's always something significant to be found.

As for this book, I want to begin by thanking my family for believing in me and supporting me through all of the time I've put into this project, starting in 2005. To my husband, Blaine, for supporting me in my decision to be a writer, and to my parents, Ciry and Hugh, for never doubting me, I am truly thankful—as I am to Rune, my son, for keeping me on my toes, inspiring me every day, and constantly reminding me of what's important in life. Additional thanks go to my grandmother, Audrey, who taught that every wish paints life a brighter color, and to dream and keep on dreaming even when you think it isn't possible, and to my grandfather, Francis, for teaching me that hard work and perseverance pay off.

I want to thank editor and publisher Rick Lovett for all of his expertise and willingness to go the extra mile. The care he's put into this book has been incredible. Thanks also to everyone who has given me feedback and encouragement: to Judy Slater for her expertise and advice; to Mary Krienke for believing in the project; and to Tom Hart for his willingness to read the Dickensian book this project began as and his help in cutting it down to size. Thanks to former high school 5k record holder Caitlin Chock for supplying details about what it's like to qualify for the World Junior Championships and to Rich Benyo, editor of *Marathon & Beyond*, for his advice on how to make this story even stronger. Thanks to Maya Nerenberg for her expertise in German, to Kelly Scott, for her knowledge of internal medicine, and to ultra-distance phenom Jenn Shelton for her honest opinion and genuine feedback. Thanks to Chris Byers for her eye for detail and in catching those little things I might otherwise have missed, and to Kristen Dedeaux for proofreading and enthusiastic support. It has been an 11-year adventure and I deeply appreciate all the help I've received in every form.

About the Author

The daughter of a wildlife-refuge manager, Holly Hight grew up in remote locations much like the high-desert towns and landscapes she so vividly depicts.

She ran cross-country in middle school, but pursued other interests in high school and college. After graduation, she returned to competition, racing (and often winning) everything from road runs and trail races to track meets and a masters national championship, sometimes beating all the guys in the process.

In college, she got degrees in criminology and political science and interned for the FBI. She then worked as a congressional staffer before winding up in Ashland, Oregon, where she now writes, runs, enjoys her family, and works in a running store owned by two-time Western States Endurance Run champion, Hal Koerner.

A journalist, essayist, science writer, and short-story writer, Holly has appeared in *Running Times, Competitor, Marathon & Beyond, Cosmos, Analog Science Fact & Fiction, and Apex.* She has also worked as a professional illustrator (including the cover drawing for this book).

Gina and her story have been an eleven-year labor of love. This is her first novel.

Strange Wolf Press

Strange Wolf Press is dedicated to the proposition that one-time genre boundaries are meaningless and that in today's Internet-driven market, authors should be free to pursue their passions, however diverse those might be. The world, we believe, is a far too interesting place to confine our reading to a single field.

In addition to *Wishing on My Father's Star*, our growing list of titles includes:

• *Million Dollar Marathon*, by Philip Maffetone and Richard A. Lovett.

• *Phantom Sense and Other Stories*, award-winning science fiction by Richard A. Lovett and Mark Niemann-Ross.

• *Patches Catches the Sargo County Cattle Rustler*, children's literature by Mark Niemann-Ross and David Brandt (illustrator).

• *Here Be There Dragons: Exploring the Fringes of Knowledge, from the Rings of Saturn to the Mysteries of Memory*, by Richard A. Lovett.

Visit us at www.strangewolf.us, or on Facebook at Phantom Sense and Other Stories.

CPSIA information can be obtained
at www.ICGtesting.com
Printed in the USA
FSOW02n1014160317
31987FS